FINDING MATT

JD RUSKIN

Dreamspinner Press

Published by
DREAMSPINNER PRESS

5032 Capital Circle SW, Suite 2, PMB# 279, Tallahassee, FL 32305-7886 USA
http://www.dreamspinnerpress.com/

Finding Matt
© 2014 JD Ruskin.

Cover Art
© 2014 Brooke Albrecht.
http://brookealbrechtstudio.com
Cover content is for illustrative purposes only and any person depicted on the cover is a model.

ISBN: 978-1-63216-276-2
Digital ISBN: 978-1-63216-277-9
Library of Congress Control Number: 2014948406
First Edition December 2014

Printed in the United States of America
∞
This paper meets the requirements of
ANSI/NISO Z39.48-1992 (Permanence of Paper).

To Kristen and Brit, for always making my books better.

CHAPTER 1

MARNIE BECKER tapped her thumbs against the steering wheel, her thoughts racing as fast as the beat. *How long had they been in the hospital? Five minutes? Ten minutes? How long did a therapy-dog visit take? What if someone gets suspicious and calls the police?* She peered into the back of the hollowed out van. She had taken out most of the equipment her brother had crammed in the back, but not all of it. *What if the police search the van and find drugs?* The sour stench permeating the van made her sick to her stomach, evidence of her brother's depravity. She hadn't had a choice. She'd never replaced her demolished car after the accident. *Don't think about it. Don't think about it. It was all a lie. Lie. Lie. Lie.* Eighteen months Brandon had been in the hands of strangers. Her child was alive.

She smacked her palms against the steering wheel hard enough to send a jolt of pain up her arms. *How could I have believed them? The skinny bastard pretending to be Brandon's father must've bribed the doctors.* She remembered Dr. Roberts had switched her meds the week before the accident. *Tired. So very tired that day.* She'd never so much as been in a fender bender before, let alone hit a curb and crash. They must have replaced her lithium with sleeping pills. It was the only thing that made sense. After pulling down the hood on her black jacket, she lifted her sweaty brown hair off her neck, then let the frizzy curls cascade down her back.

The sound of a car passing by made Marnie jump in her seat. She couldn't afford to be spotted! Seeing a crumpled ball cap on the floor of the van, she reached down and picked it up. The dismal excuse of a park was empty for now, but she needed to be prepared to move if needed. She twisted her hair into a bun before tucking it under the cap.

Her gaze drifted to the side window, the urge to get out making her body twitch. Her muscles ached with the need to move, move, move. *Can't leave. Need to stay and watch.* The nurse had told her last week that volunteers with therapy dogs show up on Saturday at 4:00 in the afternoon, and he'd been right. *Just need to keep it together for a little while.* She'd follow the skinny bastard home. Once she had a name and address, she'd find a way to rescue Brandon. They'd run away together. *Go to Mexico or Canada. Travel the world.*

Matt. The skinny bastard had called Brandon "Matt." Last week, Brandon had walked right by his momma and not recognized her. *The doctors must have done something to him. Drugged him. Brainwashed him.* Brandon would be afraid at first, not realizing what was going on. He wouldn't understand that she was rescuing him. *I'll make him understand. I'll make him remember.*

Marnie's body tensed as she noticed a kindergarten-aged child exiting the side door of the hospital with a little white dog in tow. *It couldn't be.* The boy walked briskly through the back parking lot and stopped at the street separating the hospital from the park. After carefully checking left and right just like she'd taught him, he crossed the street and headed toward the park. *Brandon.* Her eyes burned at the sight of him and her heart began to race. It was a sign. Some part of Brandon must sense that his momma was near. She bit the skin around her pinky finger. There were a lot of preparations that still needed to be made before she could act. *Money, passports, an untraceable car—*

Brandon stumbled and Marnie found herself out of the van and walking toward him without conscious thought.

"Are you okay, Br—Matt?"

Frowning, the boy rose to his feet, his little dog yapping several times. A small bag of chips had fallen out of his coat pocket and spilled onto the grass. Marnie had never let Brandon eat that kind of junk food.

"I'm okay," Brandon said, looking suspicious. She realized the brainwashing's hold was still too strong and Brandon's "stranger danger" alarm was likely blaring. She'd taught him to be cautious. Not like the skinny bastard that let her precious child walk to the park alone.

The dog moved between her and Brandon. It was another sign. Kneeling, Marnie picked up what she thought was a shih tzu or possibly a Maltese dressed in a pink dog vest. Its little heartbeat thundered against her hand as she tilted up the heart-shaped tag on the collar.

"Matt," she said, pouring urgency into her voice, "there's something wrong with Pixie."

Brandon's brown eyes widened. "What's wrong?"

"Her heart is racing and I'm afraid she's going to have a heart attack." Marnie rose to her feet, cradling the dog in her arms. "I'm a vet, and I need to treat her right away or she'll die."

Tears welled in Brandon's eyes, but he didn't close the gap between them.

"You can either come with me and try to keep Pixie calm or go back to your dad. Either way, I'll call your dad and tell him to meet me at the animal hospital."

Turning back toward the van, she wasn't surprised when Brandon decided to follow. Deep down inside he knew who his momma was.

CHAPTER 2

THE HYSTERICAL yapping of a dog could be heard through the thin walls separating the small office from the main business area. It must be bath time for the Pomeranian. Resisting the urge to sigh, Jaron Greenberg gave his prospective client what he hoped was a reassuring smile. "I'm sorry about the noise. Most dogs love getting the full spa treatment at Pampered Pooches, but a few are nervous about getting their paws wet." A chorus of barks joined the Pomeranian in doggy solidarity.

The old woman's eyes widened behind her thick glasses as Jaron's Newfoundland poked his massive head up to see what the racket was all about. The dog's thick black coat and calm demeanor meant more often than not he blended in as he sprawled half underneath the desk on the black tiled floor.

"Don't worry," Jaron said, scratching Bear's ears. "He's a furry ball of mush."

Mrs. Reynolds smiled politely but clutched her leather purse to her flower-covered bosom. It was hard to blame her. Bear really was a bear of a dog. A hundred-and-sixty-pound teddy bear.

Jaron leaned over and asked loudly, "How can I help you?"

The piercing screech of Jaron's name from within the salon drowned out her response. Wincing, he could only imagine what the high-octave sound did to sensitive pooch ears.

"I'm sorry." Jaron rose to his feet. "If you could excuse me for just a minute." It only took three steps to get across the cramped office space. He took a moment to center himself before opening the door. He wouldn't be any help if the dogs sensed his growing annoyance. His shadow nudged his hand with his big wet nose. After patting Bear on the head, Jaron opened the door and entered the hallway. The vibrant pink walls made him slightly nauseous as he moved quickly toward the salon area. When his best friend's parents had decided to escape the harsh Illinois winters for sunny Florida, they had handed over the keys to Stephen's childhood home. Rather than sell it, Stephen opted to remodel the three-bedroom ranch home, since its proximity to downtown made it relatively easy to switch the zoning from residential to commercial. The living room, spare bedrooms, and dining room were gutted to make room for the main salon and reception/boutique area. The garage was converted to storage and a kennel for dogs waiting to be groomed.

Jaron stifled a laugh as he scanned the main salon. Stephen's team of well-trained bathers, assistants, and groomers were running around like kindergarteners during recess. At the cutting and styling stations, a lab, a golden retriever, and a poodle wiggled and twisted on the slip leads attaching them to the waist-high stainless steel platforms. Only one of the three large-dog tubs along the back wall was occupied. A disgruntled Old English sheepdog sat unattended in the tub with a blob of suds on her shaggy gray and white head.

"Mel." Jaron spoke loud enough to be heard over echoing barks. Grabbing the dark-eyed woman by her sturdy shoulders, he turned her toward her charge. "Finish washing Buffy."

Melissa brushed her sweaty brown bangs off her forehead. "I swear I'll quit if he lets that Pom come back." Turning back toward the sheepdog, she weaved around a poodle whose hair was pinker than the walls. *Why on earth do people do that to their pets?* Jaron wondered. Stephen swore the dye was nontoxic, but Jaron doubted it was good for the dog's self-esteem.

Jaron spotted Stephen patting the back of a short blond woman in her early twenties that Jaron didn't recognize. *They served the Pom fresh meat? What had Stephen been thinking giving a new employee the Pom as a client?* Chaos was contagious in a pet salon. When a dog became agitated, the rest of the clients sensed the distress. The woman was crying in big gasping sobs and clutching her hand against her pink Pampered Pooches T-shirt. His best friend handed the woman off with alacrity to one of the cutters when he caught sight of Jaron approaching. Putting his hands on his ample hips, he said, "What took you so long?"

"I want you to promise…," Jaron said before being distracted by Stephen's hair. *Had his hair been like that this morning?* Jaron liked to think he would have noticed his friend's hair looking like a snow cone, with segments of red, yellow, and blue. Last he remembered, Stephen had bleached his hair to match Jaron's white-blond locks. *Maybe that had been like applying a basecoat before you paint?*

"Stop staring at my hair and save us from that shark."

Jaron held up a hand to touch his friend's closely cropped hair. "I can't help it. It looks delicious."

Stephen batted the hand away. "I did her nails and cut without any bloodshed. Just turn on your mojo and get her calm enough to finish the wash and style before she kills us all."

Jaron crossed his arms across his chest. "You said last time would be the last time you let that Pom come here." The Pom's name was Sweetie. There ought to be an award for most inappropriate name. Her reign of terror included ten different bite wounds and four stitches. She gave sharks a bad name.

Stephen looked over at the two assistants who were holding a towel up, preventing the shark from jumping down from the waist-high small-dog sink and slaughtering everyone. "The owner said he had gotten Sweetie therapy. He had a vet's note and everything."

"Banned for life, Stephen. I want you to promise."

Stephen jutted his bottom lip out like a toddler instead of the owner of a successful dog salon. "The owner is so apologetic. I just can't say no to him." He waved his hands. "And I think exposure to your psychic mojo is helping her. She barely broke the skin this time."

Looking at the mutinous faces of the staff, Jaron said, "Tell the owner to buy clippers and offer to teach him how to cut the hair himself."

Stephen blinked his big brown eyes. "Private lessons?"

Jaron nodded slowly. "You could offer to teach him after hours at his place. Just the two of you and a bottle of organic shampoo." *With the shark as a chaperon,* he thought. "You could light one of those doggy candles to set the mood." He left Stephen debating which candle scent would be better: "Splendor in the Grass" or "Friends to the Rescue." Jaron personally thought his friend should go for "Fart & Away," as in faraway, but that was probably the annoyance talking. He appreciated Stephen allowing him to run his pet psychic business from within the salon, but lately Jaron spent more time dealing with the salon's clients than his own.

Stepping over to the deep-set sink, Jaron gestured for the assistants to step back and took their place. Bear pressed against his hip. Attempting to ignore the assault on his ears from barks and yaps, Jaron focused his concentration on the pulsing energy around him. "Be calm," he requested, closing his eyes, not because he needed to, but because it unnerved people to watch his blue eyes stare vacantly into the distance. Stephen had tactfully described him as a creepy white-haired doll with glass eyes.

All of the dogs except the Pom complied. Her stuttered barking sounded like the rapid fire of a machine gun with helium bullets, making him wonder how a five-pound dog could be so freaking loud. Jaron opened his eyes and stepped closer. She looked like a drowned rat with her sable and white hair hanging in wet clumps. She lunged forward with her needle sharp teeth, almost taking a chunk out of his hand.

Bear nearly knocked Jaron to the ground as he nosed his way to the sink. The Newfie was just over three feet tall standing. When he placed his front webbed paws on the edge of the sink, he was nearly as tall as Jaron's six feet. Bear looked down at the Pom and made one deep bark that roughly translated to "be nice to my owner, you little shit." What did the Pom do when faced with a hundred and sixty pounds of irritated Newfie? She sneezed and then went back to barking.

"Let me give it a try, big guy," Jaron said, nudging Bear out of the way.

A year ago when the Pom first reacted so violently toward a groomer without warning, Jaron had taken a reading on the dog's diamond studded collar, fearing abuse. In reality, the owner (more like servant) overindulged and tolerated the dog's random rages without the slightest bit of reprimand. It wasn't at the same level as abuse, but it wasn't healthy for either party. Jaron felt a little guilty suggesting Stephen try to woo the guy with doggy candles. Stephen would eat the man alive.

Jaron zeroed in on the vibrating energy emanating from the Pom, isolating it from the other dogs. For most animals he could get a surface read of their emotions just by being in close proximity. To delve deeper he needed to either touch the animal or touch an object of emotional significance. His only option at the moment was to risk his fingers.

His concentration wavered when a woman asked, "Is he performing witchcraft?"

Looking over his shoulder, Jaron saw the blonde woman who'd been bitten on her first day at the salon.

"Shut up, Chrissy," Stephen said, making a sharp gesture at her.

Chrissy raised her chin. "I'm a good Christian and I can't be present for a satanic ritual."

Jaron shared a look with Stephen before snatching a towel from the glass shelves above the sink and scooping up the Pom. She gave one more yapping protest before settling down in his arms. "I'm calming an upset dog, not performing a satanic ritual."

Making the sign of the cross, Chrissy said, "You're attempting to draw on occult powers to commit an unnatural act."

Stephen jerked his head toward her. "Unnatural," he said, his voice rising to screeching levels. "Tell me you did not just call my best friend unnatural."

Chrissy's blue eyes widened as her boss stalked toward her. People had a tendency not to notice Stephen's broad and muscular frame until they pissed him off.

Looming over his employee, Stephen said, "He likes dick, too. Does that double his unnatural quotient?"

"Bear," Jaron said, making the big dog's ears perk up. He visualized what he wanted the Newfie to do. "Go babysit Stephen."

Bear gave him a doggy grin before trotting after Stephen. Message received.

"I didn't mean it like that," Chrissy squealed, and Jaron wondered if he would find his client hiding under the desk. He wouldn't blame Mrs. Reynolds. Lifting the bundle in his arms, he looked the Pom in the eyes. "See the trouble you caused."

The Pom licked the tip of Jaron's nose, and Jaron saw an image in his mind of her owner holding a bag of gourmet dog treats. Rolling his eyes, he walked over to his friend, who was complaining bitterly about being pinned against the wall by Bear.

"He's drooling on my five-hundred-dollar Gucci jeans!"

"You seriously spent five hundred dollars on jeans? And they call *me* crazy?"

Stephen glared. "We can't all get away with Goodwill chic."

Jaron looked down at his long-sleeved T-shirt and jeans. "Only the shirt is Goodwill. I splurged and got the jeans at Wal-Mart for ten dollars."

Stephen made a sound of disgust.

Chrissy's pale cheeks were blotchy as she looked away from her red-faced boss and glanced at Jaron. "Discriminating against a person for their sexual orientation is wrong. I wouldn't do that." She sounded like she meant it.

Jaron blinked. "Gay is okay but acting like Dr. Doolittle is the Devil's work?"

"Communicating with the Devil is a choice."

Jaron took a deep breath, resisting the urge to have Bear *accidentally* dump Chrissy into the tub. "I guess you're right. I chose to calm a dog you failed to control, because she's stressing out the other dogs and putting them at risk for injuries."

Glaring, Chrissy pointed a finger at the Pom. "I did everything I was supposed to for that hateful little dog."

Jaron held out the Pom for Stephen to take. "Dogs don't hate. People hate. Dogs can sense people's emotions and that's not voodoo talking. Scientists have studied it. She bit you because she was afraid that you wouldn't take care of her. Your fear and nervousness made her not trust you."

Chrissy bit her lip. "I'd... never hurt her."

Jaron nodded. "It's not entirely your fault. Her owner needs to grow a pair and make it clear that biting isn't an acceptable reaction. His overindulgence is making her insecure. But if you're going to work here, you need to learn to spot the signs of stress *before* the dog bites."

Jaron returned to his office with Bear in tow and apologized again to Mrs. Reynolds for making her wait so long. She unzipped her big leather purse, took out a Tupperware container of what looked like ash, and placed it on the desk. "I want you to do a reading on my cat, Mr. Pickles."

Jaron rubbed his forehead. "I'm sorry, but I'm not a medium. I can't get a reading on a deceased pet."

Her paper-thin hands trembled slightly as she picked up the container and placed it on her lap. "I had him for sixteen wonderful years, Mr. Greenberg. I just need to know that he's happy and at peace."

"There are pet psychics that... claim to be able to speak to deceased animals," Jaron told her reluctantly.

"You mean the ones who do it over the phone? Do you think they're real?"

Jaron winced. "I know my own abilities only work if I'm in close proximity to the animal or an object of importance. It's not my place to disclaim someone else's ability, but be careful if you use the phone. You can rack up a high bill quickly when the psychic is charging five or more dollars a minute."

"Even though you've only been open for a couple of years, you've gotten quite the reputation. Everything I've heard says you're the real thing. That God gave you a gift and you're using it with integrity."

Jaron felt his cheeks warm. "I'm glad some people think so."

"If you can't reach out to Mr. Pickles, then no one can," she said sadly.

"I have a theory about why," he started, unsure if he should voice it. When she leaned forward eagerly, he decided to continue. "I sense a kind of electromagnetic field that radiates from the animal. When the animal passes on, I think the people who were important to the pet absorb that energy. And when they think about the moments they shared with their pet, they can feel that energy pulsing through them," he said, placing his hand over his heart.

Mrs. Reynolds's eyes welled and Jaron scrambled to find a packet of tissues in his desk, kicking himself for opening his big mouth.

Accepting the tissues, Mrs. Reynolds said, "Thank you." She dabbed her eyes. "That's a beautiful theory and a great comfort." She wiped her nose and chuckled as Bear laid his enormous head on her lap. Petting Bear's head, she asked, "What do I owe you?"

Jaron shook his head. "I don't charge for a consult." He rose and helped her to stand.

She patted his arm. "I'll have my grandson bring by some of the chocolate caramel fudge I made this weekend."

"Homemade?" Jaron asked, his mouth watering.

She smiled. "I guess the rumors about you being a chocoholic were true too. I don't know how you manage it, being so trim, but all bakers love an enthusiastic eater."

"I'm definitely enthusiastic about anything chocolate." After asking Bear to stay, Jaron held the door for her and then followed her into the main salon.

The fur was flying once again and the scent of soap and wet dog permutated the air. He had escorted Mrs. Reynolds nearly to the door that led to the boutique entrance when she stopped abruptly. He followed her line of sight to a shih tzu getting her hair trimmed by Stephen.

"It looks just like Pixie," Mrs. Reynolds said.

It took Jaron a moment to realize what she meant, and then he had to agree. The white face and cream-colored ears looked very similar to the one on every news channel for the past two days. The dog that belonged to the boy who had been kidnapped.

"Such a terrible thing," she said, shaking her head. "Matt is such a sweet boy."

"Do you know the family?"

Mrs. Reynolds nodded. "The Wilsons live across the street from me. Do you know them?"

Jaron shrugged. "I went to one session of Mr. Wilson's yoga class last summer, but it turns out I have no sense of balance. He seemed like a nice person. I really hope Matt and Pixie are found safe and sound."

"God willing," she said before turning to leave.

Jaron returned from the reception area and approached the shih tzu, his thoughts drifting.

Stephen whispered, "They'll probably find that poor dog dead in a ditch."

"Pixie's not dead," Jaron said, rubbing under the dog's chin.

"How do you know?"

"I've met her. Mr. Wilson and Pixie are part of the pet therapy program at the hospital. The director has me do a reading on the animals interested in joining the program. I'd know if she was dead after doing such a close reading."

"God that's creepy."

"I guess creepy is better than evil," Jaron muttered, turning away and heading back to his office. Bear greeted Jaron like he'd been gone for hours instead of minutes, likely picking up on Jaron's irritation. "Good, boy," Jaron said, rubbing behind the Newfie's ears. He pressed the On button on his battered laptop and sat down at his desk.

A few minutes later, Stephen appeared in the doorway. He leaned against the frame. "Look, I know you're pissed, but—"

"Why should I be pissed? You drag me away from my client to rescue you from a killer Pom, and I get called a creepy devil-worshipper for my trouble."

Bear butted Stephen in the stomach, making him cry out as he lost his balance and landed on his ass.

Jaron wasn't sure where Bear got the idea to shove Stephen out the door, but the squeal Stephen made when Bear started licking his multicolored head was definitely Jaron's fault. "Let him up, Bear," Jaron said, stifling a laugh as he pushed up out of his chair.

"Get off me, Slobber Monster! I promise I'll fire the bitch."

Jaron held his hand out and pulled Stephen to his feet. "You can't fire her for her religious beliefs without asking for a lawsuit."

"I can fire her for refusing to work with you."

"I don't technically work for the salon, and we both know you need the help."

"Okay, this isn't how I was going to bring it up, but I need to talk to you about that." Stephen chewed his bottom lip. "Between the garage, the backyard, and the shed, we could start offering doggy daycare services. With a bit of a remodel, we'd have enough square footage for an indoor play area and still have room for storage."

"You think the Planning Commission would approve it? Won't residents worry about barking?"

"We soundproofed most of the house during the initial remodel. The only possible snag would be the outdoor area, but I talked with the commissioner. She doesn't think there will be much cause for objection, considering the noise from Main Street and the train, if we limit the number of dogs to twenty."

Jaron frowned, realizing how much thought had already been put into the idea. Stephen had converted the three-car garage, painting the walls, installing a tile floor, and concealing the garage door with an insulated curtain. Currently, the area was used for storage and to kennel the dogs as the groomers worked on them. Jaron started to ask where they'd put the kennels before he realized what Stephen intended. All that remained of Stephen's childhood home was the galley kitchen, which doubled as a break room for employees, Jaron's closet-sized office, and the master bedroom. The master bedroom was located to the left of the main salon, an ideal place to put the kennels once the current occupant got his shit out of there.

"It's not a big deal for me to move out," Jaron lied, trying to sound casual instead of panicked. "It was always supposed to be a temporary living arrangement. We both know the rent you're charging me for my room is borderline charity. It makes sense to use the space to expand." He attempted a reassuring smile. "And I should move into a place with some actual privacy."

"I would've gone bankrupt the first year if you hadn't been paying me that charity rent. But I don't want to kick you out. I want to make you a partner in the business. We'll draw up an agreement and split the profits sixty/forty."

Jaron stared at his friend. "Has using pet hair dye on your head caused brain damage?"

"How did you kno—" Stephen shooed away the question. "I'm serious about this, Jaron."

"What would I bring to the partnership? My two community college classes in business administration? I have almost no savings and no experience running a dog salon or a daycare. How does it make sense for you to hand over 40 percent ownership in your business?"

"You've been handling the finances and inventory for the salon since it opened, so don't tell me you don't have any experience. And you've been doing it for free."

"I would be paying four hundred a month to rent office space in town and that's in addition to renting an apartment. I'm getting the better deal, especially considering you conveniently neglect to cash my rent check when I'm short on customers." They both knew Jaron likely wouldn't be able to afford to keep the pet psychic business unless he started charging more per hour or got a second job. Feeling weary, Jaron sat on the edge of the desk.

Stephen wrapped his arms around Jaron's neck and hugged him tight. "I know how much you love helping people, and I wouldn't ask you to give it up, even though we both know you're barely scraping by. We can offer your services through the salon as one of the amenities. All you have to do is limit home visits to Sundays when the salon is closed and to give up crawling through Grandma's bushes looking for her lost cat." He kissed the top of Jaron's head. "Please don't be mad at me."

"I'm not mad," Jaron said, squeezing Stephen's arm. He sighed. "It would be nice not to have everything I own smell like wet dog."

Stephen's laugh sounded closer to a sob. "It'll take months to get building permits and approval for the expansion, so just be thinking about it. And you can always stay at my place once construction starts."

Jaron nodded in agreement, realizing there was another reason for him to move out. His official address was Stephen's apartment because it would be a zoning nightmare to have a converted residence be both a commercial site and an apartment rental. The only reason Stephen wasn't paying double occupancy on the apartment was that his uncle owned the apartment complex. If zoning officials figured out Jaron lived in the salon, they would likely slap Stephen with fines and put his approval at risk. Jaron needed to find a new address quickly.

JARON STARED at his HP laptop screen. *How can it only be 12:30?* He had three house call appointments starting at 5:00 p.m., and he needed to fill out the basic information for contract agreements for a biter, a chewer, and a howler. He would much rather hide in his room with the pound of fudge Mrs. Reynolds's grandson had dropped off twenty minutes ago.

There was a knock on the door followed by Mel poking her head in the office. "The Wilsons are here and they asked to talk to you."

"Me?"

Mel nodded. "Should I bring them back?"

"Uh… yeah." Jaron rose to his feet. "Of course."

Mel pushed the door open further and said, "He'd be happy to see you."

As they entered, Jaron gestured for the Wilsons to have a seat on the folding chairs in front of the desk. Mr. Wilson was a thin man in his early forties. His curly brown hair and matching brown eyes resembled the picture of Matt on the missing child poster Stephen had posted on the store bulletin board. Mrs. Wilson appeared to be a few years younger than her husband; she had hard features, straight black hair, and a pinched expression. The bags under her gray eyes were bloated and purple. While Mr. Wilson moved with the energy of a man on a mission, his wife settled into the seat like a broken old woman. Like a mother grieving for her child.

Mr. Wilson perched himself on the end of the chair with ramrod-straight posture and inhaled slowly, making Jaron think of the yoga package he'd ditched after only one session. Mrs. Wilson's cheeks colored as the sound of her husband breathing in and out echoed in the small office. Jaron remembered the breathing exercises and the irrational feeling of suffocation when he'd tried to complete them. Thinking about his breathing made him feel like he couldn't breathe.

"Thank you for agreeing to see us," Mr. Wilson said. "Mrs. Reynolds came by our house after talking with you and suggested we come see you. We're hoping you can help us."

The look on Mrs. Wilson's face said she didn't want to be included in the "we," but she kept her mouth shut as her husband continued. "It's not that we don't think the police are doing the best job they can under the circumstances. Chief Tucker called for assistance from the State Police right away, and he put us in contact with volunteer organizations. But we figure the more help available, the best chance of—" His voice faltered.

Leaning forward Mrs. Wilson asked, "What do you charge?" Her eyes looked like they'd been chipped out of a block of dirty ice.

Mr. Wilson made a sound of exasperation. "That's not important."

"How can you say that?" Mrs. Wilson asked, her voice rising.

"Because I'd hand over every last dime I have to get back my son."

"And you think I wouldn't?"

Jaron covered his mouth with his hand as the couple bickered back and forth. The amount of stress they must be under was unimaginable. A stranger had taken their child. Jaron could think of nothing to say to make that scenario more palatable. A deep, guttural bark made the humans in the room jump in their chairs. Bear was a much better communicator.

Jaron cleared his throat. "I charge ten dollars an hour with a two-hour minimum for a standard session and four hours for a search and recovery, plus travel expenses when applicable."

"Ten dollars? Minimum wage is eight fifty." Mr. Wilson traded a look with his wife. "Is that your normal rate?"

Jaron resisted the urge to sigh and instead handed Mr. Wilson a business card. "My rates are listed on the back."

Mr. Wilson squinted at the card before handing it to his wife. "Is this just a side job for the salon? Because I'd be willing to pay you more to focus on the case full-time."

"I do help out in the salon when I have time, but I'm not an employee. But I don't—"

"You can't possibly live off of ten dollars an hour."

Today was apparently the day for unsolicited business advice. And then Mr. Wilson dropped some astonishing information. "I get paid thirty dollars an hour to teach yoga."

Jaron's jaw dropped. *Thirty bucks an hour to teach people how to breathe?*

"I get sixty an hour for private sessions."

Jaron realized Mr. Wilson was the type of person who was convinced you had to pay more for something for it to be worth anything. "Other than a truck load of dog food every month, I don't have a lot of expenses. I guess I'm frugal by nature." When Mr. Wilson opened his mouth to speak, Jaron said, "But none of that really matters because I only accept cases where I think I can help, and I'm not clear on what you expect me to do."

"Mrs. Reynolds thinks you're the real thing. I remember when the pet therapy director had you attend the training session and evaluate the dogs. And I remember how much better Pixie got after that therapy session. Pixie is microchipped, and we sent flyers to every vet, animal hospital, and shelter within two hundred miles of here, but lots of people have shih tzus. We need a better way to find her."

"I can tell you Pixie is alive."

Placing his hands on the desk, he said, "You're sure?"

"Yes, but that doesn't mean… Matt is with her."

"You said search and recovery was one of the services you offer, right? So, I want to hire you to track Pixie. Even if it doesn't lead to Matt, it'll still be a clue that might help the police to find him." Mr. Wilson took hold of his wife's hand. "Maybe it's just the guilt talking, but I believe Matt is alive, and I want us to do everything we can to bring him home."

Jaron rubbed the back of his neck. "If the police are okay with it, I'd be willing to try."

DETECTIVE PAULO Silva added the finishing touches to the report on Dennis Peters. Peters was convicted on two counts of aggravated criminal sexual abuse of a ten-year-old girl. And he lived less than a mile from where six-year-old Matt Wilson was believed to have been abducted. Added to that, Peters's failure to notify his parole officer that he had switched jobs had put him at the top of Paulo's suspect list. However, interviews with Peters's employers and coworkers had confirmed that Peters was at work when the victim was abducted. Another dead end. This case would be a hell of a lot easier to solve if this town had street cameras.

Paulo had been surprised when Chief Tucker told him to keep tracking down the registered sex offenders even after the State Police had been called in to assist. The task force, led by Sergeant Devin Morris, had taken over the conference room on the first floor. The Stanton Police Station didn't have the numbers to handle such a complicated case without assistance. When he had moved to Stanton, Paulo had known he would eventually end up working with former ISP colleagues at some point, but why did they have to send Devin? This case was complicated enough without having to work under his ex-boyfriend.

Paulo scanned the contents of the report one last time. Like the other ten reports he had completed, there was nothing here that would help the task force and no reason for Paulo to have to deal with Devin directly. After hitting the Save button with more force than was necessary, he then sent two copies to the printer. Devin had mocked him for picking a town with less than thirteen thousand residents, where he'd be the token minority in the police department. Even knowing the demographics, Paulo hadn't been prepared for an all-white police station. He'd tried to explain that he was Brazilian, not Hispanic, to the few baffled people who asked him. They'd seemed equally baffled by the fact that he spoke Portuguese, not Spanish.

Paulo shook his head. He didn't have time to ponder the disturbing lack of diversity and cultural awareness in Stanton. He rose and walked over to the printer station. After picking up the report, he headed for the chief's office.

Knocking on the open door, he entered when the chief waved him in. Paulo handed him the report. "It looks like Peters is in the clear."

Chief Tucker ran a hand through his gray hair hard enough to make Paulo wonder if it was stress instead of genetics making his hair retreat from his shiny forehead.

"Close the door, son, and take a seat."

Surprised, Paulo complied with the request, wondering if he had missed something when investigating Peters. They had assigned a plainclothes officer to monitor Peters's activities.

"The family liaison officer has indicated that the Wilsons would like to bring in a local expert, Jaron Greenberg. Are you familiar with him?"

Paulo shook his head. "Is he a PI?"

"Of a sort." Chief Tucker gave Paulo a pained look. "He's a pet psychic."

"You are not serious," Paulo said before his better judgment could catch up with his mouth.

The chief sighed. "The statistics are telling the Wilsons the unthinkable. Their child was likely dead within three hours of the abduction. It's not hard to understand why they might reach out for any hope, no matter how implausible."

Paulo nodded. When he had worked for the State Police, he had seen enough missing child cases to know the doubts and second guesses plaguing the Wilsons. They were judging every parental decision under the unforgiving weight of hindsight. Why wouldn't they grasp for every scrap of hope? It was the scam artists that took advantage of their grief that were the real problem. "Do you need me to check the guy out? Find out if he has a record?"

Chief Tucker cleared his throat. "Sergeant Morris has asked that you be assigned to the task force in order to offer a local perspective as they work the case."

Paulo leaned back in his chair. "Patterson has lived here his whole life. I only transferred in two months ago. It doesn't make sense for me to offer the local perspective."

"I guess the fact that you worked with Sergeant Morris in the past is part of the reason. Patterson is a good cop with more seniority, but your experiences are more pertinent to this case."

Paulo knew the stats well. It was the reason he chose the Stanton Police Department. It had been three years since they had their last homicide. And while the department dealt with drugs and the Chicago gangs trying to muscle their way in, they were fortunate to see very little major crime. He had expected to be put back on patrol when he transferred to SPD, since most departments promoted from within. Nearly a decade as a detective with the ISP wouldn't matter in a new city. Instead of putting him back in a uniform, the chief had assigned him to the Investigations division, replacing a retiring veteran officer. It hadn't won him any favors with the boys in blue, but his fellow detectives had welcomed him.

Chief Tucker pointed a finger at Paulo. "Sergeant Morris asked for you and he's getting you. I'll be damned if I let this precinct be accused of not cooperating with the State Police."

"I don't mean to be disrespectful, sir." Paulo rubbed his clammy hands down his pant legs. It wasn't right to avoid working the case just because his ex-boyfriend was in charge of the task force. Matt Wilson deserved better. "I'll do whatever needs to be done to bring that child home."

The chief nodded. "Sergeant Morris wants you to appease the parents by meeting with Jaron Greenberg and giving him any assistance he needs. I've made it clear that I need you working on your other cases in addition to assisting Sergeant Morris."

Paulo wanted to ask why he had been assigned babysitting duty, but he knew the answer. His breakup with Devin two months ago hadn't been pretty. Devin had been given the perfect opportunity for a little revenge.

"You might think you're wasting your time talking to Jaron, but I don't believe that."

"You think the... pet psychic is real?" Paulo's thoughts veered in another direction. "Could he be connected to the case?"

"He isn't the perp, if that's what you mean."

"It wouldn't be the first time a perp pretended to be psychic."

"The video surveillance showed Matt Wilson left the hospital at 4:07 p.m. Jaron was twenty miles away at the time."

Paulo wasn't surprised the chief had the details of the case memorized. He might be in charge of a small time precinct, but he was sharp. "According to whom?"

"Me." The chief's cheeks flushed. "Since Heather moved in with me, we've been having trouble with my pug and her cat. Jaron was still there when I was called in about a possible abduction."

Maybe he had overestimated his new chief. "You really think this guy can talk to animals?"

"I know a week ago I had to take my pug to the vet for bite wounds." The chief pulled out his cell phone and fiddled with the buttons. "And this morning Heather sent me this," he said, displaying a picture of a Siamese cat and a pug curled together in a too-small cat bed.

It was so disgustingly adorable that Paulo had to fight not to smile. "Good with animals doesn't make him psychic."

"I've known Jaron his whole life. He was the first major case I caught as a detective. When he was four years old, his parents took him out to the forest preserve to experience the fall colors." Chief Tucker put finger quotes around the words "fall colors." With a shake of his head, he continued, "Jaron had been missing for two hours before they sobered up enough to contact the police."

Paulo had tracked down a group of liquored up teens in those woods his first week on the job. Miles of choking trees, sharp brambles, and snake holes. It was hard for an adult to navigate the twisting paths of thick foliage and tree roots, let alone a young child.

"We didn't have a K9 unit back then, so I called Nathan Jefferson and asked if we could use his hunting dogs. He tells me they've run off and his son is out looking for them. I head out to the parking lot where volunteers are being mobilized, and I see two hounds that look like Nate's dogs, a poodle, and a chocolate lab running by. I wondered about it, but with only an hour of daylight left and weather expected to drop into the 20s, I needed to get moving and find that boy before he froze to death.

"I drove the five miles to the forest preserve quick as I could. The chief started handing out search assignments. Then I see those dogs again, standing together and looking anxious. The lab stepped forward and started barking, going quiet as I approached it. I swear to God that dog stared at me like he was Lassie and I was the dumb shit who hadn't figured out Timmy was in the well. So I trotted after the dogs, and just about the time I'd decided I'd lost my mind, the dogs raced ahead, barking their heads off. I caught up to them and found them circled around this white-haired child covered in dirt and scratches. He put his little hand on the lab's head and said, 'Thanks for coming.'"

Paulo felt a chill race down his spine.

"I found that boy three miles away in the opposite direction of where his parents said they had last seen him. We would've never found Jaron in time without those dogs. I think God gave that boy a gift, probably as compensation for his good-for-nothing parents." The chief shrugged. "There are plenty of other stories." He pulled out his wallet, slid out a business card, and handed it to Paulo. "If there is even a chance Jaron can help, it would be wrong not to act on it."

The business card featured a close up picture of a man in his midtwenties and an enormous dog that looked like an all-black Saint Bernard. Jaron Greenberg had a mop of white blond hair that many boys have, but few retain as they age. Greenberg must have Photoshop skills, because no one had eyes that blue. Looking at the man's face, Paulo could understand the impulse to believe in him. The thought of someone so beautiful swindling people out of their hard-earned money was unthinkable. But bad guys came in all shapes and sizes, and from the sound of things, Greenberg's parents were likely excellent teachers.

"I think he's the real thing, but we can't have the press finding out we're consulting a psychic, even if it's at the request of the victim's family." Chief Tucker's gaze broke away from Paulo and focused on the unopened file on his desk. "There are some people who have a problem with what Jaron does, or with psychics in general. So when you go to visit him, try to be discreet."

Paulo understood the need to keep the public's confidence. Bringing in a psychic reeked of desperation, not a message they wanted to send to citizens. "I understand, sir," he said, rising to his feet.

"Talk to Sergeant Morris for the specifics."

Paulo had his phone out of his pocket before he exited the chief's office. Pulling up Devin's number, he hit the Send button. Devin picked up after only one ring, like he'd been expecting the call.

In lieu of a greeting, Paulo asked, "What is your problema, babaca?"

"Oh, he must be pissed if the Portuguese is slipping out."

Paulo could tell by his voice that Devin was smirking.

"I have ten active cases, Devin. I don't have time to babysit a psychic. Get one of your troopers to hold his hand."

"Get over yourself, Silva. Keeping the parents happy is important, especially in a case with this much media attention. Someone needs to be on babysitting duty and you're the low man on the totem pole at the SPD. You chose to hide in the land of pig shit and windmills. Now deal with it."

Paulo gritted his teeth. "I'm not hiding."

"The hell you're not. I'm one floor away, but you decided to bitch at me on the phone instead of in person." Devin sighed and his voice softened. "Eventually, everybody gets a case that gets to them, baby. But you work through it instead of running away from the job and the people who care about you."

"Maybe it was a mistake to transfer here, but staying in Springfield wasn't an option."

"You're wasted in this town and you know it. You should be thanking me for taking you away from investigating cow tippings and bootleg liquor." Devin snorted. "And from what I hear, you're the perfect man for this job."

"What are you talking about?"

"People in this town love to talk about their resident psychic. Especially since he's shacked up with Stephen Miller, the gay son of the former mayor."

Devin could perform a soft interrogation better than anyone Paulo had ever seen. He used his bleached-blond hair, pretty-boy face, and toothpaste commercial smile to his full advantage, and people willingly spilled their guts. "Are you thinking Greenberg's involved? Because the chief is his alibi."

"Just because he didn't do the snatch, doesn't mean he isn't involved. Hell, this could be some publicity stunt."

Paulo wished that was the case, but his gut told him otherwise. "What's your read on the parents? Would they be involved in something like that?"

"Mr. Wilson is trying hard to stay positive, but he's tearing himself apart with guilt. If it's a stunt, no way does he know about it. Mrs. Wilson might be a possibility. She's a real cold fish, that one." Devin sighed. "Odds are Greenberg's either a con artist or a wackjob."

"I still don't understand what you want me to do. Do you want me to investigate Greenberg?"

"I need you to put on those ass-hugging jeans I know you've got stashed in your apartment, and take the guy around town to let him soak up his supposed psychic vibes. If people see Greenberg walking around with a uniform, word will spread quickly. If tongues are wagging about their newest detective hanging out with a gay man, then they won't be wondering if the police have resorted to hiring a psychic to save Matt Wilson."

"Are you seriously fucking asking me to pretend I'm on a date with this guy?"

"Who said anything about a date?" Devin said, feigning innocence. "Though I hear there's a great Chinese place on Main Street."

"Keep it up, *babaca*, and you will get your face-to-face meeting with me when I smash your teeth in."

Devin snickered. "I love you too, Silva," he said, before ending the call.

Sighing, Paulo pressed the End button on the phone.

THE OUTSIDE of Pampered Pooches looked like an aging ranch home, with a neon pink sign attached to peeling cream siding the only evidence of commerce. It was located at the far end of what was referred to as "downtown"—a fallacy upheld vehemently by residents even as small business owners buckled under the strain of the mega-stores located twenty miles away in the next town over. As Paulo stepped inside the dog salon, it was clear that most of the original interior had been gutted by someone with an unhealthy obsession with Pepto-Bismol. Above a pink-checkered couch was a pop art dog portrait of a German shepherd. It looked like someone had used pieces of brightly colored magazines to fill in the line drawing in an abstract collage. Paulo admired the technique. Somewhere buried in his overflowing storage container was a collection of Andy Warhol prints. Behind a small receptionist's desk was a clear plastic wall that separated the boutique from the grooming area.

A guy in his midtwenties with clown hair and an impressive set of guns stretching out the sleeves of his pink sparkly T-shirt was placing bottles of dog shampoo on a set of glass shelves.

"How can I help you?" the guy asked, not even attempting to be subtle as he scanned Paulo from his dark hair to his boots. It unnerved Paulo to be dressed so casually in jeans, a black T-shirt, and a black leather jacket while working, but he wasn't about to give Devin another reason to bitch at him. This wasn't supposed to look like an official police visit.

"Is Jaron Greenberg available?"

The man's appraising look vanished, replaced with an icy glare. "Follow me." He shoved the box of shampoo at the receptionist before stomping past Paulo and through the open doorway.

Paulo assumed the man in question was Stephen Miller, owner of the dog salon. He didn't intend to scurry after him like a dog headed for a flea bath.

"I wouldn't keep Stephen waiting," the receptionist whispered. "He's in a terrible mood."

"What's got him so pissy?" Paulo asked.

She snuck a peek at the doorway and leaned forward. "He and Jaron are fighting. Bear took Jaron for a walk to cool off."

Paulo raised his brows. "Who's Bear?"

"Jaron's Newfoundland dog. He doesn't like it when people yell at Jaron."

Before Paulo could ask another question, Stephen bellowed, "I'm waiting!"

The receptionist made a shooing motion.

Seeing Stephen at the end of the hallway with his hands on his hips made Paulo wish he had a bucket of water handy.

Stephen unlocked a neon pink door on the right and entered. With great reluctance, Paulo followed him inside. The room hardly qualified as an office. Stephen grunted and twisted his plump frame to get around a black pressed wood desk that was nearly the width of the room. Paulo looked at the plastic folding chairs in front of the desk and opted to stand, leaning against the wall.

"I take it you know why I'm here."

"The Wilsons guilted Jaron into helping. After something so horrible, it's no wonder they're desperate. Why Chief Tucker is going along with it is beyond me."

"You don't think Jaron can help?"

"I know he can, but that doesn't mean he should. Tracking Pixie means tracking the sick fuck who took her and that boy. It's your job to take that kind of risk, not Jaron's."

"I happen to agree, but it's Jaron's call, not mine."

Stephen rolled his big brown eyes. "Jaron is incapable of saying no if he thinks he can help. But he told the Wilsons he wouldn't accept the case if the police object. So object already," he said with a wave of his hand.

Paulo found that condition interesting. Risky unless Jaron was relying on the chief's support or the parents' insistence. "It sounds like you know Jaron really well."

"I would hope so. He's been my best friend for nearly twenty years."

"And he lives with you, right?"

Stephen's dark eyes darted back and forth. "Yes."

Paulo wondered why Stephen was lying. Everything about the man screamed "out and proud" and people clearly knew Jaron was also gay. *Maybe Jaron lives with a closeted lover? Or their fight had been a lover's quarrel?* Pushing away from the wall, Paulo stepped forward until his legs were pressed against the desk. "Are you and Jaron a couple?"

Stephen crossed his arms, making his biceps bulge. "How is that any of your business?"

Paulo cocked his head. "Or maybe you just wish you were?"

Stephen's face said Paulo had nailed it, but he recovered quickly. "I'm not sure I can tell you. I'm pretty sure the things I did with him when he was sixteen were illegal."

Paulo's next question was sidelined when a blur of black fur pounded into the office and scrambled under the desk.

"Am I forgiven, Slobber Monster?" Stephen asked, rubbing the massive dog's ears with what appeared to be genuine affection.

The dog placed his paws on Stephen's lap and gave him a sloppy kiss. Stephen made a sound of disgust as he wiped his face.

Paulo heard a soft voice behind him.

"Does that mean it's safe to come into my office?"

Paulo turned toward the door to see a young man poke his head around the corner.

Stephen snorted. "I'll even let you lick me too, if you sit on my lap."

Stepping all the way into the cramped room with his arm extended, the young man said, "I'm Jaron Greenberg."

Paulo shook his hand, trying very hard not to stare. He bit down on the urge to say something horrifying cliché as "your picture doesn't do you justice." It was the truth, but one he was loath to admit even to himself. "Detective Paulo Silva."

Stephen made a loud sigh and rose. "I'll leave you to deal with the Chicano pig."

"Brazilian pig."

"Whatever," Stephen said with a huff.

The tight quarters made moving in the office like solving a sliding picture puzzle. Paulo stepped to the side and Jaron had to move backward to allow Stephen to exit. Paulo could feel the heat from Jaron's body as he stepped back into the office and walked around to the desk.

"I'm sorry to keep you waiting," Jaron said, sitting down. "I wasn't expecting to hear back from the police so quickly."

Paulo picked up a business card from a stack on the desk and read it. "Lost pet retrieval, pet communication, behavioral problems, and new pet integration. How exactly can you help the investigation?"

"I honestly don't know that I can, but Mr. Wilson wants me to try anyway."

"How do you know the Wilsons?"

"Pamela, the director of Healing Paws Therapy Dogs, has me come in to do readings on the dogs applying to be part of the program. I met Pixie during one of those sessions, and I've also taken a yoga class with Mr. Wilson."

"How long have you've been working with the therapy program?"

"It's been about two years, I think, but I'm not an official volunteer."

"Was Matt at the therapy training the day you met Pixie?"

"I don't actually know. I only meet the dogs. Pamela puts me in an exam room and brings in each dog to meet with me. It's easier for me to get a reading if there are fewer distractions."

Paulo opened his notebook and took a few notes, more interested in observing Jaron than remembering the conversation. People tended to get nervous when they think they've said something noteworthy. "Do you only get readings from pets or can you read people as well?"

"If I get a reading from a person, it is directly related to a pet, usually their own. The information is usually very general. For instance, I know you don't have any pets and you never have."

Paulo cocked his head. "Close, but I had one when I was a kid," he said, wanting to see how Jaron responded to being challenged.

Jaron shook his head. "Not true." His vibrant blue eyes slid shut and he pursed his cupid lips. "Your first grade classroom had a pet gerbil. It died before it was your turn to take the pet home for the weekend." The words were spoken with confidence, with no attempt to seek reassurance. Jaron believed what he was saying. There was only one problem. Paulo didn't remember ever having a classroom pet, let alone one that died. The scenario was a complete fabrication that Jaron apparently believed. Devin had been right. Beautifully delusional.

Paulo worked to keep disappointment from his voice. Disappointment for what, he didn't know. "Do I have your assurance you won't investigate the case without my approval?"

"Yes," Jaron said quietly.

"I'll be in touch," Paulo said.

CHAPTER 3

HEARING THE jingle of the door handle, Jaron groaned and dragged his black comforter over his head. "Go away."

The sounds of the salon intensified as the door opened. "It's almost eight," Stephen said. "Why are you still in bed? You can't be sick. Germs could never get past all the dog fur." He snickered. "So that's why. Bear is holding you hostage."

Jaron felt the mattress dip under Stephen's weight as his friend crawled onto the bed.

"Move over, Sir Drools-a-lot."

The bed squeaked in protest as Bear moved to the foot of the bed, draping himself over Jaron's shins and feet. Stephen settled next to Jaron and placed his arm across Jaron's chest. Between the two of them, Jaron could barely breathe. It wasn't an unusual feeling.

Stephen pulled down the comforter. "Are you hiding because I talked about expanding the salon? Nothing is set in stone. It would probably be smarter to put it off a couple of years."

Jaron rubbed his eyes. "It's a good idea, especially since Doggy Daycare will be closing at the end of the year when Mrs. Lorry retires. She would probably be thrilled to sell you some of the equipment taking up space in her backyard and shed."

"Does that mean you'll become a partner with me?" Stephen asked, sounding hopeful.

"I'm not sure about that yet, but you can count on my help either way."

Stephen didn't look satisfied with that answer, but he let the subject drop for the time being. "So why the groundhog act? Shouldn't you be making yourself pretty for the detective?"

"He won't call me," Jaron grumbled. "He thinks I'm a fraud."

"No, he came here thinking you were a fraud. He left thinking that you are a gorgeous nutjob."

Jaron's cheeks warmed. "Is that supposed to make me feel better?"

"Guys like that don't fuck frauds." Stephen clucked his tongue. "And you want him bad."

"I do not," Jaron said, even as his brain declared him a liar, bringing to mind an image of the detective. Detective Silva's light green eyes stood out against his thick black eyebrows and bronze skin. But it was his voice that Jaron remembered the most. Instead of a flat, steady rhythm, the words seemed to roll off the detective's tongue like the highs and lows of a rollercoaster.

"He'll call. He won't be able to stop himself." Looking oddly serious, Stephen leaned down, bringing their lips together in a soft kiss.

Jaron's jaw dropped in surprise and Stephen deepened the kiss. Stephen tasted like cherry ChapStick and chai tea.

The ring of a cell phone had Stephen pulling back. He snorted. "Told you so." After rolling to the side, he stood up and headed toward the door without a backward glance. "Don't keep the detective waiting."

The phone continued to ring, managing to sound as annoyed as the likely caller. Jaron answered the call. "Hold on." He covered the receiver. "Wait," he called out to Stephen.

Stephen paused with his hand on the doorknob, but he didn't turn around.

Jaron had no idea what to say. They had volumes of unspoken words between them, but outside of one drunken, teenage groping session, their friendship had been purely platonic. Until now. The idea of Stephen wanting more had never even occurred to him. "I'm sorry, Stephen," Jaron said uselessly.

"I know you are," Stephen said, sounding hoarse. He opened the door and left.

PAULO FOUND a parking space a few stores down from the dog salon and put in a call to Jaron. He hadn't been expecting the first words out of Jaron's mouth to be an order to "hold on." Listening carefully, he heard Jaron apologize but couldn't make out the reply. When Jaron came back to the phone, Paulo said, "It's Detective Paulo Silva. Are you able to meet with me this morning?"

Sounding distracted, Jaron said, "Okay, just give me a few minutes."

Paulo's gaze drifted down as Jaron exited the salon. Jaron's long-sleeved blue shirt and jeans looked worn from use rather than design, a stark contrast to his friend Stephen's wardrobe. Yesterday, Paulo had noticed Stephen wearing the kind of high-end designer jeans Devin coveted. Yet Jaron looked better than either Stephen or Devin without even trying, worn-out clothes and all.

"Morning," Paulo said as Jaron approached the Ford Explorer like he expected to be smacked in the nose with a newspaper.

"G-good morning. How can I help you, detective?"

"Let's go for a ride." Paulo opened the passenger door.

Jaron hesitated for a few seconds before getting into the SUV.

Paulo walked around to the driver's side and got behind the wheel. "According to your website, you get readings off objects that are special to pets. Is that right?"

"Yes," Jaron said, his white brows puckered.

Paulo worked to keep his expression neutral. He pulled out a toy from the pocket of his leather jacket and handed it to Jaron. "What can you tell me about the dog it belongs to?"

Jaron sighed deeply. "Nothing, Detective Silva."

Paulo cleared his throat. "I need you to call me Paulo."

"Okay," Jaron said, drawing out the word.

Paulo swore under his breath. "Uh, this is supposed to look like a dat—er—unofficial visit."

"Oh, Chief Tucker did mention it was important not to talk to the press about the case because it could be bad if the kidnapper heard the police were bringing in a psychic. I'd never do anything to put Matt's life at risk."

Changing the subject, Paulo asked, "Why can't you tell me about the dog?"

Jaron made a small, jittery movement with the toy. "It's a cat toy."

Paulo squinted at the toy. "It's shaped like a dog. How can it be a cat toy?"

Jaron brought the toy to Paulo's nose. "Cat. Nip."

Paulo snorted, getting a whiff of the sharp herbal scent. "Fine, you got me. What can you tell me about it?"

Jaron tossed the toy back and forth between his hands. "It belongs to a very confused cat who thinks her name is Honeybunch, Sweetheart, or possibly Button."

Paulo's lips twitched. "Button?"

Jaron nodded. Taking on a southern drawl that matched Paulo's neighbor perfectly, he said, "Aren't you just cute as a button?"

Paulo gaped at him, wondering how the hell Jaron knew that. He hadn't made the decision to stop off at Mrs. Smithe's apartment until he was leaving this morning. There was no way Jaron could have seen him going into her apartment, and then gotten to the pet salon without Paulo spotting him. The best scam artists had the ability to read people as well as the top police profilers could. Combined with extensive research, it made everything they said sound plausible. That seemed like a lot of effort for a guy who charges ten dollars an hour.

Paulo cleared his throat. "I've arranged to have us go by the Wilson's house to pick up whatever you need, and then we can head over to where Matt was last seen."

Jaron's shoulders slumped.

THE WILSONS' living room had an odd combination of country furniture and exotic decor. A bronze frog sitting in a yoga position was on a white painted coffee table. A throw blanket that looked like a sari was draped on a blue-checkered couch. The scent of sandalwood was so strong it made Jaron's eyes water.

"My husband is at yoga," Mrs. Wilson said, making it sound like an accusation.

"Would you like us to come back at a different time?" Detective Silva asked.

Mrs. Wilson's eyes drifted to a collection of photographs on the wall. "My husband believes very strongly that you can help. He's been researching psychics since we talked with you. He said a lack of faith can make it difficult for some psychics to use their ability because it creates a negative energy that can disrupt the reading."

"It doesn't work that way for me." Jaron smiled wanly. "Whether you believe me or not won't affect my reading."

Mrs. Wilson's shoulders sagged, a bit of the stiffness in her body releasing. Pointing to a bright red toy box, she said, "That's where we keep most of Pixie's toys."

Peering into the toy box, Jaron saw rubber bones, nylon stuffed animals, and other toys. His gaze was drawn to a blue rubber ball the size of a tennis ball. It was far too big for Pixie to carry in her mouth, but Jaron found himself picking it up.

Mrs. Wilson made a startled gasp, and then Jaron was sucked into a memory. Closing his eyes, he saw a toddler sitting on the carpet. The child's delighted laugh echoed in Jaron's mind. He watched a scene play out in slow motion over and over again. "Matt used to roll the ball on the ground and Pixie would pounce on it. He used to call her PP." As he opened his eyes, he noticed Mrs. Wilson wiping at her cheeks.

"It's Pixie's favorite toy. She bats it around the house like she's a cat after a mouse."

"Matt and Pixie have a strong connection. He takes care of her, right?"

"Matt's chores were... are to feed her, brush her, and clean up after her outside."

Jaron had seen the look in Mrs. Wilson's eyes before, of wanting to believe but not wanting to have her hopes crushed.

"Would you excuse us for a moment, Detective Silva?" she asked.

Detective Silva's lips thinned to a hard line. "I'll be in the SUV."

Mrs. Wilson waited until the detective had left to speak again. "There isn't anything I wouldn't do to get back my child, Jaron. I had three miscarriages before having Matt." Her voice broke. "I can't lose him too."

Jaron bit back on the urge to murmur platitudes. The odds of her ever seeing her son again were slim to none, if the press coverage was to be believed.

Mrs. Wilson rubbed her nose. "I have money saved that I can give you. Take the money and tell my husband that you can't work this case. I don't want the detectives chasing after non-existent leads when they should be focusing on finding my child."

Jaron felt an ache in the back of his throat. "I don't want your money. I promise you that I will walk away from this case if I'm not damn sure I can help."

"You can't help Matt." Mrs. Wilson turned away and headed down the hallway.

CHAPTER 4

THE PARK adjacent to the hospital barely qualified for the title. It consisted of a small slime-covered pond, one lonely weeping willow, and a few scattered benches. The clear skies overhead and mild spring weather couldn't chase away the bleakness. A horde of geese harassed a young woman pushing a stroller as she attempted to walk around the paved path that surrounded the pond. Park visitors either had to walk or find a parking space on Camilla Road. Paulo opted to park at the far end of the hospital lot instead.

Strangely subdued after his talk with Mrs. Wilson, Jaron exited the SUV, holding the ball in his hand in a tight grip. He walked in a slanted line toward the road that separated the park from the hospital parking lot. After a couple of minutes, he stopped. Paulo didn't need to look around to know they were at the edge of the hospital parking lot's surveillance video. The very spot Matt disappeared. *How the hell had Jaron found the location?* His department hadn't sent the video to the media, opting to send screenshots of Matt exiting the hospital instead since his visibility was better. Jaron must have connections in the hospital. *Could someone in security have talked to him?* It was doubtful Jaron had seen the footage. Officers had arrived at the hospital thirty minutes after Matt left his father's side, and secured the footage immediately.

Paulo's line of thinking derailed when Jaron stumbled. Arms flailing, Jaron would have fallen if Paulo hadn't grabbed him.

"Are you all right?"

Jaron didn't answer right away. His eyes were focused on something in the distance. Up close, Paulo could see a ring of gold around Jaron's irises. The morning sun made his long, thick lashes look like white feathers.

Jaron blinked rapidly. "I'm okay... thanks."

Paulo unhooked his arms from around Jaron's waist and took a step back.

Jaron stepped on the road, causing Paulo to grab him again and yank him backward. A station wagon came within inches of clipping Jaron. "Jesus, watch where you're going!"

Jaron looked chagrined. "Sorry, I don't normally do this without Bear."

Paulo stared at him. "The dog is in charge of making sure you don't end up roadkill?"

Jaron patted him on the arm. "I'm sure you'll do just as good a job."

Paulo wasn't sure whether to be offended by the comparison or not. Since Jaron seemed to take better care of his dog than himself, Paulo settled on feeling flattered that Jaron was trusting him.

They crossed the road and started walking on the dying grass of the park.

After about a dozen steps, Jaron stopped. "The boy fell here, spilling his treats and scraping his hand and knee."

Interest piqued in spite of himself, Paulo made an effort to make his voice sound bored. "What kind of treats?"

"It looks like chips of some kind. Doritos maybe, going by the shape and color."

"How can you tell? I thought dogs were colorblind."

Jaron shook his head. "Dogs do see in color, but they have less of a range than humans. I'm seeing a bag that looks dark yellow, meaning it's likely orange or red." He frowned. "I guess the bag could actually be brown, but I can't think of a brand that fits that description."

"So you're guessing," Paulo pressed, wanting to see how Jaron would react.

Jaron sighed. "Yes, detective. I'm making an educated guess based on what I see."

Paulo wondered if Jaron had toured the house with Mrs. Wilson. Maybe he saw a bag of Doritos on her kitchen table? The forensic team had found trace amounts of Matt's blood along with several Doritos in this very location. Looking on the ground, Paulo could make out slight depressions in the grass where trace markers had been placed. Jaron either had great vision or he'd scouted the area earlier.

Jaron knelt on the ground and placed the ball on the grass with his hand pressed against it; a deep line appeared between his white brows. "A woman came to help the boy. Pixie doesn't know her smell and she doesn't like her, but Pixie knows she is supposed to be good because she's wearing her special therapy vest."

"Why doesn't she like the woman?" Paulo asked, surprised by the gender of the supposed abductor. The news media had reported an unknown man in a white van as being in the area on the day of the abduction. He'd figured Jaron would parrot the reporters instead of implicating a female abductor, the rarest type of offender in these types of cases.

"The woman touched Pixie and said the word 'vet.'"

A female abductor was an angle Paulo hadn't considered since they'd extensively interviewed family and friends of the Wilsons during initial days of the investigation. Was there someone they missed? Matt was too heavy for the average woman to just scoop him up if he resisted. Claiming to be a concerned vet or that the dog needed a vet would be a good way to convince a boy who loved his dog to go with her.

Jaron made a noise in the back of his throat, drawing Paulo's attention back to him.

"Are you all right?" Paulo asked, crouching down next to Jaron. Jaron's face looked drained of color. When Jaron didn't respond, Paulo touched his hand. "Jesus, you're freezing."

"I'm okay," Jaron said, sounding anything but okay. His hands trembled visibly. "It's strange. I'm getting more details than usual."

"Have you eaten today? You're looking a little pale."

"There wasn't time. I was still in bed when you called." Jaron frowned. "Stop distracting me."

Paulo resisted asking why Jaron was sleeping at the salon instead of at Stephen's apartment. "What's different about this reading?"

"Normally, I only get visual or auditory impressions, but I'm actually getting smells too. The sharp scent of Matt's fear and something else from the woman. Dogs have twenty-five times more olfactory receptors than humans, so that's why I've always assumed I don't get smells and only limited hearing."

"Or maybe your blood sugar is crashing and you're craving steak and eggs?"

Jaron grabbed Paulo's arm, nearly toppling them both in the process. "Eggs!"

"The woman smells like eggs?"

"Rotten eggs," Jaron said, rising to his feet. "She smells like rotten eggs." His eyes rolled back into his head and his knees buckled.

Paulo only had enough time to keep Jaron's head from thumping against the ground. "Hey, Jaron," he said, tapping the man's cheek. "Wake up for me, pal." When Jaron didn't respond, Paulo checked his pulse, his concern rising as he felt the too-fast beat. "Dammit, so much for keeping a low profile." He pulled out his phone to call the conveniently close hospital.

Jaron opened his unreal blue eyes before Paulo could punch the Send button.

"If you tell me you're okay," Paulo growled, "I'll beat you unconscious and then call 911."

Jaron put his hands on the top of his head. "Bear is a much nicer sidekick. God, my head hurts."

"Are you diabetic, hypoglycemic, or just an idiot?"

Groaning, Jaron sat up. "None of the above?"

"*Você está louco*," Paulo muttered.

Jaron stared at Paulo blankly. "I have no idea what you said, but it sounded hot." Covering his face with his hands, he asked, "Can we just pretend I didn't say that out loud?"

Paulo wished Jaron hadn't said it. The words put dangerous thoughts in his head. "Let me help you stand," he said, hearing the gruffness in his own voice. Wrapping his arm around Jaron's waist, Paulo lifted him to his feet. "I think we should take you over to emergency care to get you checked out."

"No insurance," Jaron said, taking a wobbly step. "I'll be fine. Can you take me back to the salon?"

"You need to eat before you go back to work." Paulo grabbed Jaron's arm and steered him toward the parking lot. "Let's go to the Main Street Café for a quick bite."

"I have a client coming in this morning," Jaron protested. "There's food at the salon I can eat."

"Food or emergency room. You pick."

Jaron grumbled something that sounded like "as stubborn as Bear." After they'd slowly made their way back to the car, Paulo opened the door and ushered Jaron inside. After getting into the driver's seat, he turned on the SUV and set the heat to high. "I wasn't kidding about the emergency room. You're white as a sheet."

Jaron massaged his forehead. "Why do you care? You think I'm a fake."

"You're not faking a pulse rate in the low hundreds or skin so pale you're practically transparent. Does this normally happen when you try to get a reading? Because if it does, insurance or not, you need to be checked out by a doctor."

"Normally, I get a little tired, but nothing like this. It was like a sensory overload or something." Jaron shivered in spite of the stifling heat. "Take me back to the salon, please."

Paulo put the SUV in drive without another word. Once on the main road, he took a detour to the right.

"It's a left turn to get back to the salon."

"I need to make a quick stop," Paulo said, pulling into the drive-thru for Country Donuts.

"Are you getting donuts?"

"Who said anything about donuts?" Paulo groused. "Why can't I go here for the bran muffins or bagels? Not all cops eat donuts, you know."

Jaron's eyes widened. "I wasn't stereotyping. I was just surprised."

Paulo gave him a sideways look. "Yeah, your pal Stephen doesn't have a problem doing it."

Jaron's cheeks flushed, bringing some much needed color to his face. "I'm sorry about him calling you a pig. It was me he was annoyed with. He shouldn't take it out on you."

Paulo grinned. "I don't mind being called a pig since it stands for pride, integrity, and guts, but just 'cause I'm dark-skinned, everyone in this town thinks I'm from México." He moved forward in line until he was in front of the speaker and rolled down the driver's window. "What do you want?"

Jaron licked his lips. "A chocolate donut with chocolate icing, please."

Paulo pulled his eyes away from Jaron's luscious mouth.

When the fast-food attendant greeted them, Paulo said, "I'd like two chocolate donuts with chocolate icing… and one vanilla glazed."

Driving around to the window, he waved Jaron off when he went for his wallet. After he paid for the donuts, he handed the bag to Jaron. "Those are for you. Eat up."

"You don't want one?" Jaron asked, holding up the vanilla donut wrapped in wax paper.

Paulo snatched the donut out of his hand. "These things are terrible for you," he said, before taking a big bite of the sweet cake. *Pure Heaven.*

Jaron looked amused. "Are you sure pig doesn't stand for plain, iced, and glazed?"

"Eat your donut," Paulo said, shoving down the urge to smile.

AFTER TAKING Jaron back to the pet salon, Paulo reluctantly put in a call to Devin. Devin suggested they meet at a nearby café. The coffee at Main Street Café was always hot and the hash browns crispy, making it Paulo's favorite place to eat no matter the time of day. With burnt orange carpet, pastel colored booths, and generic Southwest artwork, the café was the height of restaurant decor if you were a time traveler from the eighties.

Paulo took a seat on the booth across from Devin, who looked oddly out of place in his thousand dollar gray Prada suit. When they'd first met, Paulo remembered being impressed that a trust-fund baby had chosen to be a cop. They had been friends back then. They should have stayed that way.

"How did it go with Doctor Doolittle?" Devin asked, pouring creamer into his coffee.

"It was strange. He took me right to the spot where we found the trace on the grass."

Devin paused with the coffee cup halfway to his mouth. "Maybe he was nearby when CSI was working the scene?"

Paulo snorted. "CSI? We have four detectives on staff, Devin. Patterson and two uniforms collected the trace. How can you be working this case and not know that?"

Devin ignored the question, taking a deep drink of coffee. "Are you thinking this guy might be the perp?"

"No, but I don't think we can rule out a leak in the department." Paulo gave Devin a brief summary of what Jaron had said. "It's possible he's paying someone for info, though I don't know how he affords it. His rates are dirt cheap. And if he's got inside info, then why was he claiming a woman was the perp?"

"Maybe he just gets off on the attention? You said it was strange. Why? Because he decided to make his bullshit different from the newspaper account of the abduction?"

Paulo took a sip of black coffee, the bitterness chasing away the sweet taste of donut from his mouth. "It was pretty warm today for March, but when I touched his hand, it was ice cold."

"Maybe he had a mini ice pack in his pocket or tucked under his shirt to give his hands that touched-by-death feeling."

Paulo shook his head. "I was close enough to know he wasn't carrying an icepack."

Devin's eyes narrowed. "Is that right?"

Paulo shifted in his seat. "He stumbled and—"

"And you swooped in to catch him."

"I'd be a lousy pretend boyfriend if I let him face-plant on the ground."

Sounding annoyed, Devin said, "He was reading you, not psychic energy."

"I figured as much, but I'm thinking he might have some sort of condition like low blood sugar. His face went sheet white right in front of me and he collapsed. It took a few seconds for him to come around."

"Drugs?"

"Maybe," Paulo agreed, not liking the idea. "Hard to imagine the chief hiring an addict to come to his house and help his dog."

Devin sneered. "You want it to be a medical condition because you like this guy even if he's a freak. I've seen the file on Greenberg's parents. They were both lowlife dopers."

"So what? Your parents are great and *you* turned out to be an asshole."

Grinning, Devin said, "Fuck you."

"I don't think today was a total loss, because it got me thinking. We need to take another look at the hospital."

"We interviewed everyone there that day or who might have come into contact with the vic previously."

"As I see it, there are two scenarios that make sense," Paulo said, falling back into the routine of verbal tennis with Devin. "Either it was a crime of opportunity, meaning the perp saw the boy alone and decided to act. Or the perp stalked the vic prior to the abduction. From the video surveillance, we know that Matt and Pixie left the hospital on their own through a side exit and no one followed for ten minutes."

Devin nodded. "I think we can safely say we ruled out familial abduction. Video surveillance of the father confirmed his story and several co-workers confirmed that the mother was at work. We also talked to the extended family and close friends in and out of the state."

"The only possible witness said she saw a thin man wearing a baseball hat in a rusted white van drive by when she was jogging near the time we think the snatch took place. But she couldn't give us much in the way of an ID. If a van like that had been lurking in the Wilson's neighborhood, we would've found someone who'd seen it. An old white van with covered back windows might as well be called the Pedo-mobile."

"The perp could've been driving a shiny SUV for all we know."

"Yeah, maybe," Paulo conceded, not convinced. "The therapy dogs are on a set rotation. I'm wondering if the perp might've talked to someone about the program in the weeks prior to the abduction. Perp asks a nurse about the program, not about the vic specifically. I bet it wouldn't be unusual for people to be interested or ask questions about dogs in bright-colored vests walking around the hospital."

"Meaning the perp could be a patient or a visitor who was there on one of the days Pixie and Matt were at the hospital." Devin shook his head. "Sounds like a long shot, considering the perp would have no way of knowing they would go outside. According to the father, it was Matt's job to make sure Pixie went to the bathroom prior to leaving for the hospital. It was one of his daily chores. I'm guessing Matt snuck out of the hospital when his father wasn't looking rather than admit he'd forgotten."

Paulo took out his iPhone and opened an Internet browser. Pulling up the hospital's website, he clicked on the name of the program, Healing Paws. "When I talked to Jaron about the program, he mentioned a Pamela. I thought the woman in charge is Alyssa Berry."

"She is. Your boy must have gotten the name wrong."

"He's known her for years." Paulo clicked on a news article for the program. "Got it."

Devin leaned forward. "What?"

"The director of the dog therapy program is Dr. Pamela Roberts. I'm guessing Alyssa Berry must be in charge of the day-to-day operations since she's the only one listed on the main program page."

"There's no mention of Doctor Roberts in the files."

Paulo read the bio on the doctor. "It gets better. Guess what Dr. Roberts's specialty is?"

Devin looked pained.

"General Adult Psychiatry."

Devin swore loudly, drawing stares from several patrons. "Did they think we were joking when we said we needed the names of all the people who came in contact with the vic?" He pulled a ten out of his wallet and tossed it on the table.

"Let me try talking to Roberts before you go ripping the hospital admins a new one."

"Keep me apprised," Devin bit out before stomping away.

DR. ROBERTS was a thin woman somewhere in her late sixties, her chin-length gray hair parted down the center in a razor straight line. She sat behind an antique wooden desk with her hands laced together in front of her.

"I'm Detective Silva with the Stanton Police Department. I would like to speak with you about the disappearance of Matt Wilson."

Dr. Roberts gestured toward the chair in front of her desk. "I'm not sure how I can help you, detective. You were given a list of volunteers we've had since Matt and his father began the program."

Paulo accepted the offer and sat down. "It's important that we talk with everyone at the hospital who might have come in contact with Matt. I've just recently learned that you are officially in charge of the Healing Paws program."

"The hospital knew I was dealing with a personal matter when Matt went missing. I only returned yesterday from out of town. And Alyssa Berry is in the process of taking over the program."

"With something this big, I expect the hospital to contact you."

"I expect they would have if they'd had the means to do so."

Paulo wasn't fooled by the doctor's glib tone of voice; she was clearly hurting. "It is pretty obvious you're going through a rough time, and I don't blame you for not wanting to spill your guts to a complete stranger, but my job is to bring Matt home to his family. I need your help to do that."

The skin around Dr. Roberts's eyes bunched, making her look years older. "Two days before Matt's disappearance, I received a call from a private investigator I hired. I've spent my career treating teens and adults with psychological disorders. But somehow I managed to miss the signs of chemical dependency in my own son. He disappeared two years ago."

"You hired the PI to locate him?"

Dr. Roberts nodded. "An arrest for vagrancy led her to Miami. She managed to find my son in a shelter not far from the police station. When she called, I dropped everything and drove straight to O'Hare."

Her eyes brimmed with tears. "Before my plane landed, he was dead from an overdose of heroin."

"I'm sorry," Paulo offered uselessly. He had heard variations of the same story dozens of times. A quick follow-up with the airline and the Miami PD would verify what his gut told him was the truth. "Can you tell me about the Healing Paws program?"

Dr. Roberts looked grateful for the change in subject. "The program began ten years ago when I conducted a study on the effectiveness of animal-assisted therapy in the achievement of patient goals." Her voice strengthened, like she was presenting her findings to a lecture hall of colleagues. "Animals are seen as nonthreatening and nonjudgmental. I found that many patients suffering from psychological disorders are more likely to open up to the therapist if an animal is present. After the study was concluded, I saw the benefit of creating a dog therapy program at the hospital. I obtained my Pet Partner Team Evaluator qualifications through the Community Partner of Pet Partners, so that I am able to train potential dogs and handlers. Ms. Berry has taken over the primary responsibilities. I mainly handle the initial acceptance of the dogs and handlers into the program."

"How does someone become a handler for Healing Paws?"

"The dogs need to have a current veterinarian exam and immunizations. They must also complete a certification course and pass a Pet Temperament screening. Technically, Mr. Wilson is the handler for Pixie, though Matt has gone through the training. A handler must be eighteen, but a child can act as a helper when the handler is present. The handler must also pass drug and TB screening and a criminal background check."

"How often is the criminal background check run?"

"Twice a year."

Thinking about the scenario Jaron described, Paulo asked, "How would Pixie have likely reacted to a stranger picking her up?"

"Was she wearing her service vest?"

"Does it matter?"

"Dogs in the service program learn that certain behaviors are expected when they are on duty. Pixie has been trained to allow strangers to handle her when wearing the vest. She would be aware of Matt's stress level, but it would likely take an act of physical aggression from the stranger to provoke a reaction from Pixie. Even then, she might not react."

"Where would someone get a service vest for their pet?"

"The vests can only be purchased on the Pet Partners's website through a secured login. You need a volunteer ID number and password to access the shop online."

Hoping to provoke her, Paulo said, "Jaron Greenberg wasn't listed on the list of volunteers."

Dr. Roberts frowned. "He's not… officially part of the program."

"Why is that?"

"I met Jaron when he brought Bear for evaluation. We ultimately determined that Bear wasn't suited for the program."

"How come?"

"During his final test, Bear growled when a schizophrenic patient wrapped his arms around Jaron's neck. Growling is an automatic disqualification."

"So, Bear failed because you're worried he'd attack a patient?"

"Bear isn't an aggressive dog. Even under extreme provocation, I doubt he would bite someone. He's more likely to use his size and bark to intimidate. But he's very protective of Jaron and that makes him a poor candidate for the program."

"What sort of contribution does Jaron provide your program, unofficially?"

Dr. Roberts's eyes narrowed. "Are you asking if I think Jaron has psychic ability?"

Paulo grinned. "You tell me, doc."

She gave him an old-fashioned "look." "Observation is a skill that I'm sure you're aware of as a detective. Jaron's above average intelligence and enthusiasm for dogs has aided his study of the different breed characteristics. But breed doesn't override experience. Jaron uses highly attuned observation skills to pick up on the behavioral clues demonstrated by the animals. Clues that most people aren't even aware of."

"So you don't believe he has psychic ability?" Paulo pressed.

"I believe he has an uncanny ability to predict which animals will be successful in the therapy program. I was sure Pixie wouldn't make it through the program because she is very protective of Matt. Jaron spent ten minutes with Pixie and suddenly she was a model student. I can think of a dozen other dogs Jaron has helped similarly. I don't believe in psychic ability, detective, but I do believe Jaron Greenberg has a gift." Dr. Roberts paused, color leaving her cheeks. "Why are you so interested in Jaron?"

"Jaron is not a suspect at this time," Paulo said, tamping down on the doctor's rising concern. "I'm just following up on the therapy program. Is the visitation schedule posted in the hospital anywhere like on a community bulletin board or a mailing such as a newsletter?"

"The volunteers have an assigned day and time, but it's not posted anywhere. Ms. Berry created the schedule to best serve the needs of patients. She sends out reminder e-mails to volunteers."

"Do the e-mails list the whole schedule or are they sent individually?"

"Time is an ever-shrinking commodity," Dr. Roberts said, sounding irritated. "Ms. Berry sends out the full schedule to all the volunteers, but it lists the dog's name instead of the volunteer."

"I'm not here to point fingers. I'm trying to figure out if someone might have known ahead of time that Matt would be at the hospital on the day of the disappearance."

Dr. Roberts took a shuddering breath. "I wouldn't wish the loss of a child on anyone, detective. Tell me what you need from me."

Thinking about the gaps he had noticed in the reports, he said, "I need the names and contact information for anyone that applied to the dog therapy program that *didn't* complete the program in the past two years. And the names of anyone else you might have brought in as an unofficial volunteer."

"I will have it to you by the end of the day. Do you need anything else?"

"Who would be the person to talk to about the hospital's security system?"

"You'll need to talk to John Epstein, the Environmental Services and Security Director for the hospital."

"Thank you for your help, Doctor Roberts."

After leaving the office, Paulo took the elevator to the first floor and made his way to the security office. Five oversized flat-screen computer monitors sat on a counter that ran the width of the room. Three black computer chairs sat in front of the counter with only two men occupying them. Paulo noticed each screen was split into three different views of various places in the hospital.

A man in his sixties with red hair going gray turned from one of the stations. "Can I help you?"

"I'm looking for John Epstein."

"That's me," Epstein said, rising to his feet. His dark eyes drifted to the security badge Paulo had been given when he entered the hospital.

"I'm Detective Silva with the SPD. I was hoping you could talk with me for a few minutes."

"Let's step into my office," Epstein said, gesturing toward a room on the other end of the main security area.

Paulo followed Epstein into a room crammed full of filing cabinets, miscellaneous electronics, and a metal desk.

Closing the door, Epstein asked, "What is it you're looking for? I've given my formal statement to the police."

"I'm following up on the disappearance of Matt Wilson, and I was hoping you could answer a few questions."

Epstein took off his wire-rimmed glasses and polished them on his blue button-up shirt. "I've got two grandsons around his age. I can't imagine what that family is going through."

"Tell me about the surveillance system." Paulo had read the reports on the system but nothing beat a firsthand explanation.

"We have time-lapsed cameras on the parking lot, the entrances and exits, the emergency room waiting area, and the hallways and nursery in the maternity ward."

"What about the elevators or the lobby?"

"Not yet," Epstein said with a sigh, "but I've made the request several times."

Paulo gave a sympathetic nod. Budget and best practices were rarely in agreement in a public facility. "I was told you made a copy of all the surveillance video images for the day Matt Wilson went missing. How many days' worth of images would that include?"

"We store the images for fourteen days before the system automatically deletes them." Epstein rubbed the back of his neck. "The officer only asked for twenty-four hours' worth of images, but I should've known better."

Paulo silently agreed. The officer should've requested all the images in their archive. But it was the kind of mistake that happened in a town not used to major crime. He wasn't looking forward to telling Devin about it. "I'm looking for footage for the week prior to the abduction."

Epstein moved over to his cluttered desk and flipped open a laptop. "There should still be eight days' worth of images in the archive." He logged on to the system. "They are sorted by date and camera." After retrieving a DVD from a pile on the desk, he placed it into the laptop. Unlocking and opening a file cabinet located next to the desk, Epstein pulled out a sheet of paper. "This lists the camera number and its location in the hospital."

Paulo accepted the paper. He pulled out his wallet. Handing Jaron's business card to Epstein, he asked, "Have you seen this man before?"

Epstein squinted at the card. "He looks familiar. Or maybe it is just the dog I'm remembering. It's a big dog."

"Have you talked to him before?"

"Not that I recall."

"Have you talked to anyone outside of the police about the contents of the images you burned? Or has someone talked to you about them?"

"The hospital administrators asked me about the images, but no one else. They also made it clear that I shouldn't talk to anyone about the case beyond the police if I wanted to keep my job."

After stepping into the main room, Paulo showed Jaron's picture to the other security man and got the same negative response.

Looking at his watch, Paulo realized he needed to hurry if he was going to make his court appearance. Hopefully, his testimony before the grand jury would ensure the accused was indicted on criminal sexual assault.

Epstein joined Paulo. "Here is the DVD."

"Thank you for your help, Mr. Epstein."

CHAPTER 5

JARON ATTEMPTED to brush off ten pounds of black dog fur clinging to his jeans and white sweater. Bear had not been happy about being left behind again, but his client tonight lived in a small apartment with an apparently very excitable Jack Russell terrier named Stewie. Adding Bear to the mix would have just complicated the situation. When he knocked on the door, a preppy-looking man in his thirties answered. He invited Jaron inside with a nervous smile.

Looking around the apartment, Jaron noted extensive damage to the couch and wooden chairs in the combination living room and dining room. The bottom of the front door looked like Stewie had been trying to dig his way out. Jaron could hear the mournful howl of the little terrier from somewhere further in the apartment. "How can I help you, Mr. Clark?"

"Please call me Mike." He ran a hand through his dark hair. "I need you to tell Stewie to stop chewing through the gate I set up for when I'm not here and to stop howling before the landlord throws us out."

Jaron handed him a basic contract. "If you find the terms acceptable, I can begin today. Usually when dealing with separation anxiety, it takes about three to four sessions depending on the severity, but you can decide to cancel the service any time."

Glancing at the paper, Mike said, "Today is only going to cost me twenty bucks. What about the other sessions if I decide to get them?"

Jaron resisted the urge to sigh. "The first visit is twenty dollars. The follow up sessions will be ten dollars a visit."

Mike opened his mouth to speak and then closed it again. When Stewie took that moment to start barking, he signed the contract and handed it back to Jaron.

"Okay, I'd like you to let Stewie out of his den. Don't acknowledge him at all. Walk back into the living room and sit down on the couch. It is really important that you ignore him."

"Okay," Mike said.

Pressing his hand against his stomach, Jaron tried to get a handle on the emotions shoving their way into his brain. The level of fear radiating from the small dog made Jaron physically ill. It was one of the reasons he tended to avoid eating before a session.

The terrier darted into the living room, his nails scraping against the hardwood floors. The little dog zoomed around the coffee table over and over again, trying to disperse his anxiety. Mike sat on the couch, equally tense.

Jaron took a deep breath, trying to center himself. "How much exercise is Stewie getting?"

"I have to be at work at eight," Mike said, his body stiffening. "I don't have time to walk him more than ten or fifteen minutes in the morning."

"How about after work?"

Mike glanced at Stewie before his eyes drifted to the far wall. "It depends on my work schedule. Sometimes I can only come home long enough to take him to the bathroom before leaving again. My schedule can be pretty erratic. I always take him for longer walks on the weekends."

"Jack Russell terriers might be medium sized, but they are high-energy dogs. They need a minimum of a thirty-minute walk in the morning and at least another twenty minutes at the end of the day of either walking or energetic play. They were bred to be working dogs. If they don't have an outlet for that energy, they take it out on the furniture."

Mike crossed his arms. "Can you help him or not?"

Jaron snapped his fingers. "Sit."

Stewie obeyed, plopping his backside on the floor. Mouth open, he panted, staring directly at Jaron.

"Jesus, how did you do that?"

"The first thing you need to understand is that you are the most awesome person in the world. You are better than bacon to that pooch of yours."

"How can that be? He won't even let me pet him when I get home. He just attacks my feet." Mike pointed to a pair of scuffed dress shoes perched on top of the entrance table, too high for Stewie to reach.

Closing his eyes, Jaron pictured the shoes in his mind and projected the image to Stewie. Stewie made a mournful howl, sending Jaron the image of the terrier devouring a shoe.

Jaron opened his eyes. "When you get ready to leave for work, what do you do?"

"I finish getting ready, put Stewie behind the gate, and say good-bye."

"What's the last thing you do when you're getting dressed to leave?"

"I… put on my shoes." Mike looked at Stewie. "So he's attacking the shoes because he doesn't want me to leave again?"

"When you leave, he is absolutely convinced you will never come back."

"That makes no sense. I come home every day."

"You're thinking like a human, not like a dog. Here's what I want you to do. I want you to put on your shoes, pick up your keys, and then sit on the couch."

After a moment's hesitation, Mike complied. "Why am I doing this exactly?"

Jaron closed his eyes, sensing growing distress in Stewie. He attempted to project feelings of calmness. *Nothing to worry about, Stewie.* "I'm trying to break the association that shoes equal you leaving him."

"I'm going to work, not abandoning him!"

Jaron hated dealing with defensive pet owners. They wanted a psychic because they didn't like what any dog trainer could tell them. They wanted an instant fix. *Why am I fighting so hard to keep this business?*

Jaron snapped his fingers, calling Stewie to him. Leaning over, he rubbed the terrier behind his ears. Stewie leaned into the touch, all but starving for attention. Lost in his own thoughts, Jaron wasn't prepared when he was sucked in deep into Stewie's thoughts. His mind zoomed from image to image at a dizzying speed. Breathing deeply, Jaron focused on one image that kept flashing by, willing it into focus. The slideshow of images stopped on a worm's eye view of a young blonde woman. "Chrissy?"

"What was that?" Mike asked, dragging Jaron back to the present so quickly he felt nauseous.

"Wow, you just went really pale," Mike said. "Do you need some water?"

Jaron swallowed thickly, the sour tang of bile coating his throat. "Do you know a blonde woman in her twenties named Chrissy?"

Mike's gaze drifted to the front door. "Down the hall."

"Does she power walk in the mornings?"

"Yeah, I usually see her as Stewie and I are heading back inside."

"Offer her twenty bucks a week to take Stewie with her. She could use the money since she's saving for a new car."

"That's a great idea! She loves Stewie and always makes a point to stop and pet him."

Thinking about the impressions he'd gotten from the Jack Russell, Jaron tried to decide which direction would work best on the high energy dog. "Stewie, bring me the Kong toy."

Stewie sprinted from the room, his nails scraping on the carpet. The terrier returned with the feeding toy in his mouth, placing the pear-shaped toy at Jaron's feet.

"Good boy," Jaron said, rubbing under the terrier's chin.

Mike made a sound in the back of his throat, drawing Jaron's attention.

"What's wrong?" Jaron asked.

The tendons on Mike's neck pulsed visibly. "A lot of stuff you do is like that dog whispering guy, but he never did that." He jerked his hand toward the toy. "And how would you know about Chrissy?"

Jaron's stomach tightened. It was a good question and Jaron had no intention of answering it honestly. He shouldn't have known about her money troubles or plans to buy a new car.

"I know 'cause Chrissy works at the salon where I have my office," Jaron said, trying to offer a plausible explanation. It might even be the truth. *Maybe I overheard her talking to one of the staff members?* They'd been avoiding each other as much as possible since Jaron had convinced Stephen not to fire her. "I don't think you should mention me to her."

Mike's shoulders tensed again. "Why not?"

Jaron tamped down on his annoyance of Mike's perfectly reasonable question. "Her boss is my best friend. She might feel pressured if she knows I suggested she walk Stewie."

Mike's cheeks flushed, like he was embarrassed to be caught freaking out. "What should I do with the toy? Stewie never plays with it."

"Give him the toy when he's in his den five minutes before you leave. I've found peanut butter works better than the premade treats, but make sure you wash it really well. And he only gets to play with this special toy when in his den."

"You think that will help?"

"Yes, I do. If you decide on having another session, we can work on how you should act when you leave and return home. But let's go over the plan."

Mike counted on his fingers as he spoke. "More exercise, talk to Chrissy, and give Stewie the toy."

Jaron nodded. "Don't say good-bye when you leave. If you have a radio, you can put it on low in the kitchen to keep him company, particularly if it's a talk radio station."

Mike rose to his feet and pulled out his wallet. Handing Jaron a twenty, he said, "Thank you for coming."

Jaron accepted the money, fairly certain he wouldn't be hearing from Mike again in spite of the help Stewie needed.

EVEN AFTER two months, Paulo wasn't used to how quiet the Stanton Police Station was compared to his old precinct. The SPD had recently moved out of a building built in the fifties to a new 18,000 square foot facility. The building was large enough to have room to grow. There were six cubicles in the detectives division, but rarely were more than two occupied at a time. Tonight he was the only one here, since Patterson was mediating a dispute between an elderly woman and a goat with a taste for Hypericum bushes.

Paulo forced himself to write up the report on the follow-up interviews with Dr. Roberts and Mr. Epstein. He would much rather be poring over the DVD of images from the surveillance video, but he would need the paperwork filed and ready if he discovered a reason to go back and reinterview employees. Devin would never allocate the limited resources without a sound reason. Two hours later, he e-mailed the reports to Devin and sent two copies to the printer.

Reaching his arms over his head, Paulo groaned as the stiff muscles in his back stretched. After inserting the DVD, he clicked on the folder for the main entrance for the hospital. He reviewed his notes, confirming that the pet therapy session began at 4:00 p.m., and opened an image taken two hours before the appointment. Shuffling through the slideshow of pictures, he wasn't sure what he was looking for. He couldn't get Jaron's insistence that the abductor was a woman out of his head in spite of the potential eyewitness claiming to see a thin man in a black hooded jacket.

Facts and details about the case bounced around Paulo's brain as he sifted through the images. How would Matt react to a stranger approaching him? Did the gender matter? Devin had called Mrs. Wilson a cold fish, but Paulo didn't see her that way. She loved her child every bit as much as her exuberant husband, but she was cynical by nature, pessimistic. She would've warned Matt about the dangers of strangers, likely men in particular. If a strange man had approached Matt, he would have been unnerved to say the least. Other than a few drops of blood, they had found no signs of a struggle. No drag marks in the dry ground or torn clothing. It was possible Matt had wandered farther away from the park, but no one had seen him, and the logic didn't make sense. He would want to get back inside the hospital quickly. Matt loved Pixie and saw it as his job to take care of her. Therefore, a threat to Pixie likely would have convinced him to leave with the perp. Even though his parents would rather that he abandon Pixie and run, Matt wouldn't see it that way. Pixie was *his* dog. The idea of the perp using that love sickened Paulo.

Several minutes later, Paulo found the image he had been looking for. The photograph showed Mr. Wilson, Matt, and a leashed Pixie. A few more clicks of the mouse found a clearer version and Paulo sent it to the printer. Making a mental note of Matt's clothing, Paulo moved through the pictures. In an eight-minute period after Matt entered the hospital, the only people to enter were a young mother with small children and an elderly couple.

Switching to the exit camera, Paulo moved through the pictures until he found Matt and company leaving the hospital. A few frames later, a person also exited with their head down. It was difficult to tell the gender of the person in the blurred image. The person had moved through the automatic door very quickly. Using the doorframe as a reference, Paulo estimated the height to be around 5'10," a bit above average for a woman, but certainly not unusually so. The bagginess of the black hoodie made the person's weight hard to guess, but he'd say average or slightly below average.

Paulo switched to the folder for the parking lot surveillance. The quality of the images decreased. Another area John Epstein likely hoped to improve if the hospital would fork over the money. He found the photographs that showed Matt and Mr. Wilson headed for their car. In the bottom corner of the image, the person in the black hoodie stood on the roadway directly in front of the hospital entrance, looking in the direction of Matt. The position of the camera gave Paulo no further details as to the person's identity. Clicking on the slideshow button, he watched the person remain motionless for a dozen frames before stepping back onto the sidewalk as a bus approached. Feeling a familiar surge of adrenaline, he sent several different photographs to the printer. Looking at his watch, he saw the time. 5:32 a.m. He could go home and attempt to get a couple of hours of sleep. By the time he returned, Devin would be at the station. *Or I could wake his ass up and make him come in early.* Grinning, Paulo pulled out his cell phone and put in a call to Devin.

"It's five thirty in the morning," Devin grumbled.

"Sorry to wake you, Dev. We country folks get up with the cows."

"It's roosters, asshole. This better be good."

"I think I might have a lead on the case."

Devin swore under his breath. "Fine, come on over and show me what you've got."

"Uh… I was just hoping you'd be willing to come in early."

Devin continued as if Paulo hadn't spoken. "They only have instant coffee in this fleabag motel. Buy me some real coffee and get over here. I'm in room 103."

"They don't have twenty-four hour anything in this town," Paulo hedged, wishing he hadn't called. The last thing he needed was to be alone with Devin in his motel room. "Why don't you get dressed and meet me at the Main Street Café? They open at six."

"You have ten minutes to bring me caffeine before I drive to the station and shoot you in your bubble butt ass," Devin said before ending the call.

Looking at his watch, Paulo figured he had enough time to run through the images one more time before heading over to the motel.

WHEN PAULO knocked on the door, he heard Devin say it was open. Entering the room, Paulo saw Devin leaning against the headboard of a full-sized bed, dressed only in a pair of blue boxer briefs, the stretchy material showing off his half-hard cock. The room smelled like mothballs and Devin's musky pine cologne.

"Have a seat," Devin said, patting the mattress. There was nowhere else to sit, besides the unmade bed.

"This isn't a booty call, Devin." Paulo smacked the folder of images on the bed. "Put some damn clothes on and let me show you what I found."

Devin lifted his arms overhead in a leisurely stretch, making the defined muscles on his tanned chest stand out. "If you're going to show up this early without coffee, you should at least make it worth my while."

Paulo snorted. "Since when did the job become nine to five?"

"Fine, be a prude," Devin said, sliding his hand down to cup his cock through his briefs. "Just stand there and look pretty while I take care of this monster." He pulled his red-tipped cock from his briefs and began to stroke. "You and me were smokin' hot, baby. You telling me you don't miss it?"

I miss my friend, Paulo thought. They should have stayed friends. It wasn't until the Jefferson case that Paulo realized their relationship of nearly a year wasn't anything more than friends with benefits. The sight of Devin pumping his dick rough made Paulo's balls heat, but it left the rest of him cold. Paulo pulled out his cell phone and snapped a picture of Devin mid-stroke.

"What the fuck, Silva?"

"Your mom is always saying she doesn't have enough recent pictures of you."

"Asshole," Devin said, tossing a pillow at Paulo's head. "Delete that picture." He got off the bed and headed for the bathroom, slamming the door shut.

Laughing, Paulo walked over to the door and leaned against the wall. "Your mom sent me her amazing homemade caramels for my birthday. She told me to remind you to call your grandma on her birthday next week." Paulo heard Devin swear loudly and then the sound of clothes rustling.

Devin opened the door dressed in jeans and a T-shirt. "I hate you," he said, shoving Paulo out of the way. Moving back over to the bed, he threw himself down, making the cheap mattress squeal like a pig.

Paulo sat on the end of the bed and picked up the folder. Pulling out the first image, he handed it to Devin. "I went over the images from the surveillance cameras from the weekend before Matt's disappearance."

Devin squinted at the image. "Is this one of the guys on the sex offenders list?"

Paulo nodded. "Dennis Peters left the hospital a couple of minutes before Matt." He had almost missed spotting the man. Peters was in his fifties with watery blue eyes, poorly dyed blond hair, and gray stubble. Paulo should have noticed him the first time he went over the pictures.

"Damn, Silva. You might have actually found a lead."

Paulo's gut said Peters wasn't the perp. Or maybe that was his pride talking since he'd interviewed the man. "If it's Peters, we've got to toss the witness ID. Peter is pushing two hundred and fifty pounds, no way someone would think of him as thin."

"Tell me about him."

"Two counts of aggravated criminal sexual abuse on a ten-year-old girl in 2002. He has a solid alibi, so either he convinced his coworkers to lie for him or he had help."

Devin frowned. "What's your take on the coworkers?"

"His boss is the religious type and thinks any man can be saved, but I doubt he'd lie for Peters. The coworkers didn't know Peters was a registered sex offender, and they weren't happy when they found out."

"Hm, something we should look in to. The Internet is making it too easy to reach out to your fellow perv. Maybe Peters did the scouting and someone else did the snatch."

"Except we're back to the problem of how they knew Matt would go outside alone."

"It wouldn't hurt to bring him in for questioning. You got anything else?"

Paulo shuffled the images in the folder, preparing himself for Devin's reaction. "I also found a photograph of a person matching the witness's statement leaving directly after Matt and his father." He placed the screenshot from the exit camera on the bed.

Devin picked up the photograph, squinting at the blurry image. "Tell me you're joking," he said, tossing it at Paulo.

Gritting his teeth, Paulo placed the parking lot view on the mattress. "The description matches. The… person stood in the middle of the road and watched Matt for over a minute. We need to reinterview the witness."

"*She's* watching for the bus," Devin said, his voice rising. He scrubbed his hands over his face. "That pretty-boy wackjob got into your head. He told you it was a woman and you went out and found one."

"That's not what this is about. Jaron just got me thinking in another direction. Police work found this lead."

"You don't need me to tell you the stats. Female stranger abductions are rare for infants. For a six-year-old, the odds are almost nonexistent. This is wishful thinking, not police work."

"We can't just ignore a possible lead." Paulo rose to his feet. "We need to go over the rest of the pictures and see if we can find a clearer image. Then we can go back to the hospital and see if this wo—person or Peters talked to someone about the Pet Therapy program."

Devin's expression looked dangerously close to pity. "I'm sorry, Paulo. I shouldn't have dragged you into this case. The last thing you needed was to deal with another dead child."

Paulo gritted his teeth. "This has nothing to do with the Jefferson case." He turned away from Devin.

"Bullshit. You're tearing yourself apart over a death you couldn't have prevented."

Paulo turned back toward him. "I was across the fucking hall," he said, the words spilling from his mouth without permission. They'd had this argument before, but it didn't change the facts.

"You were interviewing a witness on an unrelated case," Devin said, sounding so calm and reasonable Paulo wanted to slug him. He stood and walked over to Paulo. "There's no way you could have known what was going on in that apartment unless *you've* been hiding psychic abilities."

Thinking back, Paulo couldn't remember any details from the witness's interview, like a piece of his memory had been ripped out. Did he hear the baby crying in the distance? "When I stepped into the hallway, I remember smelling something burning, and thinking someone had ruined their dinner. The thought made me hungry. My mind was on food while that baby roasted in the oven."

Devin squeezed Paulo's shoulder. "Tom Jefferson was a monster, but you put him down like the dog he was."

Paulo rolled his shoulder, knocking loose Devin's hand. "It doesn't matter. He and his son are dead. But Matt Wilson is alive until we prove otherwise."

"Not you," Devin said quietly.

"What does that mean?"

"You're off the case."

"You can't do that!"

Devin raised his chin. "Yeah, I can. I'll let the chief know tomorrow. Take the time you need to get your head together."

Paulo left without another word, not trusting himself to speak.

CHAPTER 6

MARNIE HURRIED back to the motel room, carrying several plastic bags from a nearby gas station. *What if Brandon has already woken up?* She should've disabled the phone. *What if he calls the police?* She opened the door and stepped inside. She spotted Brandon on the full-sized bed farthest from the door, right where she'd left him. Breathing a sigh of relief, she secured the door and walked over to the other full-sized bed. After putting down the bags, she took a seat.

Marnie hated staying in this filthy room, but she had no choice. It was the only motel in the area that didn't require a credit card. It was only temporary.

Brandon rubbed his eyes. "Mommy?"

"I'm here, sweetheart. Are you hungry?"

Brandon sat up. "Where are we?" he asked, his eyes filling with tears.

Marnie ached to hold him, but she resisted. Those bastards had turned her precious boy against her. She'd only make him more afraid if she approached him. They'd stripped away his memories and filled his mind with lies. She would use their lies against them until she could break the brainwashing. "I bought milk and your favorite cereal." She pulled out a box of Lucky Charms and paper bowls from a plastic bag.

Brandon rubbed his face. "Frosted Flakes are my favorite. I don't want cereal. I want to go home!" His shout made the dog bark several times.

Marnie took a deep breath and exhaled slowly, trying to rein in her growing frustration. It wasn't Brandon's fault. He was a victim of the Wilsons' cruelty. He'd been such a sweet-natured child before they got their hands on him. She needed to break their control over Brandon if she was ever going to make him remember his real momma. "Brandon, this motel doesn't allow disruptive pets. If you can't keep her quiet, I'll have to get rid of her."

Brandon's eyes widened and his bottom lip quivered. "Please don't hurt her. I'll keep her quiet." He started petting the little dog and making shushing noises.

Marnie's eyes welled with tears. "I won't hurt her, sweetheart." She wiped her eyes with the back of her hand. "But you have to make sure she behaves or we'll have to leave her behind when we leave here. She needs you to set a good example. Can you do that?"

Brandon lowered his head. "I'll be good. We'll both be good."

Marnie gave him a watery smile. "Okay, how about we start with breakfast?" She opened the box of cereal and the package of paper bowls. She prepared the cereal just how he always liked it, with plenty of milk. She handed him the bowl along with a plastic spoon before getting up and putting the half gallon of milk in the ageing mini-fridge.

Brandon ate a spoonful of the Lucky Charms. "It's pretty good," he said, as if reluctant to admit it.

The sight of Brandon eating the cereal enthusiastically made Marnie want to jump for joy. Their future together was so clear in her mind. In the past she'd never even made it out of Illinois, but she and Brandon would travel the world together. They would visit the Eiffel Tower, the Taj Mahal, London Bridge, the Great Wall of China, the Roman Colosseum, and Machu Picchu; a different country every day. Brandon would become a student of the world. She'd take him to museums and all the famous places instead of forcing him to learn in a stuffy classroom. He would learn dozens of foreign languages from the mouths of native speakers.

As their future plans darted through her mind, Marnie unpacked the other supplies she'd gathered from the gas station. She stored them in the small dresser; a telephone and small television were bolted to the surface. "When you're finished eating, you can feed Pixie."

Brandon looked down at the small dog curled against him. A trace of a small smile touched his lips. "Daddy says it's my job to take care of her."

Marnie bit down on her tongue hard enough to draw blood. Brandon clung to his life with the Wilsons like he did the dog. She needed to sever the connection. "I wasn't going to tell you this, because I didn't want to upset you, Brandon." Marnie sat on the end of the bed. "The Wilsons stole you from me, but they decided to give you back to me."

Brandon stared at his nearly empty bowl of cereal. "I don't believe you," he said quietly.

"It's true. Your dad called me and told me where to pick you up. I'll prove it to you." She took out a small notebook and a pen from her purse. "Write down your home phone number," she said, holding the items out to Brandon.

Chest heaving and face flushed, Brandon stared at her for nearly a minute before he rose from the bed. He walked over to the dresser and put down his bowl of cereal. After returning to Marnie, he accepted the notebook and pen. He wrote down the number and Marnie felt a surge of pride over his neat penmanship.

"Let me see the number." When Brandon complied, Marnie took out her cell phone, entered the number into the phone, and then showed Brandon the display. "That's your number, right?"

Brandon nodded, clutching the notebook against his chest.

"My cell battery is almost drained, so write down the motel number listed on the phone in case they're not home." When Brandon scrambled over to the telephone, Marnie ended the call and pulled up the number she'd saved into the memory of the cell phone. The phone rang several times as Brandon frantically wrote down the number, nearly falling in his rush to come back over to her.

It hurt her so much to see how those bastards had brainwashed her child. "The answering machine has picked up. Come over here and leave a message." She handed over the phone just as the automated voice gave instructions 'to leave a message after the beep.'"

Hands shaking, Brandon accepted the phone and said, "Mom, Dad, it's me, Matt. I want to come home. Please let me and Pixie come home."

"Don't forget to tell them the number."

Brandon took a shaky breath and recited the number. Then, he handed back the cell phone.

Instead of hitting the End button, Marnie selected the number 3, deleting the message. She flipped the cell phone closed. She would wait until Brandon was asleep to get rid of the cell phone. She couldn't risk giving the police a way to track her. Rising from the bed, she walked over to the motel phone and lifted the receiver so that Brandon could hear the dial tone. Replacing the phone, she said, "If they've changed their mind about giving you up, I'm sure they'll call."

The look of hopefulness on Brandon's face made Marnie want to abandon the ruse. But she couldn't. God had reunited them. She wouldn't disappoint Him by taking the easier path. Brandon deserved to have an amazing life. And she would do whatever it took to give him that life.

CHAPTER 7

THE NEXT night, Paulo stood waffling in front of the Pampered Pooches' door. This plan had sounded a lot better several hours ago when he had gotten off shift. The day had seemed to drag by, the minutes stubbornly refusing to move as he tackled the paperwork from his other cases that had grown monstrous while he had worked the Matt Wilson case. *How could a ten dollar check fraud cause so much paperwork?* He couldn't get his mind off the case he was no longer supposed to be working on. After zooming in on the images on the CD, he had to admit that Devin was right about the person in the surveillance video likely being a woman. But what did that mean? Either Jaron was right about a woman being the abductor, or Paulo really was losing it. Paulo's every instinct told him Jaron wasn't involved in the abduction or a scam artist.

At nearly midnight, no one should be at the store, but Paulo was betting Jaron was here. It had taken him longer than he'd planned to put together his test for Jaron.

It took three rings of the doorbell before Jaron answered the door in paw print sleep pants and a white T-shirt. "Detective Silva?"

"Paulo," he corrected, pushing his way inside. "So you live here and not at Stephen's." He closed the door. "I wondered about that."

"What's up?" Jaron asked, wrapping his arms around himself.

Bear shifted slightly, making Paulo aware of his presence in the darkened lobby of the salon. Looking at the massive dog, he understood what Dr. Roberts had said about Bear. He wasn't growling or being aggressive. But he was watchful, ready to move if needed. Bear pressed against Jaron's hip, his eyes locked on Paulo.

"Um.... Bear is a little freaked out by whatever you've got in that canvas bag," Jaron said. "So can you tell me what you want, please?"

"Coffee," Paulo said. "Can I get a cup of coffee?"

"Okay," Jaron said, drawing out the word. "Let's go to the kitchen." He turned around, giving Paulo the view of his tight ass in the clingy sleep pants.

Bear growled as if he was the psychic in the family and in charge of his owner's chastity.

"Hey, Jaron. Can you please tell your dog to not eat me?"

Jaron walked back into the hallway and over to his dog. "Paulo is a... friend."

Paulo normally detested people who anthropomorphize pets, giving them human emotions. But damned if Bear wasn't giving Jaron an "are you shitting me?" look.

Jaron held out his arm to Paulo. "Take my hand."

With reluctance, Paulo inched closer and complied, hoping to keep all his digits.

Jaron laced their fingers together tightly, as if afraid Paulo might pull away, and presented their joined hands to Bear. Bear shoved his wet nose on their hands for several seconds, making a chuffing noise. He plopped his furry ass on the ground and offered a doggy grin, seemingly satisfied with the sniff assessment.

With a chuckle, Jaron pulled Paulo down the hallway, only letting go when they had reached the small galley kitchen.

"Have a seat," Jaron said, pointing to an all-white two-person breakfast nook. "The coffee should be done soon. It's set up to brew." He pressed the On button. It gurgled and dripped fragrant coffee into the carafe.

Paulo took a seat while Jaron rummaged in the cabinet for two mismatched coffee mugs.

"How do you like your coffee?"

"Black, please."

When the coffee was brewed, Jaron placed the mug in front of Paulo before taking a seat across from him. "So what's going on?"

"It's my birthday today."

"Oh, um, happy birthday."

Paulo paused, not sure how much he wanted to tell Jaron. Deciding Jaron deserved the full story for being pulled out of bed, he said, "My mother called me today to tell me another piece of my birth story."

"Birth story?"

"Every year she tells me something about the day I was born. It's usually something totally random, like what she had for breakfast or what TV show she watched that day. I tease her that one day she'll run out of memories, but she says she won't run out even if she lives to be a hundred."

"That's beautiful," Jaron said, his blue eyes glistening. "Like an oral scrapbook of becoming your mother. What did she tell you this year?"

"She walked to the elementary school on the day I was born and watched the kids play on the playground, so she could introduce me to my future school. She went into labor a couple of hours later."

"She sounds like a great person," Jaron said, sounding wistful.

"She is, and she has a mind like a steel trap." Paulo took a sip of coffee. "I asked her if I had ever had a classroom pet, convinced she would say no. But she didn't. She immediately launched into the story about the gerbil dying and how heartbroken it made me."

Jaron smiled wanly. "If you hadn't loved him, then I wouldn't have been able to tell you about him." He gestured toward the black canvas bag on the floor. "So you brought me another test?"

"How do you know that?"

"Bear doesn't react to the smell of strange dogs since we live in a pet salon, but at least one of the items in your bag belongs to a dog he knows."

"Can you tell me what I brought?"

"I know it's an item of importance to pets, so that usually means toys, collars, or leashes, but it can vary. I know a poodle that will pull the pillowcase off his owner's pillow every morning and carry it around all day."

Paulo leaned back on the chair. "I dragged you out of bed to put you through another test, and you're not even pissed about it?"

Jaron shrugged. "I'd rather be seen as a freak than a fraud."

"I don't think you're a fraud, but I need to be sure—"

"I'm not crazy?"

Paulo winced. "You've gotta understand, Jaron. This is Hollywood stuff to me. I've never considered psychic abilities could be real."

"I've had these abilities my whole life, though I didn't have much control when I was younger. If I hadn't grown up in a trailer park, I probably would've ended up in a psych ward." Jaron rubbed his forehead. "But what happens if I pass your test?"

"What do you mean?"

Jaron wrapped his hands around his mug but didn't drink. "I'm wondering if there's a test foolproof enough for you to believe me, Paulo. Or will you just convince yourself that I somehow rigged this test too?"

It was a fair question, so Paulo took the time to think about it. He'd taken every precaution he could conceive of to make this test foolproof, but would he be satisfied? Opting to answer honestly, he said, "I don't know if I can be convinced."

Jaron nodded. "Thank you for telling me that." He pushed aside his coffee cup, clearing the space in front of him. Closing his eyes, he took several deep breaths. When he opened those bright blue eyes, he said, "I'm ready."

Paulo noticed shadows under his eyes that hadn't been there yesterday. "Are you sure you're okay? We could do this another time?"

Jaron shook his head. "You won't trust the results if we wait."

Feeling his cheeks warm, Paulo asked, "Are you sure you can only read animals?"

Jaron shivered. "I don't want to be able to read people."

Paulo opened the canvas bag and pulled out a dozen pet collars of various colors and sizes. He'd recruited two rookies into helping collect them and to label each collar with a numbered piece of tape, so Jaron wouldn't be able to read his reactions. He'd even taken the extra step to remove any identifying tags from the collars.

Jaron immediately began sorting the collars into three piles. He hesitated over a collar with a leopard print before putting it aside. Pointing to a pile of three collars, he said, "Those dogs have died."

Paulo wrote down the information on the collars. He had no way of knowing if Jaron was correct or not. "Is there anything else you can tell me?"

"I can't get a reading if the dog has died. If the death is recent, I can sometimes tell where they died, but I'm not getting anything." Jaron placed his hand over a pile of ten collars. "These collars belong to living dogs." He picked up a small pink collar. "This belonged to a Doberman pinscher when she was younger."

Paulo wrote down Doberman and female. "Can you tell me the age?"

"Young, adult, and senior are the only age ranges I get."

"Why do you think that is?"

Jaron smirked. "Maybe 'cause dogs are lousy counters? How should I know?"

Paulo resisted the urge to grin. "What about her name?"

Jaron wrinkled his nose. "Becky's a senior dog. Who names their Doberman Becky?"

Paulo chuckled. "Who's going to give a Doberman grief about its name?"

Jaron selected a medium-sized black collar. "Adult female. Mixed breed. Her owner needs to take her in for a grooming. Her nails are too long."

Paulo stared at him incredulously. "How could you know all that?"

"Because the collar is Molly's." Jaron grinned. "I heard Stephen bitching today about her owner cancelling her appointment again."

Paulo laughed.

Jaron worked his way through the remaining collars and Paulo copied down his responses. If even half of the information was accurate, Jaron had an amazing ability.

"What's the deal with that one?" Paulo asked, pointing to the leopard-print collar Jaron had set aside.

Jaron picked it up, his brows bunching. "I can't get a reading on it."

Paulo noticed a slight tremble in Jaron's hands. He heard the jingle of Bear's collar and his nails clicking on the linoleum floor. Bear poked his head against Jaron's side, whining.

Jaron dropped the collar, the color draining from his face. "Nothing," he said, sounding strained. "I get nothing."

"I think you're crashing again." Paulo scrambled to his feet and pulled open the refrigerator, snagging a carton of orange juice. "My mother is diabetic and you act just like her when her blood sugar is low." Grabbing a glass from the dish drainer, he filled it with juice. He held out the glass. "Drink it slowly."

For once, Jaron didn't argue, which only heightened Paulo's concern.

"Thank you." Jaron took a sip from the glass. "I should have had juice instead of caffeine. Go ahead and check the results."

"Fine, but keep drinking the juice." Paulo paused, looking at the piles of collars. He hadn't realized until this moment how much he wanted Jaron's abilities to be real. Pulling out the sheet the rookies had prepared, he compared it to his results. After a couple of minutes, he dropped his pen to the table. "You got them all right."

"You mean except for the leopard print one?"

"No, you got that one too," Paulo said, feeling his cheeks flush. "I bought it at PetSmart and scuffed it up to make it look used."

Jaron looked up through his long, white lashes. "Have I graduated from fraud to freak?"

"My mother would call your abilities a gift."

Jaron shrugged, staring at the scratched surface of the table.

"Hey Bear, give Jaron a sniff." Paulo nudged the dog toward his owner. "Let me know if he's okay."

"What's with the furry first aid?" Jaron asked as Bear hoovered his stomach.

"When my mother was diagnosed, I remember reading about how dogs can be trained to alert someone when their blood sugar drops. I think Bear has taught himself."

Jaron rubbed behind Bear's ears, making the dog's tail thump on the linoleum floor. "You think he tried to stop the reading because he could sense my blood sugar dropping?"

"Scientists think a person's smell changes. I think when you tap into your abilities it somehow drains you, making your blood sugar drop. Have you been tapping into your abilities more often lately?"

"You make me sound like a beer keg," Jaron grumbled.

Paulo snorted and took a seat across from Jaron. "You know, irritability is another symptom of low blood sugar."

"Kisses, Bear."

In a split second, Bear's front paws were on the table and Paulo's face was attacked by a doggy tongue. Paulo made a sound disturbingly like a yelp and attempted to push the dog off of him.

"That's enough, Bear," Jaron said, mirth coloring his words.

"You coulda just flipped me off instead of passive-aggressively covering me in dog slobber."

Jaron widened his big blue eyes dramatically. "I didn't know he'd kiss *you*."

Paulo snorted. "You're not fooling me."

Jaron's laugh ended in a yawn, his eyes watering.

"Time for bed," Paulo said.

Jaron sighed. "Sorry, I haven't been sleeping too well lately. I keep dreaming about Matt and Pixie."

Rising, Paulo said, "Do you work tomorrow?"

"No, so I should probably try going back to the park." Jaron looked up at Paulo through his thick lashes. "Assuming you still want me investigating."

Paulo emptied their coffees in the sink, rinsed out the mugs, and placed them on the dish drainer. Turning back toward Jaron, he said, "Devin Morris—the guy in charge of the task force—has pulled me from the case." He held out his hand.

"Why?" Jaron took Paulo's hand and rose.

"He thinks I'm losing it, because I found evidence that might support your visions. And before I talked to my mother, I was wondering if he was right."

"So this test was for you too." Jaron touched Paulo's arm briefly. "To see if you'd caught my crazy?"

Paulo scratched the back of his neck. "Yeah." Picking up the glass of juice in one hand, he asked, "Do you have a bed in this place?"

"Stephen's parents' bedroom is still intact." He clasped his hands together. "For now, anyway. He's planning a remodel to expand the salon."

Paulo placed his hand on the small of Jaron's back, ushering him out of the kitchen. "What happens to your business?"

Jaron exhaled, sounding so drained that Paulo regretted asking the question. "Never mind, let's get you vertical."

"Are you tucking me in?" Jaron sounded amused.

"Least I can do."

They made their way through the darkened salon to Jaron's bedroom. His bedroom was simple and unadorned. A temporary living space. Seeing the drab room made Paulo think of his own apartment. Temporary. A place to retreat and recoup. Wasn't that what Devin was accusing him of?

Jaron pulled back the dark covers and slipped into the bed. Bear joined him, claiming the other half of the bed. Paulo chose not to see that as a sign.

Sitting on the edge of the mattress, Paulo said, "How about I take you to lunch tomorrow? And then we could go for a stroll at the park."

Jaron stifled another yawn. "Won't you get in trouble? I could call you and let you know what I find."

Hell no, Paulo thought. No way was he risking Jaron working this case alone. "I have tomorrow off. Devin can't bitch about me going on a date with a hot guy."

Jaron's cheeks flushed. "So it'll be a pretend date?"

Paulo brushed his knuckles across Jaron's cheek. "When this case is over, I want to take you on a real date. And it won't end at a crime scene."

Jaron smiled, his eyes drifting closed. "I'd like that," he murmured.

Paulo placed the glass of juice on the nightstand in case Jaron needed it. Jaron fell asleep quickly. Leaning over, Paulo lightly kissed Jaron's forehead. "*Doces sonhos, anjo*," he whispered.

JARON'S BUDGET didn't allow him to dine out very often, so eating at Dink's Bar and Grill was a treat. Its proximity to the salon meant it would be easy to pick up Bear after lunch. He wondered what Paulo would think of the place. The décor was an odd combination of biker bar and Grandma's dining room. There was Harley-Davidson memorabilia blended with an antique cabinet with blue china and a grandfather clock. Multiple flat-screen TVs displayed different sporting events. All but one table in the center of the dining area was filled with people eating what smelled like deliciously greasy food.

Frowning, Paulo looked back and forth between the entrance and the table.

"We could sit at the bar," Jaron offered, wondering at the issue.

"The table's fine," Paulo said, taking a seat.

Jaron sat across from him. "The bottle caps are really great."

Paulo raised a bushy eyebrow. "Bottle caps?"

"Oh, sliced jalapeño and cheese poppers. They're shaped like… um… bottle caps," Jaron said, resisting the urge to smack himself in the forehead. *Can we say duh?*

"Sounds delicious," Paulo said.

A blonde waitress in her early twenties approached the table with menus in hand. Her gaze glued to Paulo, she said, "I'm Ashley. How can I serve you today?" She handed both the menus to Paulo.

Jaron wanted to be annoyed with Ashley, but it was hard to blame her. Paulo's long-sleeved black shirt and fitted gray vest highlighted his broad chest to perfection. Waking up this morning, he'd half thought that he dreamed Paulo's late night visit. Even though today was pretend, it felt foreign not to talk to Stephen about his date with Paulo. Not to have Stephen scowl at Jaron's limited wardrobe or to try to put styling mousse in Jaron's white-blond hair. A distance had crept between them that Jaron didn't know how to bridge.

"*We* would like the bottle caps to start. I'd like an iced tea with lemon. What would you like, Jaron?"

Jaron held up his glass of water. "Could I get some bottled water and a new glass?"

Ashley sighed loudly and took the glass.

Paulo peered at his glass of water. "What's wrong with it?"

Jaron laughed. "It's not poisoned or anything, but they use well water. It tastes like sucking on a fork to me."

Paulo pushed his glass aside. "I'll take your word for it." He offered Jaron a menu before opening his own. He examined the menu like there would be a test later. After a couple of minutes he asked, "What are you getting?"

Without bothering to open the menu, Jaron said, "The potato and leek soup."

Paulo frowned. "You need something with more lean protein. It should help to stabilize your blood glucose levels. What about the chicken fajitas?"

Paulo's concern was touching, even if he saw Jaron as a human bloodhound. "I actually don't eat meat."

"Seriously?"

Jaron nodded. "Trust me when I tell you that you don't want to know why."

Paulo tossed up his hands. "Now I have to know."

"Not if you ever want to eat bacon again."

Paulo bit his bottom lip. "I really love bacon. I go to Baconfest in Chicago every year in April. They have this maple bacon donut that's to die for."

Jaron snorted. "You're a cop who goes to a bacon festival to buy donuts. Seriously?"

"What can I say? I'm a walking cliché." Paulo looked at the menu. "What about cheese quesadillas? We could share."

Jaron smiled. "Okay."

When the waitress returned with their drinks and appetizer, Paulo ordered the quesadillas, ignoring the simpering looks Ashley kept throwing his way.

Jaron dipped a jalapeño popper into the ranch dipping sauce before eating it. The cool sauce mixed with the spicy kick from the pepper made for a delicious combination. "You said you were Brazilian, right?"

Paulo nodded before popping a bottle cap into his mouth. "Damn these are good." After snagging another one, he said, "I was born in Chicago, but both my parents were born in Brazil. They went back to Brazil after I was born. I lived there until I was fourteen."

"That must have been a hard transition to come back just in time to start high school."

Paulo shrugged. "I had my older brother, so that made it easier. He's a year older than me. Mostly, I missed the beaches and the hot dogs."

Jaron raised an eyebrow. "You couldn't find a hot dog in Chicago?"

Paulo laughed. "They make them wrong. In Brazil, they put green peas, corn, and parmesan cheese on them. It's delicious."

Jaron shook his head slowly. "I've never been happier to be a vegetarian."

They kept the conversation light as they plowed through the appetizers, talking about living in Brazil versus Illinois. The summer vacations Paulo described made Jaron want to visit the country even though he didn't even have a passport. Only after their quesadillas arrived and they began devouring them did Paulo ask about the salon remodel.

"Stephen wants me to be a partner in the salon with him. He hasn't told me to give up the pet psychic business, but the reality is I couldn't manage both. He wants to add doggy daycare services in addition to grooming. My only alternative would be to find an apartment and invite clients there."

Paulo frowned. "That doesn't sound very safe."

Jaron shrugged. "It beats working at Wal-Mart."

"Why not charge more for your services?"

Jaron stared at his plate, his appetite waning. "Because what kind of scam artist charges ten dollars an hour?" Hearing his name, he looked over at a couple in their fifties arguing in whispers. He recognized the woman as Mrs. Barnes, owner of the too-pink poodle. He was pretty sure the man was her husband.

Mrs. Barnes smiled politely. "Hello, Jaron. I hope you're enjoying your lunch."

"Don't talk to him," Mr. Barnes whispered.

Jaron wondered what was the most scandalous about him: being gay, psychic, or a Greenberg.

"Is there a *problema*?" Paulo asked, his accent thickening.

Mr. Barnes's eyes narrowed. "If you choose to dine with a Satanic sodomite from a no-good family then that's your business." He tossed his napkin on the table. "But I've lost my appetite."

Apparently, Mr. Barnes objected to all of the above. Jaron was painfully aware that the argument had drawn the attention of the entire restuarant, workers and patrons alike.

While Mr. Barnes dug through his wallet, Jaron glanced at Mrs. Barnes, who showed no signs of leaving.

Mr. Barnes tossed money onto the table and rose. "We're leaving," he said, sounding exasperated.

"You go on, then." Mrs. Barnes waved at him. "I haven't finished my lunch."

Mr. Barnes placed his hands on his hips. "How can you sit there? People like him shouldn't be allowed to mix with regular people."

Paulo turned his body so that the holster for his gun was visible. "That sounded like a threat, sir."

Mr. Barnes bristled. "I'm entitled to my opinion, Mister—"

"Detective Paulo Silva, SPD. We take threats real serious."

"So help me, Howard, if you get me on Stephen's banned list, you will regret it. No one cuts Precious's hair like he does. I will invite my mother to stay with us indefinitely."

Jaron stifled a laugh at Mr. Barnes's hangdog expression. Guns didn't intimidate Mr. Barnes, but apparently an angry wife and mother-in-law did the trick.

Mr. Barnes sat back down. "My apologies for disturbing your lunch, gentlemen."

Mrs. Barnes's smile was a little frightening.

A couple of minutes later, Paulo watched the Barnes leave. "Does that happen a lot?"

"It's mostly the older folks that remember my parents, since it's been just over a decade since they left town."

Paulo squinted. "That would've made you how old? Fifteen?"

Jaron nodded. "I came home from school and our trailer was gone." He pushed his plate aside. "I never really got along with my dad, but I think maybe my mom thought I'd be better off."

"Better off being abandoned?" Paulo asked, sounding angry.

"Chief Tucker helped convince Social Services to let me stay with Stephen's family, so in a lot of ways I was better off than when I was living in the trailer park. A lot of the people who hire me figure I'm just good with pets, not psychic. And I'm cheaper than a dog trainer."

"I can think of a dozen cases I worked when I was with the state police where your abilities would've been invaluable. I can't tell you how often the only witness to the crime was the furry kind. If the SPD was smart, they would hire you as a consultant. And the consultant rate is better than ten bucks an hour."

Jaron's cheeks warmed. "Let's just get this case solved first."

PAULO DROPPED Jaron and Bear at the park while he hunted for a parking space. Keeping his mind clear, Jaron walked along the edge of the algae-reeking lake, giving Bear the chance to find the perfect spot to do his business. Psychic mojo would have to wait. Jaron used a lavender-scented disposable scoop bag to pick up the steaming pile. He noticed Paulo approaching, his stride quick and purposeful. Jaron found it difficult to look away.

Paulo rubbed his nose. "Are you sensing anything?"

Jaron dragged his gaze away from Paulo's firm chest. "Let's start at the point Matt met the woman." He headed toward the location, Bear walking along side of him. Picturing Pixie in his mind, he sent the image to Bear.

Bear snorted and then began sniffing the ground in earnest. Even nearly a week later, Bear should still be able to catch the scent of the little dog. Jaron had made a point to let Bear sniff Pixie's favorite toy before they left the salon to give him a point of reference.

"She was standing here when she picked up Pixie."

"How much detail are you getting? Enough for me to sketch her?"

"I can see that she's wearing a ball cap, but her face is fuzzy. It's something I've seen before. It's like when a dog sees a stranger, it doesn't register details about the person's face."

"But if this woman has Matt, then she's been around Pixie for a week. Are you saying Pixie isn't with Matt?"

"I have no idea. I can't skip forward."

"What does that mean?"

"It's like I'm following a trail of breadcrumbs. I can't skip ahead to the destination without getting lost." Jaron sighed. "I'm sorry, Paulo. What I do is very limited. It's meant to find cats stuck in trees, not locate kidnapped children."

"Imagine a person were to call you because their dog got lost at the forest preserve. What would you do first?"

"I would start by looking at the person's house."

"Why there and not the forest?"

"Home is a beacon to pets. They don't need to be able to read road signs to find their way home. It's instinctual. It's the reason pets that are lost on vacation miles away are still able to find their way home. The first thing I tell people who call about a lost pet is to check their yard. At least half of the time the pet is back before I even get to the house. The main reasons pets don't make it home on their own are fear, injury, or sometimes a physical barrier such as being trapped. But pets can be damn resourceful. There was a Beagle that snuck onto a ferry in order to make it home."

"So if the kidnapper had released Pixie soon after taking Matt, odds are that Pixie would've made it back home or at least headed in that direction?"

"Exactly."

"And you think Pixie is alive?"

Jaron hesitated, remembering the flash of images from his dreams. Were they just dreams? Or something more? "She... has to be alive. It's the only reason I'd still be getting readings on her."

Paulo looked thoughtful.

"God, that smell is awful," Jaron said.

"No shit. What are you feeding that dog? Liverwurst?"

"I don't mean that." Jaron began to walk along the grass. "I'm getting that rotten egg smell again. And it's getting stronger." He continued to move forward until he reached Camilla Road. Pointing to the street, he said, "The van was parked here." Flashes from inside the van poured into his mind. *The back of the filthy van. Thick stench. Too-tight grip. Tears. Angry barks.*

"Momma," Jaron said. He heard Paulo's voice, but it sounded far away, like whispers across a lake. A tight grip on his shoulders had him snapping back to the present. He pressed a hand to his mouth, his lunch threatening to make another appearance.

"Are you okay?"

Jaron took a deep breath and the feeling faded. "That was intense, but I'm okay."

"What happened exactly?"

"The woman put Matt and Pixie into the back of an old-styled van. There were no seats in the back, like someone had just torn them out. It was really dirty and had what looked like empty two-liter bottles of pop. It was difficult to tell from Pixie's perspective. Pixie was mostly focused on Matt since he was crying and clinging to her."

"You said momma."

Jaron blinked several times. "I did?" He didn't remember saying or hearing that. "I'm not sure what that means. Maybe Pixie thinks of herself as Matt's momma?"

"I don't suppose you saw a license plate number?"

Jaron shook his head. "Sorry, the only other thing I can tell you is Pixie is south of here."

"Can you tell how far away?"

Jaron cocked his head, recalling the feeling. "It's strange. A part of me thinks Pixie isn't too far away, like within fifty miles. But at the same time, it feels like she's three times as far away." He rubbed his forehead. "It might help if I go back to Matt's house and use it as a point of reference."

"All right, let's head back to the SUV, and we can give the Wilsons a call."

When they'd reached the SUV, Paulo double-clicked the key fob and opened the back door.

Jaron unclipped Bear's leash and the Newfie jumped into the backseat. He closed the door. "Give me a minute to get rid of this," he said, brandishing the doggy bag.

"Good plan," Paulo said.

Jaron walked toward the end of the block and ducked into a side street. The alley smelled strongly of stale beer and mold. Empty beer bottles and broken glass were shoved to the sides as if someone had made a half-hearted attempt to sweep. He wasn't surprised to see it so neglected. This part of town was relatively tourist free in the summer months, let alone early spring. This area was the closest thing Stanton had to a slum. Covering his hand with the sleeve of his jacket, Jaron lifted the lid on the dumpster and tossed the bag inside. Instead of heading back to the street, he found himself walking forward, not sure why. The hair on the back of his neck rose as he approached the side exit of what he thought was a sports bar. The door flew open and a man rushed out, shouting obscenities to someone inside.

Jaron took a step back. "Sorry." He started to turn away, but the man grabbed his arm.

"You look like you're hurtin'. You looking for something to make everything better?" The man looked like a human scarecrow with frizzy brown hair and stick-thin arms poking out of a dirty T-shirt. In spite of his fragile appearance, Jaron couldn't pull away from his tight grip.

Jaron shook his head. "Let go of me, please." For a moment he thought he heard a small dog barking, but the sound faded away before he could be sure.

"Did you hear dat?" A glob of spit hit Jaron in the face as the man turned his head back and forth as if searching for something. "Fucking hate that fairy dog. Won't shut up."

Fairy dog? Could he be hearing Pixie bark?

Was this man able to sense animals too? Or was he just drugged out of his mind? Jaron had never met anyone else who could communicate with animals the way he could. Could there be another reason this man could sense Pixie? A high-pitched bark drew Jaron's attention to the entrance to the alley. A small white blur appeared.

"Pixie?" Jaron yelped when he was yanked sidewise. His head impacted with the brick wall with a thud.

Pressing against Jaron, the man asked, "What did you say?"

"Oh, shit," Jaron said. Pixie had clearly led him to this man for a reason. *Too bad I'll be too dead to tell anyone about it.*

CHAPTER 8

THE NEWFOUNDLAND panted heavily, slobber clinging to his black fur. The big dog had jumped into the passenger seat the moment Jaron was out of sight.

Hoping to avoid drool on his seats, Paulo lowered the driver's side window all the way down and the passenger's side half way. He didn't want to give Bear any ideas about escaping the SUV.

Paulo noticed a tan-colored van with blacked out windows across the street. The paint looked thick and bubbled, like someone had slapped it on without sanding first. Along the edge of the sliding back door, Paulo could see white under the chipped paint. Someone had covered the back window with what looked like duct tape. Grabbing his radio, Paulo put in a call to dispatch. When Megan responded, he rattled off his location and status. "Can I get a 10-27 check?"

"Go ahead, Paulo."

Paulo recited the plate number, noticing it had Illinois plates.

"No outstanding warrants," Megan said.

Bear stiffened, making a low huffing sound. Paulo realized Jaron had been gone too long. "Let me call you back, Megan."

"10-4."

Paulo looked down the road, seeing no sign of Jaron. A black blur had him jerking backward in his seat. Bear's back feet landed right on Paulo's groin as the dog leapt through the opened window. The pain in Paulo's balls streaked up to his stomach, making him hunch over in the seat. "Fuck," he croaked. He opened the door and got out in time to watch Bear head in Jaron's direction.

Paulo ran toward the alley, cursing the dog with every painful step. Bear's frantic barking had Paulo pulling to a stop just as he reached the alley's entrance. Pressing close to the wall, he peered around the corner, taking in the details rapidly before pulling back. A man was backed against the brick wall of the alley, using Jaron as a human shield from a very angry Bear. The perp had what looked like a switchblade pressed against Jaron's neck. The man was shouting something, but the words were drowned out by Bear's rapid-fire barks.

Paulo took out his cell phone and put in a request for back-up. Taking another look around the corner, he debated his options. The odds were the knife was the only weapon the man had. If he had a gun, he'd be pointing it at the massive dog. Paulo could see a trickle of blood on Jaron's throat. It was a shallow cut, but one deep push could sever his carotid, making the blood spurt like a fire hydrant. If Bear decided to attack, this could turn ugly in a heartbeat. Decision made, Paulo stepped into the alley and shouted, "Police, drop the weapon!"

The perp shoved Jaron forward before turning to run.

Jaron fell to his knees. "Stop him."

Bear seemed to think this order was for him. He raced down the alley and tackled the man to the ground like a K9 pro.

After seeing that Jaron's neck wound was superficial, Paulo ran down the alley after them. Underneath Bear, the perp lay motionless in a fetal position with his hands covering his head. "Get him off me," he said, his voice shaking.

Paulo kicked away the discarded knife before approaching him. Bear gave a doggy grin, clearly proud to have thwarted the man's escape.

"Don't move or the dog might go for your throat," Paulo said, taking pleasure in the man's whimper. He patted Bear on the head. "Good boy."

Bear licked Paulo's hand once before running back toward Jaron. A siren in the distance signaled the imminent arrival of backup.

Kneeling down, Paulo pulled back the man's arms and cuffed him. He rose, dragging the man with him. Frisking the perp, Paulo found a wad of twenties totaling around five grand and a dime bag of crystal meth in the pockets of his over-sized jeans. He also found a license with the name Martin Becker.

An exclamation of "Oh, shit" drew his attention back toward Jaron. Jaron had slumped over, lying curled up on the filthy ground. Bear was straddling Jaron's body. His low growl reverberated against the brick walls of the alley. Officer Connors had arrived on the scene and drawn his weapon.

"*Merda*," Paulo swore. "Don't hurt the dog, Connors. He's just protecting the vic."

"He's a big fucking dog, Silva," Connors said, not looking away from Bear. "And he looks cranky."

"Dog's fuckin' nuts," yelled Becker.

Connor's expression said he agreed with the assessment.

"Come take care of this guy, and I'll handle it," Paulo said.

Connors walked backward until he reached Paulo. "Ambulance is on the way provided you can get Cujo to back off."

Paulo approached Bear slowly, resisting the urge to rush to Jaron's side. In the span of a couple of minutes, Bear's demeanor had shifted dramatically. The dog had enjoyed playing fetch the criminal. Now he stood stiffly, his skin twitching. Blood had dripped down Jaron's neck, staining his shirt. Could Bear sense that Jaron was unconscious? He could certainly smell the blood.

Fingers curled, Paulo held out his hand to Bear.

"*You're* fuckin' nuts," Becker said before Connors shut him up.

"It's okay, boy. I'm here to help him."

Bear whined, leaning down to lick Jaron's cheek.

Jaron sputtered awake, his arms flailing.

Paulo wrapped his arm around Jaron's shoulders and helped him to sit up.

Jaron's eyes widened. "Bear," he said, moving his hands over the dog frantically. "Is he hurt?"

Bear wiggled in excitement, attempting to lick every inch of Jaron he could reach.

Paulo wasn't surprised Jaron's first thoughts were for his dog. "We need to check his paws for glass, but he's fine."

Jaron's face crumpled and his eyes filled. "The guy had a knife, and I sent Bear after him." He brushed a stray tear from his cheek. "How could I do that?"

Paulo wanted to cradle Jaron in his arms, but now wasn't the time. "Hush, *anjo*. Bear is fine." He unzipped the front pocket of his vest and pulled out a travel-sized plastic tube. Popping off the lid, he dumped one glucose tablet into his palm. "Open up," he ordered Jaron. When Jaron obeyed, Paulo slipped in a watermelon-flavored tablet. "Chew it."

Jaron made a face. "God, that's awful."

"So I've heard, but it will help stabilize your blood sugar." Looking over his shoulder, he noticed Connors and Becker were headed toward them.

Jaron grabbed Bear's collar right before the dog began to growl. "It's okay, big guy."

Bear watched intently as Connors led the man toward his patrol car.

"Are you hurt anywhere else?" Paulo asked, moving his hand over Jaron's hair. "You've got a bump on the back of your head."

Jaron winced. "I banged it on the brick wall, but I think I'm okay."

A siren signaled the ambulance's arrival. It parked behind the patrol car. A young man and woman exited the van and approached. Paulo stood and stepped back so the EMTs could get to Jaron. "I've given him glucose, but you still need to check his blood sugar. He also has a head injury."

"I don't need an ambulance," Jaron grumbled, standing up.

When he swayed, Paulo grabbed him and dragged him over to the back of the opened ambulance. Jaron sat on the edge of the step rather than climb inside. *Stubborn little shit.*

The male EMT shined a penlight into Jaron's eyes and began asking him response questions.

Connors returned carrying an evidence kit and camera. He smirked. "You looked awfully cuddly with the vic, Silva. He your boyfriend?"

"How are your shorts, Connors? You looked like you were about to piss your pants."

Connors scowled. "It's common sense to be cautious with a dog like that."

The female EMT who was checking Bear's paws laughed when the dog licked her cheek.

"Yeah, Connors, he's a real monster," Paulo deadpanned. "You're lucky he didn't lick you to death."

Connors's ears turned red. "Whatever man, let's do this." He handed Paulo a camera before heading into the alley.

During Paulo's first few weeks at SPD, he learned how diversified officers had to be in this small town. It wasn't unusual for a unit to have to collect evidence at the scene. Paulo had been spoiled at ISP. "Can I get a shot of his neck?" Paulo asked the EMT.

The EMT leaned sidewise, and Paulo took a picture of the cut on Jaron's neck. It was small considering how much it had bled. "When was the last time you had a tetanus shot?"

"Last summer," Jaron said, blinking rapidly, "when I got into an argument with a garden hoe."

By the stubborn set of Jaron's jaw, Paulo knew Jaron wouldn't be riding in the ambulance unless someone knocked his ass out. Paulo would have to settle for taking him home and keeping an eye on him. "Once you give your statement to Connors, I can drive you home."

Jaron grabbed Paulo's hand, suddenly more alert. "You need to interrogate that man."

"I have time to take you home. Connors will book the guy for an assault with a deadly weapon."

Jaron shook his head and then looked like he regretted the action. "You don't understand. You need to ask him about Matt and Pixie. He's involved somehow. I know it. Stephen can come pick me and Bear up."

"You think this guy is involved in the abduction," Paulo said, before being nudged to the side by the male EMT.

Jaron hissed as the EMT wiped down the small cut on his neck. "I don't know how, but he's connected somehow. You have to talk to him."

"Sir, did you lose consciousness at any point?" asked the female EMT, sounding annoyed.

"No, I didn't," Jaron said, winning the award for the worst lie Paulo had ever heard.

"You should go to the hospital," she said, giving him a disapproving look.

"No thank you." Jaron stood up and walked over to a cast-iron bench facing the street. Holding out his hand, he asked Paulo, "Can I borrow your phone to call Stephen? I left mine at the salon."

Paulo handed over his phone and the tube of glucose tablets. "You need to take another tablet in fifteen minutes."

Jaron smiled. "Thank you; now get going and call me later. I want to know what you find out from that man."

Paulo hated walking away from Jaron, but he did it, heading to the alley to help Connors document the scene.

DEVIN DRAGGED Paulo into a conference room moments after arriving at the station. "You were told to stop working this case. Do you want to be suspended?"

"It was my day off. If I decide to spend it with my new friend, that's my business."

"Bullshit, you were dragging Dr. Doolittle around and nearly got him killed."

Paulo wondered how Devin had found out so quickly. Connors apparently had a big mouth. "You told me I was off the case, not off babysitting duty."

"That's enough, you two," Chief Tucker said as he entered the conference room. He closed the door. "Now, someone explain to me what the heck is going on."

"We might have a lead. I spotted a van that had been hand-painted to hide its white paint. I got interrupted before I could get any more details from dispatch."

The chief handed a folder to Paulo. "Megan printed this for you. She said the man you arrested, Martin Becker, is the same man the van is registered to. He's had a dozen arrests ranging from disturbing the peace to possession with intent to sell."

"So, he heard the news about the police looking for a white van," Devin said, "and decided to paint his van. He's probably got a mobile meth lab crammed in there." He waved his hand. "Hand the case over to Vice."

Paulo gritted his teeth. Devin knew damn well the SPD was too small to have specialized departments. Paulo was getting sick of Devin's "welcome to Mayberry" jabs. Picking up the file, he pulled up the public records on Becker. "He has a sister, Marnie Becker."

Devin pointed a finger at him. "Don't fucking start with that shit."

Paulo ignored him. "Jaron thinks a woman took Matt, and I found what appears to be a woman watching Matt and his father as they left the hospital parking lot the week before the disappearance."

The chief's eyes bulged. "Is that right?"

"Jaron also mentioned smelling rotten eggs when we were at the park, which is what meth smells like when it's being made."

"He smelled," Devin said, his voice rising. "Do you even hear the shit coming out of your mouth? Psychic smells!"

"Marnie Becker," the chief said, running a hand over his receding hair. "How do I know that name?" His face fell. "Oh, hell."

"What is it?" Paulo asked, turning away from Devin's furious expression.

Chief Tucker moved to a computer workstation located near the back of the conference room. "We had a case maybe one or two years ago. A mother fell asleep behind the wheel and crashed. She spent about two weeks in the ICU." His fingers moved over the keys with practiced ease. "Brandon Becker, aged six, was DOA."

Knees feeling weak, Paulo sat on the corner of the table. He could practically hear Devin grinding his molars to dust. Paulo cleared his throat. "Did she test positive for drugs or alcohol?"

The chief paused, likely reading over the details in the database. "It was ruled an accident. Her doctor had recently switched her medications to lithium."

Devin unlocked his jaw with an audible click. "Lithium is used to treat mental illness, right?"

Paulo walked over to the computer station. The chief had pulled up a newspaper article on the accident. It featured a picture of a thin woman with dark curly hair. Next to her was a young boy with matching hair and coloring. Paulo felt the surge of adrenaline race through his veins. "Jesus, he looks like Matt."

"According to the article she was being treated for bipolar disorder by Dr. Pamela Roberts." The chief swore. "She was in a medically induced coma when they buried her kid."

"She never saw his body, Devin," Paulo said, willing his friend to see the connection right in front of them.

"What are we thinking here?" Devin asked, sounding exhausted. "That the brother and sister snatched the kid together?"

"If she dangled enough money in front of him, he'd help her," Paulo said. "Let me go talk to the guy."

Looking toward the chief, he said, "Would you be willing to talk to the D.A., sir? I want us to be prepared if Becker starts yelling for his lawyer."

"I'll take care of it," Chief Tucker said.

"Thank you, sir." Devin looked at Paulo long and hard before coming to a decision. "Let's make Becker stew in lockup for a while. We need to gather as much information as we can before you talk to him."

Paulo nodded, resisting the desire to smile. "It'll also give Becker time to sober up."

THE INTERROGATION rooms at SPD were smaller than Paulo was used to, but he preferred the setup. Martin Becker sat at a small white table that was attached to the wall. His chair was set to the side so that he would be facing Paulo and the two-way mirror on the opposite wall. The cramped quarters and all-white décor was unnerving, an ideal environment to interrogate a suspect. The florescent lighting made Becker's gaunt appearance all the more apparent.

"Please be advised, Mr. Becker, that this is an audio and video recorded room."

Becker stared at the can of Pepsi in Paulo's hand like a man dying of thirst. "Whatever man, hand over the pop."

Paulo introduced himself and stated the date and time for the record. Then he said, "Please state your full name and address."

When he complied, Paulo placed a Pepsi in front of Becker before taking a seat on a white chair.

Becker snatched up the drink and popped the tab, guzzling the contents.

Paulo pulled out a sheet of paper from his leather portfolio and placed it on the table. "I'd like to ask you a few questions."

Becker belched loudly. "Can I get 'nother?" he asked, making Paulo wonder when he'd had his last hit of meth. Sugar cravings were common among methheads.

"Sure, I'll get you another one as soon as we go through your Miranda rights." After handing the sheet over to Becker, Paulo Mirandized him.

Paulo held out a pen to Becker. "If you understand each of those rights, I need you to initial each line and sign and date the bottom."

After Becker signed the document, Paulo rose and knocked on the door.

Devin handed Paulo another can of Pepsi and a manila folder.

As Becker attacked the drink, Paulo looked inside the folder. *Full Immunity contingent on the safe return of Matthew Wilson.* It was a better deal than Paulo had been expecting from the D.A. The chief must've worked some serious magic.

Paulo returned to his seat. "Where do you work?"

"I used to fuckin' work at the Fire 'n Ice bar, but that bastard cheated me out of my money."

"What happened?" Paulo asked, trying to sound concerned.

"Just 'cause I missed work yesterday, he fired me and refused to give me my paycheck."

Paulo leaned forward. "How do you get paid? By the week?"

"Yeah, and I worked those fuckin' hours." Becker threw up his hands. "It's not right."

"If you worked the hours, it sounds like he owes you money."

"Damn right he does." Becker smacked the table with his palm. "You should arrest his fat ass."

"I'll definitely be talking to him." Paulo scribbled down some notes to distract Becker from his next question. "Why did you miss work?"

Becker blinked several times. "I... had shit to do. I was gonna quit anyway."

Paulo noted the evasion but opted to let it go for now. "What was happening when I came across you in the alley?" He had learned that perps often had a harder time lying if forced to retell their story backward. Before coming in, he had read the statement Jaron had given to Connors. He'd also tried calling Jaron, but Stephen had hung up on him. Twice.

Becker shivered. "Damn dog was tryin' to kill me. I was just defendin' myself. I didn't mean to cut that guy."

Paulo decided to turn up the heat on Becker. "Your sister has put you in a tight spot."

"What the hell are you talking about?"

"We found Matt Wilson's blood in your van," Paulo said. When Becker's eyes widened, Paulo silently thanked the TV cop shows that have DNA tests in minutes instead of days.

"It was that crazy bitch! Not me!" Becker shook his head vigorously. "I'm not sayin' nothin'."

"I don't think it was your idea to abduct Matt Wilson," Paulo said, deliberately repeating the victim's name, "but the evidence is stacking up against you."

When Becker remained mute, Paulo said, "All we want is to bring Matt Wilson home to his family. You help us make that happen and the D.A. will drop the charges against you. Otherwise, you're looking at some serious time."

Becker scratched a crusty sore on his neck. "She won't hurt him. Crazy bitch thinks he's her kid just 'cause he looks like him. I tried to tell her." Becker's eyes softened, showing a flicker of the man he might have once been before meth sunk its claws into him. "Brandon was a good kid. Smart, you know? He coulda been somethin'. But that's fucking life," he snarled, slamming the door on his humanity. "She offered me money to get her a car and stuff." He ran a hand through his greasy hair. "Money she knew I couldn't refuse. It took me nearly a week to get her a fake ID and birth certificate since I couldn't risk doing nothin' local."

"Where did you get the IDs?"

Becker sucked on his rotting teeth. "A guy I know gets them from China."

Paulo wasn't surprised. Fake IDs were the newest commodity coming out of China. The fakes were so good the hologram and bar code both worked when scanned. "What were the names?"

"Maria and Barto Fernandez. The details on the car are in my phone. I don't know where she is now, but I know she's headed for Mexico. She's fluent in Mexican."

"When did you last see her?"

"I dropped off the car and shit to her yesterday at 'round ten in the mornin' and got back my ride. She was at a motel about an hour away."

"Did you see Matt Wilson when you dropped off this stuff?"

"Yeah, I seen him. He's fine. She wouldn't do nothin' to hurt that kid."

Paulo hoped that was true. "What about his dog, Pixie?"

Becker tucked his left arm against his stomach. "Didn't see it. She musta ditched it somewhere."

Paulo noted the change in his demeanor when Pixie was mentioned. Becker was closing himself off. That wasn't a good sign for the little dog. "Tell me again what happened when you first encountered the man in the alley."

AN HOUR later, Paulo joined Devin in the conference room, telling him what he'd learned from Becker. "Martin believes his sister left soon after he dropped off the car, so around ten in the morning. I tried to get him to give me specifics about where she's headed, but he claimed he didn't know beyond Mexico. She likely didn't want him to know."

"If she went through Texas, she could reach Del Rio Crossing within thirty hours," Devin said. "But with a young kid, I'm guessing it would take closer to forty hours. In either case, I don't think she's made it to the border yet. Unless this is all bullshit and Becker is just fucking with us."

Ignoring Devin's cynicism, Paulo said, "I'm guessing she's close to Texas by now, assuming she went through Missouri and Oklahoma.

We need the warrant for the house to include a computer if she has one. She might have plotted her route."

Devin made a sour face. "We're going to need to call in the Feds. They have more sway with the border patrols. But I'd rather have more confirmation before I call them in for assistance."

"Call them now, Dev; we'll have the evidence by the time they get here."

The conference room door opened and the chief walked in. "I sent an officer over to Marnie Becker's house. There was no response. She works at home as a Spanish-speaking customer service representative for an insurance company. According to her employers, she's been on medical leave since the day Matt Wilson went missing."

Devin nodded. "I'll take my team to the motel. Paulo, I want you to handle the warrants for the van, residence, and financial and phone records. Then I want you to talk to Dr. Roberts and find out what she knows."

Paulo bit down on the urge to object. He wanted to be searching that motel instead of pushing paperwork. It was his damn lead that had brought Becker in. "Dr. Roberts is too by-the-book to give us anything about her client without a subpoena."

Devin huffed. "So write the subpoena, but while you're waiting to get it in front of a judge, put a little pressure on her."

Chief Tucker shook his head. "How about I contact the feds and put out the Amber alert while you two boys duke it out?"

"Thank you, sir," Devin said, putting his hands on his hips. When the door closed, he said, "I'm in charge of this task force, Paulo, which means I decide who does what. And I'm taking *my* team to the motel. We'll find out if this lead is worth anything."

"You're being petty, Devin, relegating me to the sidelines out of spite."

"You found a junkie willing to sell out his sister, not the find of the century. Now, it's a lead we can't afford to ignore, but it's no slam dunk. This guy could just be jerking us around."

"You used to trust my instincts."

"Your instincts didn't used to be led by your dick," Devin said, exiting the conference room.

Paulo leaned against the side of the conference table, feeling drained. Through the anger, he could hear the worry in Devin's voice. Paulo hadn't broken any regulations. Yet. But the potential for this case to blow up in his face was seriously high. If that was what it took to bring home Matt, then so be it. He sure in the hell wasn't walking away from the case or from Jaron.

CHAPTER 9

PAULO KNOCKED on the door to Pampered Pooches. All his earlier attempts to talk to Jaron had been intercepted by Stephen. Hopefully, Jaron's meddling best friend had gone home for the night.

Stephen yanked open the door. "What the hell do you want?"

"I wanted to check on Jaron."

"He's resting," Stephen said, gripping the edge of the door hard enough to turn his knuckles white. "It was so nice of you to drive him home after that psycho nearly cut his throat. Oh wait, that was me!"

"I offered to drive him home," Paulo said weakly, knowing that answer wasn't good enough. He hadn't even waited for Stephen to arrive before heading to the station. He'd gone chasing after the lead, leaving Jaron sitting on that bench. "I should've insisted when he turned me down."

Stephen snorted. "You know what's sad? I think you're starting to believe your own bullshit. You're not here to check on Jaron. You're here to make sure the key to solving your case is in working order. He handed you the bad guy on a silver platter. You don't need his help anymore."

"Jaron wants to solve this case as much as I do. He was planning on going to the park without me. At least if he's with me, I can try to keep him safe."

"You did a bang up job today, detective."

When Paulo opened his mouth to retort, he heard a soft voice in the background.

Stephen whirled around. "You should be in bed."

Jaron walked through the salon in dirty jeans, likely the same ones he'd had on earlier. The blood-stained sweater he'd been wearing was thankfully gone, replaced with an oversized Pampered Pooches T-Shirt.

Paulo shoved the door open and stepped inside. "How are you doing?"

Jaron wrapped his arms around his chest. "I'm fine," he said, directing the answer to Stephen with a hint of exasperation. "I have a bump on the head, a small cut, and some bruises. I've gotten worse trying to retrieve cats from trees."

Paulo cocked his head. "You can't just tell them to come down?"

Jaron flapped his hand. "Just because I can communicate with cats doesn't mean they'll actually listen to me." He beckoned Paulo forward. "Come back to my room and tell me what happened with that guy."

"No fucking way," Stephen said, his voice wavering. "He is not staying."

Jaron's head flinched back slightly at Stephen's tone. "I'll be fine. I'll see you tomorrow."

"You know what? I fucking own this salon." Stephen pointed a finger at Paulo. "And he's not staying."

Paulo had no desire to get between two men that had a twenty-year friendship. The tension in the room had reached suffocating levels. "I can give you a call later, Jaron."

Jaron stared at Stephen as if Paulo hadn't spoken. "I suddenly need your *permission* to have someone in *my* room?"

"Let's be honest," Stephen said, his chin quivering. "You're more like a squatter than a tenant. You've been living off the break room scraps for years."

"Go to hell," Jaron said, his voice breaking. Looking at Paulo, he said, "Give me a minute." He turned around and headed for his room.

Seeing Jaron's devastated expression, Paulo was tempted to make Stephen's face match his multicolored hair. Until he got a look at Jaron's best friend. Stephen's shoulders sagged as if the guilt radiating from him was weighting him down.

"You're a fool," Paulo said, finally understanding. He'd thought Stephen's jealousy was behind the wheel, but a far more powerful emotion was in the driver's seat. Love.

"You're using him, whether you realize it or not. I'll be damned if I'll stand by and do nothing about it." Stephen looked back toward Jaron's room for a moment before heading down the hallway toward the galley kitchen.

Jaron emerged from his room dressed in a clean pair of jeans and a blue V-neck sweater that made his eyes shine like cobalt. He was holding a clear plastic container of dog food. Bear trailed after him, carrying his own leash. When he reached Paulo, he said, "Could I get a ride to the motel? I need to get a room and drop off Bear, and then we can talk."

"Why don't you come back to my place for tonight? You can figure out what you're going to do in the morning." Paulo couldn't stand the idea of Jaron staying in that shitty motel.

"Okay," Jaron said as if his brain was processing at half speed. "Thanks."

PAULO UNLOCKED and opened the front door to his apartment, motioning for Jaron and Bear to step inside.

Jaron looked around the barren living room. "Were you robbed?"

Paulo's living room décor consisted of an elliptical machine, a small collection of hand weights, and a crooked standing lamp. "My old furniture was too big to fit, so I put it in storage." He waved his hand. "I just haven't gotten around to finding new stuff. I managed to fit my bed and flat-screen TV in the bedroom." Paulo walked over to the room and flicked on the light. "Barely." The king-sized bed took up so much space he'd had to remove the door to the bedroom. Accessing his closet required crawling over the bed, but at least it had a pocket door. The built-in shelf on the headboard eliminated the need for an end table. Claustrophobic chic.

Jaron blushed. "I sort of assumed I'd be sleeping on your couch...."

Paulo stared at him, feeling his cheeks warm. "I didn't even think about it. I just didn't want you staying at that shitty motel Devin is at. You can have the bed."

Paulo heard Jaron swallow hard, a dry click in his throat. "The bed looks big enough to share."

Paulo rubbed his face with both hands, trying to drive away the image of Jaron sprawled naked in his bed. *This was such a bad idea.* Especially since Jaron was now a witness in an ongoing investigation, not just a consultant hired by the family of the vic. A defense attorney would have a field day with a detective who slept with one of the witnesses.

Jaron cleared his throat. "You mentioned Devin before. He's in charge of the investigation, right?"

Needing distance, Paulo walked over to the small kitchen that faced the living room. "Yeah, Devin works for the State Police in my old unit." He paused, not sure how much he wanted to explain. When it would no longer put his badge at risk, Paulo had every intention of taking Jaron out on a real date. Opting to be upfront, he added, "We were... together for about a year, but we broke up a couple of months ago."

Jaron followed him into the kitchen and placed the container of dog food on the counter. "Is it awkward having to work with him now?"

Paulo opened the cabinet, pulled out two bowls for Bear, and placed them on the counter. Was Jaron considering giving Stephen what he wanted? If things went wrong, it would definitely make working together at the salon difficult. "Devin is more pissed about me leaving the ISP and moving here than he is about us breaking up." Which pretty much explained why they'd broken up in the first place. "Stephen implied that you'd been together when you were kids."

Jaron looked confused for a moment before he spoke. "It's never been sexual unless you count the time we jacked off together during a WWF wrestling match."

Paulo smirked. "All those muscular guys covered in oil and spandex? Who could blame you?"

Laughing, Jaron shook his head. After opening the container of food, he filled the bowl. His expression turned serious. "He kissed me the morning you called. I was so shocked I didn't know what to do."

Paulo didn't like the idea of Stephen kissing Jaron, even though he knew he had no right to complain. Why the hell had the guy waited until now to make a move? Jaron was way too hot to have not dated before. But Paulo hadn't given much thought to the Stanton gay scene. In a town of thirteen thousand residents, how many would be gay? Twenty? Thirty? Maybe sixty if you include the college town twenty miles away and the surrounding smaller towns. Without a car, Jaron would be dependent on others to get him there. Paulo doubted Stephen would lend Jaron his car to go cruising bars for a hookup. He was surprised Jaron and Stephen hadn't dated, considering they were both gay and close to the same age. Stephen seemed a little too high strung for Paulo's taste, but he was attractive even with the extra pounds padding his waist. "You've never thought about the two of you getting together?"

Jaron scrunched up his nose. "I love Stephen. I love his parents. I love all four of his brothers, even the one who's one step away from being a televangelist. If they needed me, there isn't anything I wouldn't do for them." Turning on the faucet, he filled the other bowl with water, the contents spilling over without him seeming to notice. "They've treated me like family since I was a teenager." He shut off the water. After picking up the bowls, he found a clear space on the floor to place them.

Paulo could see black smudges on the back of Jaron's neck from where Becker had held him. Jaron must've crashed hard if he hadn't bothered to wash after having that methhead's hands on him. "Why don't you take a shower?"

Jaron pressed his palms against his eyes for a moment. "I'd like that, thanks."

Realizing Jaron had grabbed food for his dog but not clothes, Paulo said, "Hold on and I'll get you something to sleep in." He walked over to the bedroom. Climbing over the bed, he rummaged through a basket of clean clothes. He pulled out a tank top and drawstring shorts before maneuvering backward out of the bedroom. He handed the clothes to Jaron.

"Are you hungry?" Paulo asked.

"Not really," Jaron said, right before his stomach declared him a liar.

Paulo rolled his eyes. "I'm ordering a pizza. There are four spare toothbrushes under the sink, because the only dentist in this town is terrifyingly diligent."

Jaron grinned. "So I've heard. Stephen calls him the Cavity Nazi. He actually writes the date on the toothbrush packages to switch to them. And he sends out e-mail reminders weekly to floss."

"You don't go to see him?" Paulo asked, wondering if maybe he had missed a non-insane dentist in the phonebook.

"He's never really been in my budget." Jaron tapped his bottom lip. "But I've been lucky to not have any problems beyond crooked bottom teeth."

Reminders of Jaron's current and past poverty were jarring. Paulo wasn't sure why. He'd known plenty of people who barely scraped by. Maybe it was the lack of bitterness in Jaron's voice. Like he never expected to be more than the white trash Stephen accused him of being. That seemed unbelievably wrong. "There's a first aid kit and other toiletries in there too. Help yourself to whatever you need." Paulo took out his phone as Jaron headed for the bathroom.

Pulling up his contacts, Paulo selected the number for a nearby restaurant. One of the benefits of this apartment was its proximity to a pizzeria owned by a retired cop. He never waited more than ten minutes for his order. Unfortunately, they were going to have to eat it picnic style on the industrial gray carpet. Most of his meals were eaten in bed or while standing in front of the sink. They were going to take away his gay card if he didn't stop living like a straight frat boy. After this case, he'd try to find a place big enough to fit his furniture.

When the call was answered, he ordered a large veggie supreme and an order of breadsticks. Then he headed for the bedroom to change out of his suit and into jeans and a Chicago Blackhawks sweatshirt. Moving back into the main living area, he shoved his gun into an empty drawer in the kitchen. He doubted Jaron would be happy with the gun's usual home, the shelf above the bed.

When Jaron emerged from the shower, Paulo couldn't keep from staring. *Fucking hell.* Jaron's skin was flushed pink from the heat of the shower, his skin glistening with moisture. The too-big tank top showed his long, lean neck and delicate collarbone. A small, circular Band-Aid was the only indication he'd nearly gotten seriously hurt today. Paulo wanted to feast on all that warm, wet skin.

A knock on the door forced Paulo to drag his gaze from Jaron. He answered the door, paid the deliveryman, and then accepted the pizza and breadsticks.

With a doggy grin, Bear head-butted the door closed.

Amused, Paulo asked, "But can you lock and chain the door?"

Jaron laughed. "Don't give him any ideas." After surveying the room for a moment, he grabbed three twenty pound hand weights and set them on the ground. When Paulo handed him the pizza, Jaron rested the box on the weights, creating an Asian-like table. No one would be revoking Jaron's gay card.

Paulo got himself a beer, and Jaron requested water. Sitting Indian-style, they dug into the pizza and breadsticks. As they ate, he explained what he had learned from Martin Becker. He left out what they'd found in the van. Blood, vomit, and urine wasn't a good dinner conversation topic. It would take the lab a couple of days to get back the results, but they had found what was presumed to be white dog hair.

Lost in thought, Jaron nibbled on the end of a breadstick, seemingly oblivious to the effect it was having on Paulo's libido.

"So she thinks she's Matt's momma. That means she probably won't hurt him, right?"

"I hope not," Paulo said. "I'm going to talk to Marnie's psychiatrist tomorrow."

"Dr. Roberts."

"How did you know that?"

Jaron frowned. "She's the only one there I know?"

Paulo wondered at the scope of Jaron's abilities. Every time he thought he had them pinned down, they seemed to zigzag in another direction. "What you did today was amazing."

Jaron ducked his head. "I don't know about that. You found Martin's van. You would've tracked him down. And I doubt he would've pulled a knife on you."

"How did you know I found his van?"

Jaron froze for a moment before taking a sip of water. "One of the officers must've mentioned it. Or maybe I'm just remembering the van from my vision?" He shrugged and picked up another piece of pizza. "Will I be able to go to the motel they stayed at?"

Devin hadn't officially released the crime scene, but that didn't mean they couldn't take a look around. Now that they had a suspect, the investigation would change, particularly since the Feds were scheduled to make an appearance tomorrow. With the strong possibility of Marnie heading for Mexico, the Feds were likely to take the lead, even if, officially, it was a joint operation. The SPD didn't have the resources needed to conduct a country-wide search for a suspect. Paulo hated the idea of being relegated to the backseat in the investigation. "We might not be able to enter the motel room, but I can get you close if you're interested. We could go after I meet with Dr. Roberts in the morning."

"Sounds like a plan," Jaron said.

Jaron looked so distracted that Paulo asked between mouthfuls of pizza, "Are you sure you're okay?"

Jaron shrugged, but something crossed his eyes that Paulo couldn't identify. It almost looked like pain. "I don't know if it's because Pixie has physically moved so far away or what, but the connection feels frayed. Like it's unraveling in my fingers when I try to tug on it."

"You've been pushing yourself hard. Maybe you need to just let go of it and let your body recover."

Jaron closed his eyes briefly. "I'm not sure I know how. Using my abilities comes as naturally to me as breathing. How do you tell yourself to stop breathing?"

Paulo considered the question. The answer was you didn't. Because even if you tried holding your breath, eventually the instinct to breathe would override your will. And Jaron's abilities didn't come without a cost. How long before his bouts with low blood sugar caused him permanent damage?

Jaron smiled wanly. "You paid for dinner, so I'll clean up."

Paulo knew better than to argue. "Thanks." He rose and headed for the bathroom to get ready for bed.

When he emerged, Jaron took his turn. Paulo stripped down to his boxer shorts and climbed onto the bed. It was earlier than he normally went to sleep, but he didn't want Jaron to feel obligated to stay up. He pulled down the gray comforter for himself and Jaron.

Paulo set the alarm clock for 7:00 a.m. rather than watch Jaron crawl on his hands and knees onto the bed. How the hell was he supposed to fall asleep with Jaron within groping range?

Jaron lay down on the pillow with a weary sigh.

After turning on his side, Paulo brushed a damp strand of hair off of Jaron's cheek. "Stephen's right about you helping enough. Now that we have a name and a face, it's only a matter of time before we track Marnie down." He brushed his thumb across Jaron's bottom lip. "I'll make sure the Wilsons know how helpful you've been on this case."

Jaron reached up and touched the side of Paulo's bristled face, drawing him into a sweet kiss. "It's not over for me until I find Pixie," he whispered, before deepening the kiss.

Paulo lost himself in the sweetness of Jaron's mouth. It was so different from Devin. Kissing Devin had felt more like a competitive event than foreplay.

A loud sigh had Paulo pulling away to look at the end of the bed. Bear sat in front of the bed with his leash resting on the mattress. "You've got to be joking, mutt."

Bear sighed again and nudged the leash with his nose.

Jaron sighed. "It must be ten, his walk time." He sat up. "It won't take me long to take him out."

Placing a hand on Jaron's chest, Paulo shoved him back down. "Don't get up. I'll do it."

Paulo scrambled out of bed and threw on his clothes. After attaching the leash to Bear's collar, he made a quick stop in the kitchen before heading outside. His apartment complex wasn't big on outdoor décor. It had a few sad-looking flowerboxes and a patch of grass in front of the building. The icy cold concrete made him wish he'd stopped to put his shoes on.

Paulo held up a hotdog. "Do you know what this is?"

Bear wiggled his butt against the grass like he was a weed whacker.

"I've got one delicious bribe for you to hurry up." He tossed the hotdog to Bear, who gobbled it up in two bites. "Okay, now go pee, so I can get back in there before my balls freeze off."

Bear looked over at the small patch of grass and then back at Paulo's hand, undoubtedly waiting for another hotdog to magically appear.

"Rookie mistake, Silva. Bribe comes *after* you get the perp to do what you want." Paulo shoved his hands in his pockets. "Go pee, Bear," he said, trying to sound stern.

Bear licked his chops.

Paulo shook his head. "You're so lucky you were the big hero today."

Bear had certainly done a better job at protecting Jaron than Paulo had. Stephen's condemnation had hit too close to his own internal censure.

Twenty minutes later, after Bear had sniffed every inch of the six foot lawn in front of the complex at least five times, he had finally chosen the perfect spot to take a piss. They headed back inside, Bear attempting to lick Paulo's hotdog hand as many times as possible.

They made their way back into the apartment. Pointing to the living room carpet, Paulo said, "Go to bed."

Bear gave Paulo one more lick before lying down.

Paulo shucked his jeans and sweatshirt before crawling back into bed. He found Jaron curled up in a ball under the covers fast asleep. Paulo wasn't even surprised. That damn dog was better than a chastity belt.

CHAPTER 10

THE UNEXPECTED ring of the doorbell startled Peggy, making the calico cat on her lap leap to the floor while complaining loudly. Wondering who would come calling so late, Peggy dragged her old bones from the comfort of her La-Z-Boy recliner and walked to the door. She tightened her white robe and peered through the peephole, seeing a familiar face.

After unlocking and opening the door, she said, "Marnie, what a surprise. You should've called so I could've given you a proper welcome." Peggy frowned, taking in Marnie's appearance. Her long, curly hair had been cut short and dyed red inexpertly. "Are you okay, child?"

"I'm sorry I didn't call," Marnie said, tripping over her words as they rushed out. "Something amazing has happened, and I knew you'd understand."

Manic, Peggy thought, her concern rising. "Come inside, child, and we'll talk."

"I have a surprise," Marnie said, waving her hands. "Go inside and have a seat, and I'll bring it to you."

"Okay, Marnie," Peggy said, knowing from experience it was better not to argue when the woman was in this state. She moved back inside and sat on the couch. Outside of a card at Christmas, Peggy hadn't attempted to contact her former employer and friend since Brandon's funeral. She'd babysat Brandon five days a week from the time he was a babe. His death felt like losing one of her own grandbabies. When Peggy's daughter had urged her to move to Missouri, Peggy had jumped at the chance to move closer to her family. *Who had been there for Marnie in her grief, with her parents dead and her brother an addict?*

Peggy had always admired how hard Marnie worked to give Brandon the best life she could. The furniture in her home might be worn and tattered, but it was clean and safe. Marnie's return drew Peggy's attention back to the present. Peggy's heart hammered against her chest as she saw who was with Marnie. "Brandon?"

"Ha," Marnie said, punching the air. "I knew you'd see it." She began rambling about the accident and lying doctors so quickly Peggy could barely follow a word. The initial shock fading, Peggy took a closer look at the silent boy at Marnie's side. His arms were wrapped around himself and his dark eyes looked haunted. The resemblance to Brandon was uncanny, but as the adrenaline drained from her system, Peggy saw the differences, his cleft chin and small delicate ears. Most importantly, Brandon would have been nearing eight years old had he lived. *Who is this child, and why does Marnie have him?*

Chapter 11

When Jaron entered the salon, he saw four cardboard boxes stacked on the couch in the lobby. Next to the couch was a large, clear container of dog supplies. From the look of it, Stephen had shoved half of the salon's treat inventory in with Bear's stuff.

"He's not here," the receptionist, Amber, said, looking embarrassed. "He won't be back until late tonight."

Jaron knew that wasn't a coincidence. They'd fought in the past, but this felt different. Stephen had started ragging on Paulo from the moment he had picked Jaron up at the crime scene. It wasn't unusual for Stephen to disapprove of someone Jaron was interested in romantically. Given Jaron's track record with relationships, Stephen's concern might even be justified. But Stephen rarely turned that vicious tongue of his on Jaron.

Mel handed off her scissors to Chrissy before approaching Jaron. She yanked on Jaron's hand and pulled him into a tight hug. "What happened?"

It was bad enough that Stephen was throwing him out, but the whole staff had likely seen him shoving Jaron's stuff into boxes. "Stephen decided to evict his squatter."

Mel pulled back and cupped Jaron's face. "We won't last a week without you."

Jaron kissed her forehead. "You guys will be fine without me."

Dropping her hands, she shook her head, making her too-long dark bangs cover her eyes. "You help out more just sitting in your office than Saint Chrissy manages in the salon all day," she said loud enough for the saint to hear. Chrissy hadn't made many friends at the salon.

"Don't be mean," Jaron whispered. "A lot of people have a problem with regular psychics, let alone the doggy kind."

Mel rolled her eyes. "The dogs are calmer and better behaved when you're here. And everyone loves the dog communication videos you made."

Jaron cringed. "Please tell me they aren't posted on YouTube." Stephen had promised they would only be used in house.

Mel grinned evilly. "I put all ten of them on the Pamper Pooches YouTube channel. The one with Bear and the Chihuahua has, like, fifty thousand hits. After I posted the link to my FB page, it went vir—"

Jaron held up his hand to make her stop. "If you finish that sentence, I'll drown myself in one of the tubs." Comparing the popularity of a video to the spreading of disease was just plain wrong. He'd taken several workshops with Stephen on business and accounting software, but he was social network illiterate. Maybe it was because he'd had limited access to a computer growing up. Or more likely, it was because all his friends worked at the salon. The salon was his social network. At least, it had been.

Mel squeezed his arm. "Wait here and I'll pull my car around front. You can stay with Gary and me until Stephen gets his head out of his ass."

"I wouldn't say no to a ride, but I already booked a room at the Lakeside Motel. It could be a while before I figure out what I am going to do."

Mel frowned. "You're not thinking of giving up the psychic business, are you?"

"I don't know," Jaron said honestly. "I think I'll take a break for a little while after I finish my active cases." When Mel opened her mouth to object, he said, "I'm tired, Mel. I just need time to get my head together." Ever since starting the Matt Wilson case, Jaron had felt drained, emotionally and physically. His budget wouldn't allow a very long break, but at least Bear wouldn't starve thanks to Stephen raiding the supply closet.

THE LAKESIDE Motel wasn't located anywhere near a lake. The original owner claimed the lake had been there when the building was built in the 1950s. No one cared enough to contradict the old coot. When he died, the motel got a new owner but kept the name. The first heavy rainfall showed the new owner why the property was so cheap. The drainage was so bad that the parking lot became a shallow lake. It also had that reputation because inevitably some idiot would dump a bucket of minnows in "the lake" just to be an asshole. As a consequence, Jaron's room smelled like dead fish, mold, and desperation. But at forty bucks a night, it was the cheapest motel in town.

Bear sneezed three times, making Jaron happy to have his inferior olfactory perception. The room didn't look any better than it smelled. It had dun-colored carpeting, a queen-sized bed with a camouflage print, and a stuffed deer head on the wall. The deer's hide looked bleached and molted in several places. *Why do people put dead carcasses on their walls?*

Jaron placed the two boxes he carried under the deer, pulled off his gray corduroy coat and tossed it over the poor deer's head.

"What a shithole," Mel said as she entered the room carrying the container of dog supplies.

Jaron took the container from her and set it next to the boxes. "Everything I own smells like wet dog. I fit right in here." He ducked back outside to retrieve the last of the boxes before Mel could badger him into staying with her. Jaron might be on friendly terms with her husband, but he doubted Gary wanted him sleeping on their couch indefinitely. After grabbing the remaining boxes, he returned to the motel room and placed them with the others.

"I don't like you staying here," Mel said.

"It's only temporary," Jaron assured her.

"You're damn right. I'll drag you out of here myself if I have to." Mel gave him another bone-crushing hug before leaving. After locking up, Jaron stretched out on the scratchy comforter. Bear jumped onto the bed and laid his head on Jaron's stomach. Jaron rubbed his furry head, trying to ease the Newfie. Two days away from home had stressed Bear out. *What happens when I have to get a job?* The idea of Bear spending all day inside alone was unbearable. He would have to convince Stephen to let Bear stay at the salon when Jaron was at work. He was sure Mel would agree to let Bear into the backyard a couple of times during the day.

Jaron knew his twenty-year friendship with Stephen wouldn't crumble under the weight of one fight. But he also knew he couldn't go back to living in the salon.

Since Stephen had mentioned the remodel, Jaron had been scouring the want ads. The places he could afford didn't bother with an online ad. There were two apartment complexes in town that had studio apartments in the four hundred dollar range. He didn't know much about them beyond that they were old and cheap. He could handle outdated, but it had to be clean. He'd never managed to get a cockroach to talk to him, let alone get it to leave.

Being the owner of several apartment complexes, Stephen's uncle Simon would be able to tell Jaron the places to avoid. But then Simon would insist on Jaron staying at one of his complexes in the surrounding towns. No doubt, Jaron would end up with a special rate, which was one step above being a squatter.

Jaron had around five hundred dollars in savings, enough to cover a deposit. He had earned the money a few years ago, before he opened the Pet Psychic business. He'd seen a flyer for a missing hard-of-hearing show dog. Finding the Cavalier King Charles spaniel had been the catalyst to open his own business. Jaron didn't have many expenses when he'd first started beyond business cards. Stephen's parents had given him their old laptop when he graduated high school, and Stephen had added a tag line for Jaron's pet psychic services in his paid advertisements for the salon. Jaron had been living off Stephen's generosity for too long. It was no wonder Stephen had finally snapped.

Jaron should get up and make use of the motel's free Wi-Fi and see if Wal-Mart or one of the other big retailers had job openings. It was more likely than finding something local. Though how he'd travel the twenty miles to get there, he didn't know. His bike, which he just realized he had left in Stephen's backyard, wouldn't do him much good in bad weather. Grabbing the spare pillow, he smacked it over his face.

Not one to tolerate such a pathetic display, Bear shoved his cold, wet nose under the pillow and deployed a tongue attack.

Jaron tossed the pillow on the floor and wiped the slobber from his chin. "You're right. I'm being a drama queen. What's a little black ice to keep you in kibble?"

Bear leaped off the bed and walked over to the door.

"You're definitely the smart one in this relationship." He would take Bear for a long walk. Then, Bear would sleep while Jaron went to the crime scene with Paulo. Thinking about Paulo made Jaron's cheeks heat. Paulo had looked like he wanted to make a meal of him. Yet his kiss was sweet and gentle. Jaron loved the way Paulo's accent thickened when he got turned on.

He shoved those thoughts away. Romance would have to wait until he'd found a new job and a place to live. Homeless and jobless wasn't very sexy.

Jaron scrambled off the bed and reached for his coat. He halted when he felt a strange sensation on his back. It felt like a static shock had moved down his spine. After a brief pause, he felt it again. Not painful exactly, but definitely odd. It had almost felt like someone was petting his back with a static-charged brush. When he attempted to concentrate on the feeling, it disappeared. What could have caused that?

He examined the comforter and the sheet below, relieved when he didn't see any creepy crawlies moving around. Was the mattress the kind that vibrated? An examination of the headboard didn't reveal a place to shove in a quarter.

Jaron moved into the bathroom, turned on the light, and pulled up his shirt. Turning around, he looked over his shoulder at the mirror. The skin along his spine appeared red and blotchy. He could also see several small scratches. They hadn't been there yesterday when he showered at Paulo's place. Could his life get any weirder?

CHAPTER 12

PAULO PULLED out the documents from his briefcase as he rode the elevator to Dr. Roberts's floor. The scope of the subpoena might be limited to information pertaining to the death of Marnie Becker's child, but Paulo marveled at the speed with which it had been issued. Was it the small town factor? Or the media frenzy over the case? Either way, he had the means to get Dr. Roberts to talk about one of her patients. He'd opted to show up unannounced rather than give her time to bring in the hospital lawyers.

Exiting the elevator, he headed for the doctor's office. He'd confirmed with the front desk that Dr. Roberts didn't currently have a patient. He knocked on the door.

"Enter," Dr. Roberts said, her voice curt.

Paulo entered the office. Dr. Roberts's gray hair was pulled back into a severe bun. She didn't look happy to see him. Paulo wasn't surprised. Without asking for permission, Paulo took a seat on the plush chair in front of Dr. Roberts's antique wooden desk. "I arrested Martin Becker yesterday. Are you familiar with him?"

"Martin Becker is not one of my patients," she said, evading the question effectively. The tightness of her mouth telegraphed her familiarity with him.

"He's the brother of one of your patients, Marnie Becker, correct?" When the doctor didn't respond, Paulo handed her the subpoena. "Based on information obtained from Martin Becker, his sister has become a person of interest in the disappearance of Matt Wilson. I need to ask you some questions about Marnie and the death of her son, Brandon."

"Doctor/Patient confidentiality pre—"

Paulo put his hands on her desk, pushing down hard enough to make the old wood creak. "We both know there are exceptions to that rule when innocent lives are at stake. And I've got a court order to back it up."

"Yes, detective. But your only evidence Ms. Becker is involved seems to be the unreliable testimony of a drug addict looking to avoid jail time." She tossed the paperwork into her outbox. "I'll have the hospital's legal team review the subpoena and get back to you. Good day, detective."

Paulo had no intention of giving up that easily. "Martin's plea deal is contingent on the safe return of Matt Wilson. He has no motivation for lying."

"I wouldn't be surprised if he was punishing her for refusing to give him money. He has an expensive habit to feed, but she has—rightfully so—been unwilling to fund his drug use."

Paulo resisted the urge to smirk. He might not have Devin's honeyed tongue, but he had his own ways of dragging the truth out of people. People loved to contradict you. "I'd like to ask Marnie about it, but no one knows where she is. She hasn't logged on to work her shift on the customer service line since two days before Matt Wilson was abducted. And she's not at home."

Dr. Roberts looked startled. Opening up a small laptop, she said, "Her work is supposed to contact me if she misses two consecutive days."

Paulo heard the sound of Microsoft Windows loading on her laptop. "When we talked before, you said that the hospital didn't have a way to contact you when you were in Florida. Maybe Marnie's work tried to contact you while you were there?"

Dr. Roberts's hands hovered over the keyboard. "A colleague was supposed to be handling my patients while I was gone."

Paulo heard the unspoken censure in her voice. Considering the chaos that followed Matt's disappearance, it wasn't surprising if one failure to show up to work was shoved aside. That was assuming

Marnie's employers had even bothered to contact the hospital. Paulo sincerely doubted it.

Dr. Roberts turned toward the laptop screen. "Did you check with the Gordon Center to see if she'd checked herself in? She spent several weeks there after the death of her son."

It was clear Dr. Roberts wasn't convinced Marnie was responsible for Matt's disappearance. She just thought her patient had gone AWOL, not abducted a child. Paulo needed to take another approach with her. "You admire Marnie."

Dr. Roberts turned toward him. "Why shouldn't I? The media eviscerated Marnie, painting the picture of an unstable monster. The public demanded to know why Social Services hadn't taken her child away from her. Marnie gave her child a safe and loving home, all the while overcoming tremendous obstacles. But somehow she's unfit? One in five adults has a mental illness in this country, but the media and Hollywood would have you believe they are all one step away from being violent psychopaths."

Paulo happened to think stealing a child away from his parents was pretty damn monstrous, but he kept his opinion to himself. He also knew how easily the media twisted and sensationalized a story to ramp up the hype. Marnie might've been stable once, but the death of her child had obviously been the catalyst for her mental decline. Needing to understand her disorder better, he said, "Her brother said she's bipolar, but the way he described her paranoia and delusions, it sounded more like schizophrenia. Could she be suffering from both?"

Dr. Roberts shook her head. "A person can't be suffering from both. Bipolar disorder affects a patient's mood, emotions, and behavior. They experience depressive episodes, manic episodes, and mixed episodes."

"Depressive episodes are when they are depressed, right? And don't have much motivation to do stuff."

Dr. Roberts nodded. "Manic is the polar opposite state. Many patients describe feeling very happy and report increased activity and decreased need for sleep. It is also where patients report changes in behavior such as grandiose thinking and racing thoughts. Some patients have psychotic symptoms such as delusions and hallucinations."

Dr. Roberts was giving him the textbook definition of the disorder, staying away from anything personal. Paulo needed her to focus on Marnie. "Meaning it is possible that a person suffering from bipolar could convince themselves that a loved one wasn't really dead, especially if she was denied a chance at closure and being blamed for the death."

Dr. Roberts folded her hands on the desk. She didn't speak for over a minute. "My sister died when she was twenty years old from a head injury she got from a skiing accident. Thirty years later the last thing my mother said to me before she died was that mothers should never outlive their children."

Paulo shifted in his seat, painfully aware that Dr. Roberts had also outlived her own child too. "I can't imagine what that's like."

When she spoke, her voice sounded like she'd acquired a two pack a day smoking habit. "All good parents who experience the death of a child suffer guilt regardless of the circumstances. Add to that the community and media bombarding Marnie with blame, and I wasn't surprised when she checked herself in for treatment."

Paulo leaned back in his chair. "But the delusion makes that all better, right? If Brandon isn't dead, then she doesn't need to feel guilty anymore. But how long does the delusion last?"

"The duration of mood episodes typically last a couple of hours." Dr. Roberts sighed. "But it can last several months for some patients."

Paulo could see that Dr. Roberts still didn't want to believe Marnie was involved in the abduction. "I'm not at liberty to give you specifics, but I can tell you we have more evidence than just her brother's testimony. Marnie has Matt. I would bet my career on it."

Dr. Roberts stared at Paulo, her dark eyes seeming to gauge his sincerity. "I have no knowledge of Marnie's whereabouts, detective. What information are you looking for? She has never talked about Brandon still being alive."

"Her brother attempted to convince her to let Matt go, and I would assume that Matt has as well. How would Marnie react to someone challenging her delusion?"

Dr. Roberts pondered the question for a moment. "There's no way for me to predict definitively. But I can tell you that Marnie abhors violence. I can't see her physically harming Matt. She would be more likely to seek validation that Brandon is alive from someone who knew him."

"Is there anyone specifically you think Marnie might contact?"

"Marnie has an aunt in Texas, but they're not close. And Brandon's father was never involved in his life. She would more likely seek someone who knew Brandon, such as a family friend or maybe a teacher. She would want someone to tell her she's right about Brandon being alive."

Paulo was almost afraid to ask his final question. "What if Marnie believes the police are going to take her child away? Do you think she'll still be nonviolent?"

Dr. Roberts looked away. "I don't know."

"Thank you for your time." Paulo stood. "If you hear from Marnie or think of anything else that might help us find her, please contact me immediately."

Paulo exited her office and headed for the elevator. As he hit the button, he heard his cell phone ring. He pulled out his phone and answered the call when he saw it was Jaron. "How's it going?" he asked, hearing what sounded like traffic in the background. "Where are you?"

"I decided to take Bear for a walk." The sounds in the background faded, as if Jaron was moving away from the street. "I didn't know how long he'd be cooped up in my motel room while we visit the crime scene."

Paulo exited the elevator and headed for the main entrance. "I thought you were going back to the salon to talk to Stephen."

Jaron sighed. "Stephen wasn't there, but he'd boxed up all my stuff. That sent a pretty clear message that he wants me out."

Paulo gritted his teeth. "He can't legally evict you without giving you at least a ten day written notice."

"I'm not really a tenant. He let me stay there because he's my friend. I don't want to drag the court into it."

Paulo dropped the issue for now. "How about I meet you at the motel in an hour?"

"I'll see you then."

STOPPING IN front of his motel room, Jaron dug into the front pocket of his jeans to find the keycard. No luck. He'd hoped to have enough time to jump in the shower before Paulo showed up. He and Bear had had a serious power-walk. The Newfie was still panting. While hunting for the card in his back pocket, he noticed an attractive blond man coming from the opposite direction. The man's expensive suit looked like it had been custom-made to fit his broad shoulders and narrow waist.

The man stopped in front of Jaron. "What are you doing here?" he asked, sounding surprised rather than confrontational.

Jaron frowned. "I'm staying here?" He didn't recognize the man. Feeling uneasy, he continued to hunt for his keycard until he found it in the inside pocket of his jacket.

There was a spark of some indefinable emotion in his blue eyes. "You're Jaron, right?"

"Um, have we met?" Jaron couldn't imagine forgetting someone that looked like a male model.

"I'm Sergeant Devin Morris with Illinois State Troopers." He grinned, showing off teeth that would make the Cavity Nazi proud. "You can call me Devin." He held out his hand.

Jaron dropped Bear's leash and shook Devin's hand. "Nice to meet you," he said, feeling incredibly awkward. Like any second he'd accidently blurt out, "I made out with your ex." With the exception of his blond hair, Devin couldn't be more different from Jaron. He looked sophisticated in a way Jaron could never manage even if he owned a suit.

Curling back his fingers, Devin offered his hand to Bear, but Bear showed no interest in sniffing. *Weird.* "I just swung by the motel to pick up a folder I'd forgotten, but I'd been hoping to talk with you. We have a task force meeting later today with the Feds. Do you have a few minutes?"

"Um, I can talk for a little while, but then I need to leave for a case." Jaron wasn't sure if the visit to the crime scene was official or not. He didn't want to get Paulo in trouble. Devin seemed friendly, but something about his smile seemed a bit off.

Jaron unlocked and opened his door. When he stepped into the room, he gave Bear the mental version of "be good," and released him from the leash. "Just give me a second." He focused on getting Bear's bowl from the container and bringing it into the bathroom. He filled the bowl with water and placed it on the floor before returning to the main room.

Bear looked tense as he tolerated Devin petting his head. Was Jaron responsible for Bear's unfriendly attitude or was Bear picking up negative vibes from Devin?

Seemingly oblivious to the doggy cold shoulder, Devin said, "One of the officers at the station showed me a video of this guy being walked by a tiny dog. It was freaking hilarious."

Jaron suppressed the urge to sigh. In retrospect, the scenario had been pretty silly. But he'd been trying to show people that positive training, not brute strength, ensured a dog heeled during a walk. A little kid would've worked better as a demonstration, but the Chihuahua was easier for him to get a hold of.

Bear grumbled, sending Jaron an image of Devin's jacket and an oily smell.

"Huh," Jaron said. "A gun."

Devin raised his sculpted brows. "Pardon?"

Once Jaron assured Bear everything was okay, the Newfie trotted into the bathroom to get a drink. "Sorry, I just realized Bear can smell the gun oil or maybe the gun itself. He reacted the same way when we were at Pau—um… when we were talking to the police officer."

Devin's friendly persona disappeared. He closed the distance between them, stopping only to pull the bathroom door closed. "That's not how you were going to end that sentence."

Jaron found himself pressed against the wall, stuck between the deer head and Devin.

Devin placed his hands on the wall, boxing Jaron in. "I'll bet your pooch reacted to the scent when you were in Paulo's kitchen. Did he force you to eat that horrible Fuba cake he loves so much for breakfast?"

Jaron wondered how the hell Devin knew that. He had to agree about the cake being disgusting. Cornmeal and coconut? *Yuck!* He'd eaten it anyway. He had worried it would be awkward in the morning with Paulo. But he felt comfortable with Paulo in a way he couldn't remember feeling before.

Devin must've read something in Jaron's expression because he looked decidedly smug. "Paulo hides his gun in the kitchen when he doesn't want to scare off a trick."

Jaron raised his chin. "I'm not his trick." He pressed his palms against Devin's remarkably firm chest and shoved, barely managing to move the man an inch. "We didn't do anything." Technically a lie, but a couple of kisses didn't make him into a trick. "I got into a fight with my friend and I needed a place to stay for the night."

Devin's face hardened. "Do you think I'm a moron?"

Bear barked and butted his head against the bathroom door.

Devin looked at the flimsy door warily before taking several deep breaths. "Martin Becker will be charged if we don't bring home Matt safe. Sleeping with a witness would earn Paulo a serious reprimand at a minimum. If a defense attorney or the media found out, it could be a hell of a lot worse. He could be prosecuted for witness tampering. If that happens, I'll make damn sure you're charged with impeding a police investigation."

Jaron realized Devin genuinely wanted to protect Paulo. "It's good that you look out for him even though you guys broke up. I won't do anything that will put him in a compromising position."

"We aren't broken up. I'm not his goddamn ex."

"What?"

Devin laughed; the sound devoid of any humor. He pushed away from the wall. "We were never a couple. He's been my friend since the Academy. The sex was stress relief, friends with benefits. That's all it was."

The cold dismissal made Jaron angry. "He said you were together, not fuck-buddies. Are you the reason he left ISP?"

"I'm not the reason he left."

Jaron couldn't resist asking. "Then why?"

Devin turned on his heel and strode to the door. He opened it but paused in the threshold. "If you want to know the real reason he's hiding in Stanton, ask him about the Jefferson case."

Jaron watched Devin leave. He let out a disgruntled Bear from the bathroom before taking out his cell phone. Pulling up Paulo's number from his contacts, he hit the Send button. Paulo answered on the third ring.

"We can't go to the crime scene." Jaron had no idea how he'd get there on his own. Car rental? Borrow Mel's car?

"What happened?"

"I ran into Devin outside of my motel room."

"That's another reason you shouldn't stay at that rathole. Stephen needs to get over himself and let you move back in."

Was Jaron seriously having this same conversation again? "Would you be quiet a second and let me explain?"

Paulo's silence was very loud. His long sigh had Jaron inexplicably admiring his lung capacity. It was distracting as hell. And annoyingly hot.

Paulo's voice dipped down low, and then raised again, his accent sounding almost musical. "Tell me what's wrong, *anjo*."

Jaron made a frustrated noise. He wanted to say "Your porno voice is giving me pervy thoughts, and I don't want to get you in trouble." They would definitely end up having seedy motel sex if he did. "You can't go with me to the crime scene. Devin will have you reprimanded."

"He's bluffing," Paulo said, sounding confident.

"And have me arrested."

Paulo didn't have a snappy comeback for that. A jail cell would certainly solve Jaron's housing dilemma.

Paulo made another pornographic noise. "I'll understand if you don't want to come with me. But I need to go there."

Jaron bit his bottom lip. He was fairly sure the chief wouldn't toss his butt in jail. Mostly. "Are you sure Devin's bluffing?"

"Yes," Paulo said without hesitation. "He might try to kick my ass for going behind his back, but he won't rat me out to the chief."

Paulo had a lot of confidence in his ex-boyfriend's loyalty. Was it the cop thing? Or were stronger emotions in play? Jaron sighed. "I'm staying at room 106. We can leave whenever you want."

Paulo's grin was audible. "I'll be there in ten."

JARON HAD been shocked to learn the motel Marnie had stayed at with Matt was only an hour away from Stanton. He'd been staring at the picture of Marnie and her son that Paulo had given him for most of the drive. She and Brandon looked so happy in the photograph.

Paulo pulled the SUV into the parking lot of a run-down motel and parked near the front office. The motel was located off the highway at more of a way station for travelers than an actual town. The motel was one long line of rooms. The kind of place that offered rooms by the hour, something even the Lakeside motel didn't do. According to Paulo, Marnie had been staying in room 102 for nearly a week. The idea that she'd been only fifty miles away was maddening. If Jaron had gotten on his bike, would he have been able to track the motel down? It was a little far, but he'd ridden farther in one day.

After they exited the vehicle, Paulo popped the trunk. A wide variety of equipment was stored in there that Jaron couldn't identify. Paulo began rummaging through the containers of equipment and putting items into a black backpack, calling it a portable evidence kit.

Jaron pulled up the hood of his red hoodie to combat the spitting overcast sky. He felt like a kid standing next to Paulo in his suit and trench coat.

Paulo zipped up the backpack and closed the trunk. "I'll talk to the manager and get us access to the room."

"Wait a second," Jaron said, looking down at his right hand. His fingers were tingling like his arm had fallen asleep. The air around him grew colder as the strange sensation crept slowly up his arm. *What the hell?* He opened and closed his fingers, trying to shake off the disturbing feeling.

"Tell me what's going on, Jaron," Paulo said, a slight tremor in his voice.

Jaron struggled to clarify the sensation. "It's hard to explain."

Paulo dropped the backpack. "Try, because I can see your breath, but I can't see mine."

Jaron shivered as if his body only just recognized the cold seeping into his bones. He regretted only wearing a fleece hoodie, but the temperature had been in the midfifties when he left Stanton. Now, he felt like he had been dropped into the middle of the Arctic. "I'm feeling pressure on my arm, almost like something is pulling me." He took a step forward and the intensity increased. "I think maybe I'm being drawn towards Pixie." It felt like he was walking an unruly dog Bear's size, not a ten-pound shih tzu. But maybe physical size didn't matter since he was being drawn to Pixie's energy. Stumbling on a pothole, he lost his balance. He swore as his knees slammed against the asphalt with a bone-jarring thud.

Paulo swallowed visibly. "You're moving," he said, pointing at the ground.

"What?" Jaron asked, looking down. With the initial shock of the pain fading, he could feel it. His jeans scraped against the parking lot, as some unseen force slowly moved him forward. "What the fuck?"

"Is that... normal?"

"Normal?" Jaron said, his voice sounding hysterical even to his own ears.

Paulo threw up his hands. "I'm a little out of my depth here, Jaron. It's not like I can shoot it." He licked his lips. "Right?"

Jaron held out his hand. "Help me stand before I get road rash."

Paulo hesitated for several painful seconds before offering Jaron his hand.

Great, Jaron thought bitterly. *I've officially qualified as a freak.*

Jaron waved Paulo away. "I've never been normal," he said quietly. With a groan he rose to his feet. His jeans had torn at the knees and blood was oozing through the holes. *It had to be the new ones.* "Nothing about this case has been normal." From the moment the Wilsons had stepped into his office, his life had been in a tailspin. He took a couple more steps toward the street and away from the motel.

"Dammit," Jaron said as he lurched forward.

Paulo wrapped his arms around Jaron's waist. "I've got you." He grunted, his arms tightening. "But not for long."

"Enough," Jaron said, louder than he intended. Closing his eyes, he pictured Bear's leather leash. He imagined the handle of the leash wrapped around his hand, pulling it taut. The pressure eased enough that Jaron no longer felt like his shoulders were in danger of dislocating. He kept his arm to the side gripping an invisible leash. "I've become a freaking mime," Jaron griped.

"That's what bothers you?" Paulo asked, sounding incredulous. "Not the unseen force reeling you in like a fish on a hook?"

"It doesn't feel evil or anything." Jaron stepped away from Paulo and continued walking. He barely resisted the urge to verbally praise his imaginary dog for heeling. *How can this be my life?* "It just feels really enthusiastic. Like how when you have a ball in your hand and the dog is just vibrating with excitement. You are the center of its world in that moment."

After they had walked for about ten minutes, Paulo asked, "Why this way and not toward the highway?"

The area had turned more industrial. The small collection of gas stations and fast food restaurants had given way to warehouses and factories.

Jaron suspected he knew the reason. "Pixie isn't with Matt." He pressed a hand against his churning stomach. The next words spilled from his mouth without conscious thought. "Pixie barks at Marnie for making Matt sad." An image formed in Jaron's mind: Matt huddled on the floor of the motel, tears streaming down his cheeks. He kept repeating words Pixie knew. Mommy. Daddy. Home.

"Marnie offers Pixie peanut butter, likely to get her to be quiet. But Pixie refuses and keeps barking, barking, barking." Images slammed through Jaron's mind like a slide show set on high speed, making him dizzy. When he swayed, Paulo grabbed his arm. There had to be a way to focus the visions. After taking a steadying breath, Jaron said, "Show me Matt."

Jaron could see Matt lying motionless on a floral bedspread. A small plastic cup and a bottle of what looked like cough medicine sat on the end table. He realized the view was from above, as if someone was holding Pixie. "I think Marnie might have given Matt something to calm him down and make him sleep. It looks like cough medicine gauging by the shape and color, but I can't be sure."

Paulo's expression darkened. "Matt's old enough to know he's in danger, but young enough not to understand the threat."

"I thought Dr. Roberts said Marnie wouldn't likely hurt Matt."

"Maybe not directly, but what if Matt is hurt trying to escape? Or a cop IDs her and she runs? We could end up with another child dying in a car crash."

On the ride to the motel, Paulo had shared with Jaron Marnie's tragic history. Jaron couldn't help feeling sorry for her.

Feeling the pressure yield, Jaron stopped and looked around. He saw two red brick buildings with a narrow alley between them. Barred windows lined the alley on either side. Toward the far end of the alley was a torn garbage bag. The sight of it made Jaron's chest ache. Any sympathy he might've had for Marnie evaporated. "What I've been seeing is an echo of Pixie's last day." He gestured toward the bag.

"Stay here." Paulo pulled out a camera from his backpack and snapped several pictures. He then examined the ground in front of the trash bag before approaching it from the right. He took several more pictures.

Turning away, Jaron pressed his hand against his mouth. Acid licked at the back of his throat as the images shoved their way through his mind. He saw a nervous-looking Marnie handing Pixie to her brother and unlatching Pixie's collar. Wishing he could read lips, Jaron watched her explain something to her brother. *Did she say shelter?* He couldn't be sure.

Looking grim, Paulo walked back over to Jaron. "I don't want to disturb the scene, but it's definitely a small white dog. It's not wearing a collar, but if it's Pixie a scan for her microchip will confirm it." Paulo's voice sounded cool and controlled, but his clenched hands and the bulging veins on his neck hinted at anger boiling beneath the surface. "Did Marnie do this?"

Jaron shook his head. "Marnie gave Pixie to her brother. And Martin tossed Pixie into the back of the van. Pixie found a bag of what I'm guessing was drugs. She bit it and then spit it out. Could that have killed her?"

Paulo nodded. "For a ten-pound dog, it wouldn't take much if she inhaled it or ingested it."

Jaron closed his eyes, willing the images away. "Why would Marnie give Pixie to her brother? She had to know he wouldn't take good care of the dog."

Paulo wrapped his hand around the back of Jaron's head and pulled him into a tight hug. "I can guess at the reason. If she's trying to run away with Matt, then Pixie makes it more likely that people might recognize them. The dog's also a connection to his old family."

Jaron pressed his forehead against Paulo's shoulder. He swallowed hard, a hot tear slipping down his cheek. "Why not just leave Pixie behind in the motel room? She has to know how much Matt loves his dog. How could she be so cruel?" His stomach felt like it was on fire. "Matt's name is ping ponging around in my brain because that's all Pixie was focused on. Matt was her boy and she failed him. It was anger and frustration that made her bite that bag of drugs."

Massaging the back of Jaron's neck, Paulo said, "We're going to find Marnie. I promise you. We're going to bring Matt home."

Jaron pulled back from him and wiped his eyes. "I know you will, but I've reached the limit of what I can do to help."

"What do you mean?"

"Pixie is dead, Paulo. The trail died with her. There's nothing more I can do."

"I don't believe that. I think your abilities are changing... evolving. You said yourself nothing about this case has been normal. It's like that day in the forest when you were a kid."

"How do you know about that? Did the chief tell you?"

Paulo nodded. "Those dogs were ten or fifteen miles away, but you reached out to them, drew them to you. Because a part of your subconscious knew you wouldn't survive without them. If you could do that at aged four, imagine what you could do now. You just have to find a way to control your abilities, so it doesn't keep draining you physically."

Jaron smiled wanly. "You'll find Matt. I know you will, Paulo."

"Marnie handing over Pixie to a brother she doesn't trust changes everything. She's in panic mode and that's dangerous for Matt." Paulo's gaze darted around the filthy alley. "How do you find pets that have died if you're not a medium?"

"I sense an electromagnetic field that radiates from the animal. I think that energy must linger for a time after the pet dies. I've found deceased pets before, but it's never been this intense. I get a few images from their last moments, not a complete replay." Jaron hoped to never feel anything like it again.

"There's got to be more to it if you can get readings off their collars. Some of those dogs on my test had died years ago. Have you ever tried to get a reading from a dead pet?"

Paulo's questions felt disturbingly like an interrogation. "I only got readings from the live dogs," he insisted. "I could only tell the dogs were dead, nothing more. I've had these abilities my whole life. I think I woulda noticed if I'd suddenly become a dead doggy whisperer."

Paulo said something that sounded like "*merda*." "Pixie was dead when you confronted Martin in the alley. You weren't following the trail to her body then. You were tracking her killer."

"W-what do you mean her killer?"

"There's no way Pixie got into Martin's stash by accident. It was a convenient way to get rid of the dog." Paulo grabbed Jaron's arm, drawing him close. "I know you're freaked out, but we have a chance to bring Matt home. You just need to eat and rest. I need to call in the local police to help secure the scene. I can get one of them to drive you back to the motel."

Was that the reason Martin could hear Pixie? Was she haunting her killer? Feeling numb, Jaron pulled away from him. "I can walk." There was no way he was spending another minute in this alley. "I've got glucose tablets if I need them."

Paulo shook his head. "I don't want you walking back alone. It shouldn't take the police more than a couple of minutes to get here."

Jaron took a step back when Paulo reached for him. "I'll be fine."

Jaron turned away from Paulo and headed back toward the motel. Paulo didn't understand. During the flashback, Jaron had felt Pixie die, felt a part of himself die with her.

CHAPTER 13

PAULO ENTERED the crowded SPD conference room. Forty men and women were crammed into a space designed for half that number. Someone had taken out the tables and lined up the chairs like a press conference. The chief stood at the front of the room with a man in his late forties. The man had slicked-back black hair and a blank expression. Fed. Seeing as how Paulo barely recognized half of the people, the head Fed must have quite a posse.

Paulo had been worried about being late to the meeting. Fortunately, the way Chief Tucker was scowling at the ceiling-mounted LCD projector meant the meeting wouldn't be starting anytime soon.

Noticing Devin near the back of the room, Paulo weaved through the sea of sweating cops. When he reached him, Paulo stared pointedly at the blond rookie sitting next to Devin. Connors vacated the seat, muttering "asshole" under his breath.

Devin cupped his hands around his mouth and said, "Woof!"

Dozens of cops around them took up the chorus, barking and howling as a red-faced Connors made it to the back of the room where it was standing room only. The chief was seemingly too busy poking at a laptop to give a shit about the doggy chorus.

As Paulo took his seat, Devin knocked his shoulder against Paulo's. "Can't let the rookies get uppity."

Paulo refused to acknowledge Devin's unspoken apology. Devin had crossed a line when he tried to bully Jaron into walking away from this case. "I prefer uppity to threats of reprimands and jail time."

Devin lowered his voice to an angry whisper. "I'm trying to help you, asshole." He rubbed his forehead. "You honestly expect me to stand by while you commit career suicide?"

Paulo nearly said yes, which was all kinds of disturbing. Was he deliberately sabotaging his career? Not something he wanted to think about. He lifted his chin. "Shouldn't you be up there with them?"

Devin straightened his tie. "I'm sure I'll get dragged up there eventually. This is the chief's rodeo. We need to look united in front of the Feds."

Chief Tucker introduced Special Agent Ronald Fisher and thanked him for his assistance on the case. Paulo zoned out as the chief started naming Fisher's team and began bringing everyone up to speed on the details of the case.

Paulo's thoughts wandered to Jaron. He'd already confirmed with the vet that the remains he and Jaron had discovered were indeed Pixie. He only wished the discovery hadn't come at such a high cost. Jaron had been deathly pale and visibly shaking by the time they got back to Stanton. Watching Jaron gobble up the disgusting glucose tablets had made Paulo realize he needed to squash his growing sense of urgency and stop pushing Jaron so goddamn hard. Moments after Jaron had discovered Pixie's corpse wasn't the time to start poking his abilities with a stick.

The investigator in him wanted to know everything about Jaron's psychic talent. *How the hell does an intangible ghost-dog drag a full-grown man?* Paulo had barely resisted the urge to bust out a prayer, something he hadn't done since primary school. Jaron might not think he was an animal medium, but it was the only explanation that made sense.

"Are we going to find out anything new at this meeting?" Paulo asked, keeping his voice low.

Devin opened his mini notebook. "Marnie cleaned out her checking and savings account for a total of fifteen thousand."

"She gave half that much to her brother."

"We've got an alert placed on her credit card, but I doubt she'll use it. We need to get the Wilsons updated on the case. They have to be ready to make another statement to the press either tonight or tomorrow."

Paulo gave Devin a sideways look. "Are you finally convinced Marnie is the perp?"

Devin grimaced. "I still say it was the dog and not psychic vibes that led Jaron to Martin, but the evidence is stacking up against his sister. Martin's not lying about her involvement. The motel manager picked out Marnie from a photo lineup. He never saw the kid, but he did see her with a small white dog a couple of times. He also confirmed the checkout time. It matches Martin's statement. And since you broke the case, you get to break the news to the parents."

Paulo sighed, dreading having to tell the Wilsons about Pixie's death. "I should bring the family liaison officer with me."

"What? Are you worried the Ice Queen will yell at you?"

"She's not cold," Paulo said. Devin didn't seem to understand that people dealt with grief differently, especially when it was a family member. A thought occurred to him. "Did we track down any other family for the Beckers?"

Devin reviewed his notes. "An elderly aunt in Texas. We've got the local PD on it, but the aunt hasn't seen Marnie since before Brandon was born. Why?"

"Dr. Roberts mentioned the need for validation in people with delusions. Marnie didn't get it from her brother. He tried to convince her that Matt wasn't Brandon."

"Maybe Martin lied about that. If she comes to her senses, he doesn't get paid."

Paulo thought back to his interview with Martin. "The guy's brain is mush. He'd react first and take advantage second."

Devin nodded. "We could tell the hotline to be alert for callers claiming to have known Marnie or Brandon. She might have tried to contact one of Brandon's teachers or classmates."

"Marnie worked in the insurance office when Brandon was alive. She switched to working from home after his death. Do we have any information on who took care of Brandon?"

Devin shook his head. "No, but someone has to know about it. I'd start with the brother."

Paulo doubted Martin had any idea about who used to take care of Brandon. But he was damn sure going to talk to Martin about what happened to Pixie. "Jaron and I took a look around the motel today. And we found Pixie."

"What?" Devin said, loud enough to earn a glare from the chief. Devin squirmed in his seat like a naughty schoolboy caught talking by the teacher. "Sorry, Chief."

Paulo bit down on his lip to avoid grinning as Devin's cheeks flushed. "Check your e-mail. I sent you a preliminary report."

Devin pulled out his iPhone and opened his e-mail. He couldn't have read more than the first few lines before he said, "Son of a bitch!"

"Morris!" the chief shouted. "Get your ass up here."

Devin swore under his breath before standing up.

While the chief's ire was focused on Devin, Paulo took the opportunity to sneak out of the meeting. Let Devin find a way to explain to Agent Fisher how they'd managed to find Pixie's remains.

AFTER GAINING the very important information from Martin that the babysitter was an "old bitch," Paulo headed for the Wilsons'. He'd have to follow up with Dr. Roberts or possibly Marnie's neighbors to find out if someone knew the woman's name. He gave himself a mental note to check the financial records too, just in case Marnie was writing the babysitter weekly checks when Brandon was alive.

Martin had clammed up as soon as Paulo started asking questions about Pixie. Paulo hadn't been surprised, but it was still frustrating. He couldn't go before a jury and say Jaron had a vision implicating Martin in Pixie's death. Hopefully, there would be a way to trace the drugs in Pixie's system back to Martin.

When he reached the Wilsons', he parked in the driveway. The front door opened before he could even get out of the car. Dressed in workout pants and a tank top, Mr. Wilson hovered in front of the door.

Paulo exited the SUV, wondering if he should wait for the liaison officer to get here. "Good afternoon, Mr. Wilson."

"Do you have news?" Mr. Wilson asked, practically vibrating out of his skin.

"Yes, can we go inside and talk about it?"

Mr. Wilson opened the door and stepped inside. "We can talk in the living room."

Paulo followed him into the living room. Mrs. Wilson sat on the end of a blue-checkered couch, clutching a matching blue pillow. Her husband sat down next to her and gestured toward the other end of the couch.

Paulo took a seat. "I've been working with the man you hired, Jaron Greenberg. He led us to a man named Martin Becker."

Mrs. Wilson's grip on the pillow tightened. "Is he the one who took Matt?"

"We believe his sister is the one who took Matt. We think she's suffering from the delusion that Matt is her deceased child."

Mr. Wilson blinked several times. "Do we know where she is?"

Paulo opted to avoid answering directly. There was some information that he didn't want to be leaked to the press. "We've issued an Amber Alert that includes her information and the car we believe she's driving."

"Is this... good news?" Mr. Wilson asked. "I mean, better than a pervert, right?"

"This woman is obviously unstable," Mrs. Wilson said with a sneer. "How did her child die?"

"Her child died in a car accident."

Mrs. Wilson's expression softened. "Was she the driver?"

Paulo nodded. "I do have some bad news. Jaron searched near the motel Marnie Becker and Matt stayed at, and he was able to track down... Pixie's remains."

Mrs. Wilson's face hardened, any empathy she might have had for Marnie dissolving. "It sounds like Jaron's the one doing all the investigating. What are *you* doing to track this woman down?"

Mr. Wilson threw up his hands. "This was why we hired Jaron in the first place and got the police to agree to work with him. Why shouldn't Detective Silva use every resource he can to find Matt?" He shook his head. "I knew Jaron was talented, but I had no idea he could help so much." He got in one more dig by saying, "You didn't even want to hire him."

Mrs. Wilson stared at him, speechless.

Wishing he'd waited for the liaison officer, Paulo said, "It's important to focus on what we can do going forward. We have a press conference scheduled for this evening. We would like for you to be a part of it. Your liaison officer will be by shortly to talk about the specifics. They will help you to figure out what to say. It is crucial that we withhold certain information from the press."

"Why not tell them everything?" Mr. Wilson asked.

"Because we've been getting a hundred tips a day on the hotline. It will likely triple after the press conference. We need a way to weed out the good ones."

When Mr. Wilson frowned, his wife said, "If someone claims they saw this woman with Pixie, then we know it's probably not a legit tip."

"Exactly," Paulo said. "I would also like you to refrain from mentioning Jaron. He deserves a lot of credit, but it needs to wait until we bring Matt home. A woman suffering from delusions could react badly to knowing a psychic is tracking her."

"We won't mention Jaron," Mrs. Wilson said definitively.

Rising, Paulo said, "Thank you. Your liaison will be here within the hour. I'll see you tonight at the press conference." He shook hands with Mr. and Mrs. Wilson before heading out.

AFTER STRIKING out with Dr. Roberts, Paulo went back to the SPD. He knew that it was a long shot, but he'd hoped Dr. Roberts might know about who took care of Brandon when he was alive. At least he'd gotten her to agree to review her notes to see if there was any mention of a babysitter. He needed Devin to authorize more personnel to help canvas Marnie's neighborhood. Paulo found Special Agent Fisher waiting for him as he exited the elevator.

"Let me buy you a cup of coffee, detective," Agent Fisher said. The glint in his dark eyes said it wasn't a request.

Paulo was tempted to refuse, but playing nice with the Feds was Cop 101. "Sure. How about the Main Street Café?"

"Sounds good." Fisher punched the button for the lobby on the elevator. "I hear they have great hash browns."

"I've already had my lunch break today," Paulo said. He'd spent twice his allotted time driving Jaron to the motel. He hadn't wanted to leave Jaron in that shitty room, looking like he'd had the life drained out of him. "I don't really have time for more than coffee."

Fisher grinned. "Not to worry. It will be a working lunch. I need some details about this case clarified and you seem to be the man with all the answers."

Fisher remained silent as they exited the building and walked over to the café. The café was strictly self-seating, so Paulo snagged a booth near the entrance. He took a seat, forcing Fisher to sit opposite him with his back facing the entrance. Paulo had seen cops sit on the same side of a booth to avoid having their backs to the entrance. Some shit was hotwired into the cop brain.

"What can I do for you, Agent Fisher?"

"You guys requested FBI assistance. We can't do our jobs if we're being left out of the loop. So how about you start by explaining exactly how you tracked down Martin Becker?"

Paulo knew he had to tread lightly. His report had deliberately left out all mentions of Jaron's psychic ability. *How much does Fisher know? Had Chief Tucker or Devin talked to him?* "It was the dog's barking that drew me to Becker. I saw that he had a knife against… the vic's throat. According to the vic, he reacted violently when the vic mentioned Pixie's name."

The waitress arrived with a coffee pot, filling both their mugs at their request. She placed laminated menus on the table before leaving.

Fisher tore open three sugars and dumped them into his coffee. "I spoke with the first responder today, Officer Connors. He indicated that you and the vic were… friendly. He also said that Jaron Greenberg is the town weirdo. He runs a psychic business out of a dog salon."

Paulo considered snagging a bag of Bear's shit in the very near future. Connor's locker was in serious need of new decoration. "The Wilsons told the chief they wanted to bring in a local pet psychic. Sergeant Morris assigned me the job of keeping him out of trouble and off the press's radar."

Fisher took a sip of coffee, winced, and grabbed another sugar packet. There had to be more sugar than coffee in that mug. "I can see why Morris wouldn't want that to be common knowledge."

"I advised the Wilsons to refrain from mentioning it to the media."

Looking down at the menu, Fisher asked, "Have you been on any recent adventures with the psychic?"

Paulo took a sip of his coffee to stall. He didn't want to be caught in a lie. "Jaron was with me when we discovered Pixie's remains."

Fisher raised his dark eyebrows. "Is that right? Sergeant Morris didn't mention the psychic being there during his briefing."

"Sergeant Morris had only just received the preliminary report at the time of the task force meeting."

When the waitress returned, Fisher said, "The hash brown special, please." Turning his attention back to Paulo, he said, "Let's talk some more about the psychic."

Paulo hated the way Fisher kept referring to Jaron as "the psychic." "What do you need to know?"

Fisher laced his fingers together. "What do we know about the psychic's background?"

"Jaron has a squeaky clean record and his alibi for the abduction is the chief."

"Any connection to the suspect or the victim?"

Paulo hesitated, his gut tightening. "Jaron attended one of Mr. Wilson's yoga classes and he has worked as a consultant for the Healing Paws therapy program."

"How did the Wilsons get the idea to bring in the psychic?"

"According to the chief, a neighbor had been to see Jaron that day and she suggested to the Wilsons they talk to Jaron."

"So this neighbor talks with the psychic and somehow gets the idea to go running to the Wilsons. You don't find that suspicious, detective?"

Paulo pushed aside his coffee. "Look, I get it. Before this case I would've said psychic abilities were a load of crap. But I've seen what Jaron can do. He's the reason we've had two major breaks in this case."

"That's the problem." Fisher tapped the tabletop. "He's too damn good to be true. I've worked with other PDs that have brought in a psychic, usually at the request of relatives. The psychics offer vague visions in the hopes of claiming they helped solve the crime after the investigators solve it. Never has a psychic solved a missing child case. Never."

Paulo frowned. "What are you saying? We've got more than psychic vibes in this case. There's hard evidence to support it."

"I've seen the psychic's business card. He's got the kind of pretty-boy looks that Hollywood just loves. I think he staged this whole abduction so he'll look like the hero and get his own TV show. The Wilsons might keep quiet about him now, but they'll be gushing about the amazing psychic when they get back their little darling."

Paulo stared at him in shock. "You honestly think the Wilsons are faking this abduction?"

Fisher shrugged. "They wouldn't have to be involved. It could just be a deal between the psychic and the Beckers."

Paulo took a deep breath, exhaling slowly. "If that were the case, it would make more sense for Matt to be discovered at the motel. Or at the very least, someone would've leaked Jaron's involvement to the press." He was more than a little surprised the press hadn't gotten wind of them. "Your scenario makes no sense. There's no connection between the Beckers and Jaron."

"I have just one more question, detective," Fisher said as Paulo noticed the waitress approaching their table carrying a steaming skillet. "Are you fucking the psychic?"

The waitress lost her grip on the skillet, causing it to smack on the end of the table and crash to the floor. Hash browns and fried eggs splattered everywhere.

"Damn," Fisher said, "That looked good too."

CHAPTER 14

"YOU'RE GOING to give yourself gray hairs if you keep fretting," Jaron said, rubbing behind Bear's ears. "I'm fine."

Jaron had had every intention of putting the psychic business on hold until further notice before Mrs. Reynolds called, not long after Paulo left. She was a sweet old lady. Hearing her on the verge of tears had compelled him to go looking for her new cat. Her daughter had adopted the cat for her mother. They ought to name the cat Houdini.

Bear whimpered and the coppery scent of blood flooded Jaron's senses. The cut on the back of Jaron's head felt deep enough to likely need stitches, but his mop of blond hair had stanched most of the bleeding. Much to Bear's distress, Jaron had briefly lost consciousness when the branch snapped and he tumbled to the ground. Between his head smacking the brick wall and today's adventure, his head felt like it was going to explode. The ER staff at the hospital wasn't thrilled at letting Bear stay in the waiting room, but thankfully, Jaron had gotten Dr. Roberts to vouch for him. He didn't think he had the energy to take Bear back to the motel. And his attempt to call Stephen had gone unanswered. They'd never had a fight last so long.

Jaron always recommended waiting at least a couple of months before getting a new pet. The mind and the spirit needed time to grieve. But what if it was more than that? What if Mrs. Reynolds's deceased cat had chased off the rival new cat? He shook his head and then immediately regretted it. Bile coated the back of his throat. *Vengeful cat ghosts? Seriously? Did I scramble my brain in that fall?* He'd been distracted all evening, his thoughts unwillingly turning to Pixie. *Did I really follow her ghost into that alley?* The idea seemed absurd. But how else could he explain it? Tomorrow he would have to talk to the Wilsons and let them know there was nothing more he could do for Matt. An ounce of doubt wiggled into his brain as he remembered Paulo urging him to push his abilities further. He shivered, wishing he'd worn a warmer coat.

A buzzing vibration on Jaron's thigh made Bear lift his head with a snort. Bear lay on the floor, trapping Jaron's feet with his furry paws.

Rolling his eyes, Jaron dug his phone out of his pocket and answered the call.

"Where are you, Jaron?" Paulo sounded tense.

Jaron sighed. "I'm at the hospital's ER waiting room."

"What happened? You were supposed to go home and rest."

"I got into a scuffle with gravity and gravity won," Jaron said, feeling oddly giddy in spite of the pain in his head. He didn't want Paulo to worry, but he couldn't seem to concentrate. "I was trying… to get a cat out of a tree and fell."

"I'll be there in ten minutes." Paulo ended the call before Jaron could ask what was going on.

TEN MINUTES later, Paulo headed into the hospital with Fisher right on his heels. His attempts to ditch the man had been unsuccessful. Paulo found Jaron still sitting in the ER waiting room. At least a dozen other patients were likewise waiting to be seen. Jaron was slumped in his chair, holding a bandage to the back of his head. Surprisingly, the hospital personnel had allowed Bear to stay with him. Or maybe *allowed* wasn't the right word. They'd likely need a forklift to get him away from Jaron's side.

Agent Fisher pushed past Paulo and approached Jaron.

"Mr. Greenberg? I'm Special Agent Fisher. I would like to speak to you for a moment."

Jaron blinked several times. Beads of sweat clung to his forehead. "Hi."

"Are you all right?" Paulo asked as he neared Jaron. He sat on the empty chair next to Jaron.

"I am now," Jaron said, smiling sweetly.

Paulo didn't believe him. Brushing the sweaty hair off Jaron's brow, he asked, "When did you last eat?"

Before Jaron could answer, a nurse called out his name. He stood on shaky legs. Bear likewise rose, pressing himself against Jaron's side as if trying to keep Jaron steady.

Fisher blocked Jaron's path. "I just need a few minutes and then you can see the doctor."

"Get out of his way, Fisher," Paulo shouted, rising to his feet. "He obviously needs treatment."

Ever helpful, Bear decided to headbutt the FBI agent in the stomach until he no longer blocked Jaron's path.

"Hey!" Fisher said, sounding indignant.

Paulo ignored him and placed his hand under Jaron's elbow. "Let's get you to the nurse."

Jaron stepped away from him, heading for the exit. "Can't stay," he said, his speech slurring. "I needa find the cat." Jaron pulled off his blood-stained jacket and dropped it to the floor.

"You're not thinking clearly," Paulo said, noticing sweat stains on Jaron's T-shirt. "We need to get you checked out. The cat will be fine." He wasn't sure if Jaron meant the cat from the tree, but regardless, he needed immediate treatment. Clearly, Paulo had pushed Jaron too hard.

"Cat missin'. Havta find her."

Paulo heard the nurse calling for help. Something was very wrong with Jaron, but he couldn't be sure if it was hypoglycemia or the head injury. Paulo had had more than a few concussions that left him loopy. But Jaron's condition seemed much more severe. He had sounded fine on the phone. What had changed?

"Pixie," Jaron said, as if in answer to Paulo's unasked question.

Bear cocked his head and trotted over to the automatic door, causing the door to slide open. An orange tabby ran inside and sat in front of Jaron with an annoyed yowl. "Wow," Jaron said, before his eyes rolled into the back of his head.

Paulo thrust his hand under Jaron's head to prevent it from smacking on the floor. Jaron's muscles stiffened, and then he began to shake. Paulo turned Jaron onto his side into the recovery position as Jaron's arms began to flail.

A nurse with the nametag of Beth knelt down by Jaron's head. "Has he had seizures before?"

"I... don't think so," Paulo said. He felt like he'd taken a punch to his chest, knocking his heart off beat. "He's been having trouble with low blood sugar." He scrambled to his feet to give the nurse more room to check Jaron out.

When the tabby meowed loudly, Beth addressed Fisher. "You get the cat." Turning to Paulo, she said, "You check his phone for an emergency contact." She pulled Jaron's cell phone out of his pocket and tossed it to Paulo. "Move it, people!"

"I'm allergic," Fisher said, snatching the phone from Paulo's hand.

Paulo stood by helplessly as a wheeled stretcher was rolled into the lobby. Two male nurses lowered the bed down and transferred Jaron onto it while Beth supported his head and neck. Jaron's arms were straight as a board in front of him as Beth took his pulse. As Paulo watched, thin scratches appeared along the top of both Jaron's arms. The scratches were deep enough to draw blood.

Paulo traded a look with Fisher, not sure of what he had just seen. Fisher looked equally dumbfounded.

"What caused that?" Beth asked, placing her hand under Jaron's arm to get a better look. "I didn't notice them before."

As if in answer, Bear barked several times, directing his attention to the carpet next to the stretcher. One of the nurses looked behind himself at the empty carpet before looking back at the dog. "Will someone grab a hold of that dog? He's scaring the crap out of me." He raised the stretcher up and began to push it.

Rising, Paulo snagged Bear's leash when the Newfie tried to follow Jaron through the double doors. Bear dragged him about two feet before Paulo dug his heels in. "Sit," he said, a little desperately.

Bear grumbled before sitting down, his gaze locked on the closed door.

Fisher handed Paulo the phone, keeping his distance from Bear. "I left a message with a guy named Stephen."

Paulo shoved the phone into his pocket. He noticed the cat sitting on a young girl's lap, enjoying the attention it was getting.

"I can't believe the psychic faked a seizure to get out of talking to us," Fisher said.

Paulo took several deep breaths, resisting the urge to smash Fisher in his sanctimonious face. "He didn't fake anything."

Fisher looked at him like he couldn't believe Paulo was so dense. "Are you telling me you bought this little performance?" He snorted. "Though I have to admit training the dog to bark at nothing is a nice touch."

"And the scratches on his arms?"

A hint of uncertainty clouded Fisher's eyes. "He... must've hidden them under makeup. And then rubbed off the makeup when he was thrashing around like a beached seal. His buddy was probably the one who deposited the cat in front of the sliding door. That's probably why he didn't answer his phone."

His legs feeling like he just completed a marathon, Paulo stumbled over to one of the waiting room chairs and sat down. He ignored the curious glances and whispered conversations from the other patients.

Fisher kept his distance as if he sensed Paulo had reached the limits of his patience. Or maybe it was the guard dog that had placed himself in front of Paulo.

The cat that had started the chaos crawled onto Paulo's lap. Paulo rubbed under the cat's chin as he read the heart-shaped tag on the collar. The name Kiki and a phone number were engraved into the metal. The cat's steady purr helped to slow his racing heart. Though his pulse slowed, he couldn't control the thoughts bombarding his brain. How had Jaron gone from dizzy spells to seizures? Was it the result of finding Pixie's remains? Or maybe it really was the head injury? Paulo had no clue and he absolutely hated the feeling.

Desperate for a distraction, Paulo pulled out his phone and called the number on the pet tag. When a frazzled-sounding older woman answered on the first ring, he explained the situation. The woman's daughter agreed to come and pick up the cat immediately.

Twenty minutes later Paulo felt relief when Stephen rushed through the sliding door and went straight to the front desk. Nurse Beth had refused to tell him anything about Jaron's condition even after he had flashed his badge.

Paulo lost his grip on the leash as Bear sprinted toward Stephen. The big dog nearly knocked him to the ground as he whined and wiggled in anxiety-driven excitement. Stephen endured the sloppy greeting, clinging to the Newfoundland's thick black fur.

Paulo stood and approached them as Beth leaned over the counter and said, "Be good, Bear."

Bear planted his furry ass on the carpet and shut up. To hell with the psychic business. Jaron could make six figures as a dog trainer if the animals obeyed that well even when he wasn't around to send them psychic vibes. Paulo picked up Bear's leash and wrapped it around his hand, determined not to lose hold again. He was surprised security hadn't shown up to toss all of them out. Jaron must've charmed the scrubs off Nurse Beth.

"I'm here about Jaron Greenberg." Stephen handed Beth a manila folder, his hand visibly shaking. "This is the paperwork for my medical proxy and his insurance information. His Social Security card and birth certificate are in there too in case you need it."

Beth handed the folder to another nurse and asked her to make a copy. Turning back to Stephen she said, "Give me a minute to get an update on Jaron." She used the side door that led to the treatment area.

"I thought he didn't have health insurance," Paulo said.

"After that psycho hurt him, I enrolled him in the salon's healthcare plan. It's barely more than basic coverage, but it's better than nothing." Stephen looked at his hands. "I was waiting for the card to arrive to tell him."

Paulo knew bullshit when he heard it, but he didn't call Stephen on it. Fisher joined them when Beth returned.

Nurse Beth's grim expression didn't bode well for Jaron. "We've hooked him up to a saline drip with some potassium and we're monitoring his blood sugar. We've given him extra glucose in a bolus via the drip to get his levels back up to normal. But they continue to drop and we're not sure why yet."

"Is he awake?" Stephen asked.

The nurse shook her head. "No, but that isn't unusual after a seizure. He could remain unconscious for several hours. Once we stabilize his blood sugar, we'll CT his neck and head."

At Stephen's confused look, Paulo explained. "He fell out of a tree trying to retrieve a cat and cut the back of his head. He had a seizure while waiting for treatment."

Fisher muscled his way into the conversation. "Are you sure the seizure was real?"

"Who the fuck are you?" Stephen asked, as if just noticing Fisher had maneuvered his way into the conversation.

"I'm Agent F—"

"Do I look like I give a fuck?" Stephen snapped.

The nurse gave Fisher an equally unfriendly look. "He's not faking. Now please step away, sir. This conversation is private."

Fisher held up his hands and stepped back. He failed to see the taut leash behind him. Bear had moved to the side, creating the perfect opportunity to trip up Fisher and send him crashing to the ground.

Paulo took more than a little satisfaction in Fisher's yelp of pain.

"Let's take Bear outside," Stephen said, grabbing hold of Paulo's arm. He held onto Paulo until they reached the parking lot. They walked silently until Stephen stopped in front of a compact Hyundai in an obnoxious green color. He hit the key fob and opened the backdoor. "Get in, slobber monster, before the spook throws you in cuffs."

Bear whined, turning his head toward the hospital entrance, clearly distressed at the idea of leaving Jaron behind. Paulo understood the sentiment.

Stephen's face crumpled, his eyes glistening under the parking lot lights. "Jaron will be fine." He repeated the words as if he could will it to be so.

Bear grumbled as he climbed into the car.

Stephen closed the door. "Now tell me what the hell is going on? Why is that guy acting like he wants to handcuff Jaron to a gurney?"

"Fisher believes that Jaron orchestrated Matt's kidnapping in order to create publicity for himself. The fact that Jaron found Pixie's remains today makes him all the more suspicious."

Stephen's posture stiffened. "That's insane."

Paulo nodded. "I agree, but Fisher doesn't know Jaron the way we do. And when he was presented with evidence of Jaron's abilities, he convinced himself they were faked."

"What evidence?"

Paulo quickly described what he witnessed in the waiting room. "Has anything like that ever happened before?"

"No," Stephen said. But then he paused, his brow wrinkling. "Maybe? But we were, like, six years old. We were walking back to my house after school when he stopped and started crying. He kept repeating that Butch was hurt. That was when I noticed bloody scratches on his arms and legs. I was sure they hadn't been there before, but I was just a kid." His expression darkened. "And Jaron was hurt a lot back then." Seeming to shake off the memory, he continued, "Later his asshole father got caught hosting amateur dog fights. They found a half a dozen dead dogs buried in shallow graves in the woods."

"Okay, but why would Pixie's ghost hurt Jaron? He's been trying to help her."

"How the hell should I know?" Stephen muttered irritably. "We need to find a doggy exorcist or some shit." He snapped his fingers. "I know who to call."

Paulo raised his eyebrows. "You know an exorcist?"

Stephen glared at him. "No, but Mel is into all that hoodoo stuff. And I can get her to take Bear back to the salon." He pulled out his cell phone and typed a text. Within a couple of seconds, the phone chimed. "She's on the way."

They headed back inside the hospital to wait for her arrival. Paulo typed a text to Devin as he walked, determined to get Fisher far away from Jaron. He trusted Devin to figure out a way to lure Fisher out of the hospital.

STEPHEN SAID, "Thank God," when a young woman with long dark hair and eighties bangs entered the hospital ten minutes later.

The woman identified herself as Mel before sitting next to Stephen and taking hold of his hand. "What have you heard?"

When Stephen made no sign to speak, Paulo said, "They're giving him extra glucose to try to stabilize his blood sugar, but it's not working."

His voice thick, Stephen said, "He won't wake up, the lazy bastard." He wiped tears from his eyes. He held up a pamphlet he gotten from Nurse Beth. "This says he's in danger of slipping into a coma."

Paulo bit down on the urge to reassure Stephen that Jaron would be fine. "The doctors are trying to help him, but they don't have all the facts."

Mel frowned. "What do you mean?"

"Every time Jaron has worked on Matt Wilson's case, his blood sugar has dropped."

Stephen threw up his hands. "And that wasn't a clue to leave him the hell alone?"

"Hush, Stephen," Mel said, patting his arm. "You know Jaron wouldn't walk away from the case he thought he could help solve."

Paulo knew Mel was right, but he didn't like it. He wanted to bring Matt home, but he wasn't willing to sacrifice Jaron in the process. "What do you know about ghosts? Have you heard of animal ghosts?"

"Some people think pets can't have ghosts because they don't have souls, but I've never believed that. I would assume the pets would manifest in the same way as human ghosts. People report cold spots, feelings of unease, electrical problems, and audio and visual manifestations."

Paulo could certainly attest to the cold spots. And Jaron had reported seeing Pixie in the alley and at the motel. "How does it become a ghost?"

Mel brushed her bangs out of her eyes. "Um… all I really know is from watching Ghost Seekers on TV."

Stephen held up his hand. "Are you seriously telling me reality TV is Jaron's only hope?"

Mel blushed. Ignoring Stephen's outburst, she said, "The common belief is that ghosts are created when a person who dies has unfinished business or doesn't know they are dead. It would make sense if Pixie is manifesting to the one person who can help find Matt."

Paulo's head started to throb. He needed to understand what made this case different from others Jaron had worked if he was going to help him. "Has Jaron had fainting spells before?"

Stephen bit his bottom lip. "Not as an adult, but it has happened before as a kid. My mom was always trying to cram food down his throat when she saw him. He was skin and bones." He left the "why" unsaid, making Paulo want to track down Jaron's asshole parents. If, as the chief had suggested, God gave Jaron his abilities to compensate for shitty parents, he should demand a refund.

"How often do Jaron's cases end with him finding a deceased pet?"

Mel piped in. "Almost never. It only happens when people wait too long to contact him."

Realizing he was blatantly breaking regs by discussing an open case, Paulo described how they discovered Pixie's body.

"Dragged?" Stephen repeated, looking alarmed. "By what?" He paled. "By Pixie's ghost? Is that what you're telling me?"

Paulo understood Stephen's shock, but they needed to stay focused. "Yes, but Jaron said the force compelling him didn't feel malicious. So why is it scratching him bloody and sending him spiraling toward a coma?"

Something in Stephen's distressed expression changed. Paulo half expected to see a shining light bulb appear above his head. "Jaron had given up. He has told countless would-be clients that he isn't a medium. He tells them he can't communicate with the pet after it has died. Pixie's unfinished business is saving Matt and her only means of helping Matt had stopped trying."

Paulo cocked his head. "So, Pixie is just trying to get Jaron's attention to get him back on the case?"

Stephen addressed Mel. "Is there any way to get ghosts to stay away from a person?"

Mel sighed. "Salt is supposed to repel ghosts, but I doubt the hospital staff will let you surround Jaron's bed with a ring of salt. And I'm not even sure we should do it."

"Why not?" Paulo asked.

Mel looked down at her clasped hands. "If Pixie's ghost is reaching out to Jaron, there must be an important reason why. The ghost might even be able to sense that Jaron's the only one who can help Matt."

Stephen's face hardened. "I watched the press conference the parents made. The cops know who took Matt. They just have to get off their asses and track the psycho down."

Paulo ignored the jibe. "We're doing everything we can to find the woman who took Matt, but there's no way to know how quickly it will happen. The national coverage of the press conference will hopefully help bring in more legitimate tips. What do we do in the meantime to help Jaron?"

Paulo got twin blank stares in response.

CHAPTER 15

JARON STANDS on a cobblestone path with his hands on his hips. The trail branches off to the right and to the left. The thick blanket of trees on either side makes it impossible to see where the paths lead. Leaves cover the ground in unnatural colors of purple, pink, and turquoise. He remembers a tree. A snap. Pain. A tabby cat.

A cool breeze that smells strangely of antiseptic makes him shiver. The sun is bright, but he's freezing. A murmur of voices directs his attention to the right-hand path. Seeing no one, Jaron asks, "Is anyone there?" He shakes his head in disgust. "Like maybe a serial killer with an axe?"

A high-pitched bark draws Jaron back to the left path. Someone has committed the sin of dressing a small dog in a frilly dress and putting two blue bows on its head.

Jaron squints. "Pixie?"

The little shih tzu yaps once and then takes two steps backward.

"Looks like she wants you to follow her." The deep purr of Paulo's voice is unmistakable.

Jaron notices Paulo further down the path, leaning against an old white oak and dressed in an outfit straight out of a medieval porn flick. Tight black leather pants show off his muscular thighs. A sleeveless chainmail shirt hugs the contours of his chest. A longsword appears to be strapped to his back.

Jaron's vision flickers, and he finds himself amongst the trees with a mouthwatering view in front of him. "Hi."

Paulo's gaze drifts down his body and a smile curves his full lips. "Love the knee socks, Hansel. Is the dog supposed to be Gretel?"

Jaron looks down at himself. He seems to have been polkafied by a German folk singer. He's wearing a white shirt, suspenders, midthigh leather shorts, and knee socks. "Oh, that's fair. You get leather pants and a cool-looking sword and I get freaking lederhosen. What kind of screwed up dream is this?" The moment the words leave his lips, Jaron realizes it's true. He's dreaming. He holds his breath.

"What are you doing?" Paulo asks, his accent as thick as honey.

"I'm trying to wake up," Jaron says, closing his eyes.

The feel of Paulo's soft lips and bristled chin against him cause him to open his eyes. "You kissed me."

Paulo shrugs. "Seems to work in fairytales."

Jaron licks his lips and leans against a tree. "Maybe we should try again just to make sure."

Paulo grins and steps closer, giving Jaron another soft kiss. He puts his hands against the side of Jaron's face, holding him in place as he deepens the kiss.

The wet warmth of Paulo's mouth feels good, but Jaron hates being so constricted. He can't even turn his head. He attempts to lift his arms but fails. Straps of some sort have pinned him to the hard surface of the tree. Backboard. Neck brace. "What's going on?" Jaron asks. "Why can't I move?"

Paulo kisses Jaron's forehead before stepping back. A black stallion the size of a Clydesdale appears next to Paulo. Instead of a saddle and reins, the horse is wearing a jumbo-sized collar with a dog tag. Paulo pats the horse's head and attaches a leash to the collar. The horse whimpers, nuzzling the side of Jaron's face. The straps holding Jaron in place seem to melt away.

"What's wrong, Bear?" Jaron asks, rubbing behind his pointed ears.

"He's worried about you," Paulo says.

"I'm fine." Jaron hears someone say, "He's seizing again," which sounds very bad, but the scene in front of him holds his attention. "I need to pick a path. Do you know which way I'm supposed to go?"

"That depends," Paulo says, cocking his head. "Where do you want to end up?"

The sun is setting, turning the trees into a dark wall enclosing the path. "There was a little white dog." Jaron turns around, trying to find the dog. A sharp pain in his hand makes him gasp.

Paulo takes hold of Jaron's hand, his grip warm and firm. "Maybe you should go to the right." He licks his lips. "We could go back to my place."

Jaron steps closer to him. "Okay." A garbled bark has him turning back toward the left. Pixie has a piece of bread in her mouth. "Just give me a minute, and then we'll go."

Jaron moves down the path with Pixie yapping at his heels. Amongst the wall of trees, there is a raised door with a latch instead of a doorknob. He opens the door but doesn't step inside. Peering through the door, he sees a new location. The bright sun makes his eyes water. The area has changed in the past decade, but there is no way Jaron doesn't recognize it. He had lived at the Summer Sun trailer park until he was sixteen.

The door swings shut and disappears. Jaron turns and continues down the path. He spots Pixie further up the path attempting to drag a large bag of bread. The ripped bag leaves a trail of breadcrumbs. "I have a very literal brain," Jaron mutters to himself.

When Jaron reaches Pixie, a window appears. Jaron sees Matt sitting on a floral couch with a calico cat on his lap. An elderly woman sits next to him. There's no sign of Marnie. It looks like the woman is trying to comfort Matt. He can see them talking, but can't hear them. He lifts the window.

Matt pets the cat's back. The cat doesn't look thrilled to be touched, but it allows the petting, likely sensing Matt's distress. "I want to go home, Peggy."

Peggy sighs. "I know you do, child."

"Marnie said Mommy and Daddy stole me and that she's my real Mom." Matt sniffles. "She said they decided to give me back to her. We waited a whole week at that motel in case they changed their minds, but they never came. Why didn't they come?"

Peggy looks conflicted. "I'm trying to convince Marnie to contact your parents."

Matt gives Peggy the kind of long, assessing look that seems foreign on such a young child's face. "How do I know I can trust you?"

The window slams shut before Jaron can hear her answer. Jaron attempts to pry open the window, but it won't budge.

"That won't work," says a familiar voice.

Jaron turns around. The woods and path have faded away in the dark. Only a spotlight remains with a figure standing in the center. "Stephen?"

Stephen's pants and shirt look like they were made from candy wrappers. Instead of hair, he has blue, white, and red Jelly Beans glued to his head.

Stephen looks down at his outfit. "I guess I should be happy not to be cast as the evil witch in this fairytale."

Jaron shakes his head. "Never."

Grinning, Stephen takes hold of Jaron's hand and pulls him into the spotlight, away from the endless dark.

The warmth of Stephen's hand makes Jaron realize how cold he feels. "Are you still mad at me?"

Stephen rolls his eyes. "No, but you need to wake up or I'm going to start manscaping your duck fluff."

Jaron glances down, seeing white linoleum tile instead of a cobbled stone path. "Where is Pixie?"

Ignoring the question, Stephen lifts Jaron's hand with his palm up. "Paulo stole this from the cafeteria. You've got a cop committing petty larceny for you." He holds up a saltshaker and dumps the white grains onto Jaron's palm.

"What are you doing?" Jaron asks as his whole hand begins to tingle.

"According to Mel, salt is supposed to repel ghosts. And we need that little fur-ball to back the fuck off before you end up in a coma."

"I have to find Pixie." Jaron attempts to pull away but Stephen grips his hand tightly.

"Please," Stephen says, his voice thick. "Wake up."

The tingling sensation spreads up Jaron's arm, chasing away the cold that had settled into his bones. "I can't leave yet," he says desperately.

A blinding light surrounds him.

CHAPTER 16

IT WAS the shaking that woke Jaron. It felt like someone had shoved a vibrator under his left shoulder blade. The sensation only lasted a few seconds before disappearing. Head throbbing, Jaron opened his eyes. He blinked several times until his vision cleared. The bed he was on was barely big enough for him. It had a white plastic guardrail and footboard. He felt the vibration again under his lower back. Looking down, he saw an IV attached to his left wrist. Three red scratches spanned nearly the length of his forearm, standing out in stark relief on his pale skin.

On his right, Stephen sat on a white plastic chair, his eyes closed. He was murmuring something under his breath, but Jaron couldn't say what. He had both his hands wrapped around Jaron's hand in a death grip.

Jaron's attempt to say his friend's name sounded more froglike than human.

Stephen's eyes snapped open and his mouth dropped open in surprise. A look of unbridled relief passed over his features, quickly replaced with a scowl. "I swear you wait for me to be an asshole to pull this kind of shit."

"Huh?" Jaron said, attempting to sit up. He felt annoyingly weak. Like someone had replaced his bones with Jell-O.

Stephen hit a blue button on the guardrail, causing the head of the bed to rise. "Do you remember when we were in the sixth grade and I called you white trash? You fell out of a tree that day too and broke your arm."

Jaron's mouth spoke before his brain could get on board. "I lied about that."

"What are you talking about? My parents were the one to take you to the emergency room. You had a cast for over a month."

Jaron licked his dry lips. "No, I mean about the tree. My dad was the one to break my arm."

"Why wouldn't you tell me?"

Jaron shrugged. "It sounded too white trashy to say my dad got drunk and broke my arm 'cause I'd refused to go with him to the dog fights."

Stephen stared at him. "You've never once talked about your dad hurting you. Not once in twenty years. What did they put in that IV? Truth serum?"

Jaron's laugh sounded like it had been processed through a blender.

Stephen tilted his head toward a cup sitting on a white plastic tray-table next to the bed. "Drink some water," he said, making no move to release Jaron's hand.

Jaron carefully maneuvered the hand with the IV in it and picked up the cup. Tilting back the cup, he drank deeply. The cold moisture eased his sore throat. "When we first met, I'd convinced myself your parents wouldn't let us be friends if they knew about my family. Later, it was just easier to forget it. Mostly, my dad ignored me, and I spent more time at your house than the trailer." He paused, suddenly picturing the broken-down trailer of his childhood in vivid detail. A nagging sense that he'd forgotten something clung to his thoughts.

"My parents and my brothers love you. We fucking celebrated when your parents took off." Leaning over, Stephen kissed Jaron's forehead. "I love you, too."

Jaron smiled. "I know you do." Looking down at his scratched arm, he asked, "What exactly happened?"

"What do you remember?"

The question made Jaron uneasy. "Last I remember I was at my motel room." He had been contemplating which flavor of canned soup would taste the best cold, since the microwave in the motel's lobby was broken. He had settled on pretending his can of tomato soup would be like gazpacho. He'd been sadly mistaken. He'd also been regretting turning down Paulo's offer to stop at a drive-thru on the way home from the crime scene. The idea of food had been unimaginable at the time. A couple of hours later he was starving.

"Apparently, you got a call about a lost cat and fell out of a tree trying to wrangle the furry rat. You went to the ER of the hospital to get your head stitched up."

"Is the cat okay?"

Stephen made a pained sound. "Can you try to be a normal, self-absorbed human for, like, five seconds?" When Jaron opened his mouth to retort, he continued. "The cat is fine. Paulo tracked down the owner. And before you ask, Sir Slobbers-A-Lot is fine too."

"Oh, Paulo was here?" Jaron said, feeling his cheeks heat up. For some reason he was picturing Paulo in a pair of tight leather pants. What drugs were in this IV?

Stephen scowled. "He got called back to the station."

Thoughts seemed to be bombarding Jaron's mind, images that made no sense. A path. Trees. A metal door. The hand Stephen was clinging to felt hot and gritty. When he attempted to pull away, Stephen tightened his grip.

"Don't drop the salt," Stephen ordered.

Jaron stared at him. "Am I still at the base of that tree bleeding to death? Because you were acting less weird when you were dressed in candy." He really wished his mouth would stop showing its independent streak. "I have no idea what that means." He could picture Stephen in his mind with candy stuck on his head. "I think these drugs gave me psychedelic dreams."

"Look, Mel said that salt repels ghosts, so I got Paulo to swipe a shaker from the cafeteria. We need Pixie to stay the hell away from you."

Hearing Pixie's name made Jaron remember his dream. It had been more than his wandering psyche. Hadn't it? "I don't need protection from Pixie. I need to stop resisting and hear the message she's sending me." Details of the dream were fading, but one fragment remained clear in his mind. He needed to go home. Back to the Summer Sun Trailer Park.

Stephen didn't look convinced. "Your blood sugar dropped so low you started seizing." He squeezed Jaron's hand hard enough to hurt. "They were afraid you were going to slip into a coma. You could've suffered brain damage. I need you to take this seriously, please."

"A handful of salt won't keep Pixie away."

"How do you kn...?" Stephen lowered his voice. "Is it here?" He looked behind himself as if expecting Pixie to jump him.

Jaron shook his head. "But I doubt it's the salt."

"Then we'll get with the Scooby research and find a ghost-be-gone remedy."

"Did you just make a *Buffy the Vampire Slayer* reference?"

"Shut up," Stephen grumped. "It's a classic."

Jaron noticed a closet next to the bathroom. "Are my clothes in the closet?" It was also clear he was the only patient in the room. He didn't want to think about what a private room was costing him.

Stephen narrowed his dark eyes. "I told them to burn them."

"Why would you do that?" Jaron asked, his frustration growing.

Stephen's reply sounded strained, like he was barely keeping himself from yelling. "During that seizure, you pissed yourself and your T-shirt had blood and vomit on it. Is that reason enough to toss them?"

Jaron's complaint died on his lips. Horrified, he realized he'd wet himself in front of Paulo and a room of waiting patients. The idea shouldn't be more upsetting than a seizure or possible brain damage, but it was. And Stephen thought he was devoid of vanity. Seeing the guardrail controls, Jaron said, "Let's talk to the nurse," before hitting the Call button.

They sat in an uncomfortable silence for several minutes until a woman in blue scrubs with a candy print entered the room. She was holding a clear plastic case. "I'm Beth. How are you feeling, Jaron?"

"I'm feeling much better and wondering when I can leave."

Nurse Beth frowned. "Let me check your glucose level again." She approached the bed and placed the case on the tray table. When she opened it, Jaron saw what looked like a large remote control, cotton balls, a plastic container, and a number of small plastic pieces that looked like golf tees. Stephen was forced to get out of her way, leaving Jaron wondering what to do with the salt. Sliding his hand under the thin covers, he let go of the salt and attempted to wipe off the grains clinging to his sweaty palm.

Beth removed the remote from the case and scanned the ID badge she wore around her neck. She then scanned the ID bracelet on his arm. "This glucometer will allow me to measure your blood sugar level. I'll need a small sample of your blood." Opening a plastic container, she took out a test strip and inserted it into the glucometer.

When Jaron bent his elbow and tilted up his arm, she peered at his hand closely. "You've got something on your—"

Stephen interrupted her. "That's my fault. I was... eating... a soft pretzel earlier. I must've got salt on him when I was holding his hand. From the salt. On the pretzel."

Nurse Beth looked at Stephen like she was considering calling security. Stephen's flushed cheeks and shifty-eyed look wasn't helping. Any second he'd start blabbering about ghosts and they'd both end up in a rubber room.

"Ignore the guy freaking out in the corner," Jaron said. "He faints at the sight of blood."

The insult dragged Stephen back to his sassy self. "Says the guy too chicken to cut his own dog's nails."

Nurse Beth shook her head, her expression moving from suspicious to amused. She ripped open an alcohol wipe and began cleaning Jaron's index finger thoroughly. "You'll just feel a pinch." She pressed the plunger against his finger. She squeezed his finger and collected the drop of blood with the test strip. A cotton ball was pressed to his finger as they waited for the results. When a beep sounded, she said, "Your level is within the normal range."

"Does that mean I can leave?" Jaron asked hopefully.

"One normal reading doesn't mean your glucose levels have stabilized. It would be better to keep you for at least a few more hours, possibly overnight as an outpatient to continue to check your levels." She looked at Stephen. "Your friend can come back in the morning. Visiting hours ended several hours ago."

Stephen blew out a noisy breath. "And don't start bitching about the cost. I enrolled you in the salon's medical plan."

Jaron bit down on the desire to ask how Stephen had managed to enroll him without a signature. "I need to go to the Summer Sun Trailer Park to… investigate one of my urgent cases."

Stephen put his hands on his hips. "You want to go to the 'Not' after dark." He looked at the nurse. "Are you sure he isn't brain damaged?"

Jaron acknowledged that Stephen might have a point. It didn't help that he felt so tired. "If I stay here tonight, you have to bring me back clothes first thing in the morning and give me a ride to the trailer park. And agree to check on Bear because he's probably totally freaked out."

Stephen gritted his teeth. "Fine, but I'm buying one of those meter thingies and a carton of salt."

"Salt?" Nurse Beth asked, raising her eyebrows. "Why would he need salt? He was given potassium in his IV." She addressed Jaron. "Have you made changes to your diet lately?"

Jaron shook his head. "Stephen's just creating a mental shopping list. He needs to get toilet paper too."

The nurse didn't look convinced, but she let the matter go. "If your friend comes back at seven in the morning that should give us enough time to figure out if you've stabilized. But I'll need to take a detailed history from you. You should also schedule an appointment with a doctor to figure out why exactly this is happening. Until then, we need to talk about controlling your low blood sugar with diet."

Jaron nodded in agreement, not looking forward to the conversation.

Stephen approached the bed and leaned down to kiss Jaron's forehead. "I love you, you stubborn bastard."

Jaron grinned. "I love you too."

THE SUMMER Sun Trailer Park was unofficially divided into two sections. Residents called them the "Care" and "Not" sections. If you were in the Care section, you planted flowers in the summer, kept the trash off the lawn, and took *care* of your home. Most of the trailers were modular homes built on slabs, nearing the size of a small apartment. The Not section lived up to every stereotypical trait you could throw at them, from car parts on the lawn to filthy living conditions. Jaron had grown up in the Not section, envying those in the Care section. Years later, he often wondered why people in the Care section bothered. Townspeople treated them like there was no difference. Trailer trash.

Stephen pulled off his sunglasses. "Jesus, this place is a shithole."

"The thing I remember the most about our trailer was that it was freezing in the winter and broiling in the summer. But that was mostly because we couldn't afford the electric bill."

They'd been wandering the Not section for nearly a half an hour. While Jaron had recognized the area in his vision, he didn't know the specific location of the trailer. He hadn't had so much as a psychic twitch since he'd left the hospital. It was unnerving. He'd even resorted to checking his pockets to make sure Stephen hadn't snuck salt inside his jeans or jacket.

Frowning, Stephen watched a young child that was clinging to a filthy Barbie doll. There was no sign of her parents. "When my dad was mayor, I tried to get him to shut the Not down."

Jaron hadn't known that. "Good people live here. It's just that the bad ones are so loud they drown out the voices of the people trying to live the best life they can."

Stephen smiled wanly. "You sound like my dad. He said good people can come out of the Not." He squeezed Jaron's hand briefly. "People like you."

Jaron's cheeks warmed. Looking over to the right, he saw the trailer he was looking for. It had a clothes line connected to the side with a bright pink blanket draped over it. The design on the blanket was mini candy shapes. *Congratulations, Hansel, you found your house.* "I think that's the one."

A woman in her late thirties exited the trailer as he and Stephen approached. Her long dark hair was in a side braid, highlighting her prominent cheekbones and dusky complexion. She was wearing what Jaron thought of as church wear: a long flowered skirt and a white sweater. "Morning to you," she said, not sounding the least bit friendly.

Jaron wondered how he could question her without sounding like a crazy person. "Um, hello."

Stephen jutted his chin out. "We're helping the police with the Matt Wilson case. Have you heard about the little boy who was kidnapped?"

The woman pressed her lips together. "Why would the police be workin' with the two of you?"

Stephen lifted his chin, meeting her icy gaze straight on. "Why not us?"

Jaron stepped forward, drawing her attention. "The police have a suspect by the name of Marnie Becker. We're helping them track down people who might know her. I used to live in the Not, so I volunteered to help."

"I don't know no Marnie Becker." She walked over to a bike chained to the side of the trailer with three different chains. "And I'm late for church," she said, unlocking the bike efficiently. She rolled the bike over to the dirt road and straddled it.

Stephen stepped in front of her. "Seems like trying to help a kidnapped child would be a good excuse for arriving a couple minutes late to church."

She glared at Stephen. "I done told you I don't know her."

Jaron joined him. "We're trying to track down a woman in her late sixties. We think she might have lived in this area. Her name is Peggy."

Tying her long skirt in a knot above her knees, she said, "There was a Peggy Sampson that used to live out here. She watched my sister's babies a few times when the sitter cancelled. But she moved out of state to be closer to her daughter."

"Do you know where?" Jaron asked.

She shook her head. "Good day to you," she said, steering her bike around them and pedaling away.

"We need to find the manager's office," Stephen said.

"How will we convince him to give us private information?"

Stephen wrapped his arm around Jaron's shoulders. "How you managed to stay so innocent growing up here I'll never know."

Jaron poked him in the stomach. "I'm not innocent."

Stephen grinned. "As pure as that mop of white hair of yours."

As they approached the manager's office, they saw a red-faced Paulo exiting the building. His grim expression darkened further when he spotted Jaron and Stephen. As Paulo hurried over to them, Stephen said, "I'll leave you two lovebirds alone," before heading inside the office.

Paulo scanned Jaron from head to toes before pulling him into a tight hug. "What the hell are you doing out of the hospital, let alone here?"

Jaron pressed his face against Paulo's neck, smelling leather and something herbal like rosemary. "The hospital released me."

"That's insane." Paulo tightened his grip, warming every inch of Jaron. "You had a fucking grand mal seizure."

"I'm not convinced there's anything they can do to help me. And even if there was a pill that could shut off my abilities, I wouldn't want it."

Paulo released him. "There's got to be something they can do for you."

Jaron shrugged. "They suggested I buy a glucose monitor and go to the ER if my levels drop too low. I'm also to schedule an appointment with a doctor." Wanting to change the subject, he asked, "What are you doing here?"

"I talked with Dr. Roberts when she came to check on you at the hospital. She mentioned that Marnie's former babysitter lived in the trailer park, but she didn't know her name or any other details. I'm going to need a warrant to get that asshole manager to hand over the records. I've got someone looking over Marnie's financial records to see if she paid anyone on a regular basis by check when Brandon was alive."

Stephen emerged from the office brandishing a sheet of paper. "Look what I got. Margret-Peggy Sampson's forwarding address."

"How did you get that?" Paulo asked, sounding indignant.

"You owe me fifty bucks, detective."

"Missouri," Jaron said. "She moved to Missouri."

Stephen huffed. "Way to steal my thunder with your mojo, Jaron."

Jaron grinned. "Sixth grade geography, not mojo. I know Matt is south of here and about three hundred miles away." It wasn't until he spotted what his brain was calling the candy trailer that he'd had such a precise location for Matt.

"Why do you think that?" Paulo asked. "All of the evidence points to her heading for the Mexican border. She'd be in Texas by now if she hasn't already crossed."

Paulo's words triggered a vision. Jaron saw Matt sitting on a recliner, staring listlessly at a TV. The angle was low, making him realize he was seeing Matt from a cat's perspective. "Peggy has a cat named Snickers who's very grumpy about the new house guests. Snickers wants the loud guests to get out of *her* house."

Paulo took hold of Jaron's hand. "You're saying Matt is at this woman's house right now?"

The vision melted away. "Yes, and I need to go with you when you go there."

"No," Paulo and Stephen said simultaneously.

Paulo squeezed Jaron's shoulder. "It would take hours to get there. If I can coordinate with the local police, we could have Matt in police custody within the hour. I need to get back to the station." He looked at Stephen. "Get him something to eat, take him home, and make him rest."

Jaron watched Paulo hurry away with a ball of dread forming in his stomach.

"What's wrong?" Stephen asked. "Do I need to jab you with one of those plastic needles?"

Jaron struggled to translate the feeling he had into words. "They're not going to get to Matt in time."

"Isn't it more likely you're suffering from a little pessimism instead of suddenly becoming a precog?"

"God, I hope so."

CHAPTER 17

THE STRESS of the past several days had seeped into Peggy's bones, leaving her weak and weary. She felt like a prisoner in her own home. Marnie had taken her cell phone and disabled the house phone. It was only a matter of time before Peggy's daughter would show up to find out why her mother wasn't answering the phone, especially with the storm raging on outside. Peggy didn't know what to do. Marnie needed treatment, not a jail cell. There had to be a way to help Marnie and Matt. Watching Matt stare at the television like a zombie, she knew she needed to act now.

Peggy found Marnie in the kitchen, pacing back and forth in front of the breakfast nook. Marnie had been ranting about the car Martin got her all morning, claiming they'd barely made it to Peggy's house. If Peggy could get Marnie out of the house even for a little while, she could use one of her neighbors' phones to contact the police. "My truck would be able to make it to Mexico if you changed the oil. Why don't you take it over to the Quickie Lube and then get it gassed up while I make some sandwiches for the trip?"

Marnie's smile looked like it would shatter her face. "You'd give me your truck?"

Peggy forced herself to smile. "I want to help you," she said, speaking the truth.

"Daddy!" Matt shouted.

Peggy and Marnie moved quickly into the living room in time to see a photograph of Marnie flash on the screen. It looked like a news bulletin.

Eyes brimming with tears, Matt said, "You said they didn't want me. You said they only wanted Pixie back. I believed you!"

The boy sounded so heartbroken Peggy ached to take him into her arms and comfort him, but she didn't get the chance.

"Get your things, Brandon." When Matt failed to comply, Marnie said, "Now," her voice rough and angry.

"I hate you," Matt said as he left the room and headed for the den, his temporary bedroom.

Peggy's legs felt like they'd been replaced by warm butter. She couldn't let Marnie leave with Matt. "You can't keep running, Marnie. It isn't good for Matt to be under so much stress."

Marnie stiffened. "You mean Brandon."

"Sweetheart, I understand how you could get confused. He looks a lot like Brandon, but Brandon would've been nearly eight years old. Matt is only six years old. He needs to go home to his family and you need to get back into treatment."

"They've gotten to you too," Marnie said, her voice hardening.

"What are you talking about?" Peggy's pulse began to beat erratically, sensing the danger before Peggy could wrap her brain around the change in Marnie. Marnie had gone unnaturally still, her posture more like a lifeless mannequin than her usually endless motion.

"How much did they pay you to keep quiet about Brandon? Was it enough to buy this house? What was the price tag to steal a child from his mother?"

Until this moment, Peggy hadn't realized how far gone Marnie truly was. The kidnapping should've been the first clue, but this paranoid, angry creature wasn't the woman who so lovingly cared for her son amongst such adversity. The grief had twisted something in Marnie. "You were a good mother. Brandon was lucky to have a mother who worked so hard to give him the best life possible. But Matt isn't your child. Somewhere deep inside you have to know that."

An unreadable emotion flickered across Marnie's face. "They removed his birthmark. The mark on his arm that looked like a butterfly. I used to kiss that butterfly every night after I read him a story."

"I told Martin to wait until you were better to have the funeral. But he was more interested in the money the church offered to pay the funeral director. He selected cremation so he could pocket the difference."

"Brandon isn't dead," Marnie snarled. "He can't be dead."

Looking toward the den, Peggy heard the sound of Snickers meowing loudly. She walked toward the back of the house. "Matt?" She quickened her pace when the boy didn't respond. Marnie made no move to follow her. Entering the den, Peggy scanned the room quickly, seeing no sign of Matt. Snickers sat on a wooden chair in front of an opened window. Rain splattered the windowsill.

"Oh, God."

CHAPTER 18

FIVE MINUTES after Stephen left, Jaron sighed when someone knocked on his motel door. He'd hoped to be wrong about Matt, but his every instinct screamed otherwise.

Bear scrambled off the bed and scooped his leash off the carpet as if determined to win back his role of psychic sidekick.

When Jaron opened the door, he was surprised to find Devin on the other side. "What's happened?"

"There's been a complication," Devin said, looking grim. "Will you come with me?" He looked down at Bear. "You should bring the dog, too. He'll help with the cover story."

Jaron turned back toward the bed and grabbed his jacket. He hadn't bothered to take off his shoes after getting brunch with Stephen. Picking up Bear's leash, he followed Devin out of the motel room.

Devin walked quickly toward a white Chevrolet car with a yellow stripe identifying it as a State Police vehicle. He clicked the key fob and opened the back door for Bear. "Paulo's on his way to Missouri. He left not long after you saw him at the trailer park."

Jaron released Bear's leash and the Newfie jumped into the back seat. He noticed the car didn't have a cage blocking access to the front seat. "I take it the police didn't find Matt at the babysitter's house?"

Devin shook his head. "Get in and I'll explain on the way." He went around to the driver's side and got in.

Jaron complied, barely getting his door closed before Devin was backing out of the parking space. He wanted to demand an explanation, but Devin's icy façade made him hesitate.

They sat in an uncomfortable silence until they reached the ramp for I-55 S toward St Louis. His gaze locked on the road, Devin began to speak. "Peggy Sampson lives in Missouri, near a small town that butts against the Washington National Park." He snorted. "They're even smaller than Stanton."

"Matt is in the woods," Jaron blurted out, the details of his dream pouring through his mind.

Devin tightened his grip on the steering wheel, his knuckles turning white. "Why do you think that?"

Jaron had no intention of telling Devin he dreamed it. "It makes sense. If you'd found Matt at the house, there would be no need to bring me there."

Devin grunted in agreement. "When the local PD got to the house, they found Peggy tied up in the backroom with duct tape. Peggy said that Matt had run away and that Marnie had gone after him."

"How long will it take us to get there?"

"We'll be there in about three hours."

"Three hours," Jaron repeated. "Meaning Matt would be out there for hours on his own." He ran a hand through his white-blond hair. If he hadn't agreed to stay at the hospital overnight, the police might have gotten to Matt before he went into the woods. He swallowed, trying to banish the sudden ache in his throat. "The police will find him before that, right?"

"The area is pretty remote, so it'll take time to organize a search. We've requested assistance from their County Sheriff, but that will take time too. They've also had a lot of rain." As if summoned by Devin's words, a light rain began to fall, and he turned on the windshield wipers. "The fact that Matt isn't wearing shoes, and his age, make the search more difficult. Kids his age don't always respond to searchers calling out for them, but they can manage to run several miles. And if Marnie finds him first, there's no telling how she'll react."

Jaron could understand Matt hiding from searchers since he was trying to run away from Marnie. "Why didn't you go with Paulo?"

Devin's jaw twitched. "I agreed to coordinate with Agent Fisher before heading out, because the less time Paulo spends with Fisher the better. I don't want him losing his badge because he knocked Fisher's teeth out."

"Who's Agent Fisher?" Jaron asked, surprised. He didn't remember Paulo talking about this person, but Devin had mentioned a meeting with the Feds when they first met. He assumed that included Fisher.

Devin gave Jaron a sidewise look. "You met him yesterday at the hospital."

Thinking back, Jaron couldn't remember any details from being in the hospital ER. Bear grumbled from the backseat, sending Jaron an image of a man in a suit sprawled on the ground. Whoever this man was, Bear didn't like him one bit. "I don't remember much beyond waking up in the hospital bed."

"Fisher is with the FBI. He was convinced you were working with Marnie and her brother. And that the kidnapping was nothing more than an elaborate plot to gain you publicity."

"That's horrible! How can he think that?"

Bear pushed his head between the gap in the seats and licked the side of Jaron's face. Jaron wiped his cheek and patted Bear on the head.

"Apparently, Fisher went over to the Wilsons to question them about it. Mr. Wilson went ballistic and threw him out." Devin smirked. "Since Chief Tucker insisted Fisher be the one to bring the Wilsons to Missouri, it's bound to be a fun trip. They should arrive there a little before us. Or a lot, depending on how many speed barriers Fisher breaks."

It was a small comfort that Mr. Wilson believed in him. Mrs. Wilson had accused him of being a fraud, but that wasn't an unusual reaction. He doubted Mrs. Wilson shared her husband's outrage at the accusation. She might even agree with Fisher. The thought made Jaron nauseous. "You don't believe in my abilities either, so why are you playing chauffeur?"

"I don't think you're involved with the Beckers. I don't care how good a fuck you are. Paulo's too smart to be conned that completely."

Jaron resisted the urge to correct Devin. *I'm such a good lay I fell asleep in the middle of it.* "That doesn't explain why you're bringing me to Missouri."

"It doesn't matter what I believe. You've got Mr. Wilson convinced, even if all your discoveries can be chalked up to lucky coincidences."

"I wouldn't call nearly getting my throat slit lucky," Jaron said dourly.

"First, Martin Becker regularly gets thrown out of that bar where you encountered him. And second, Peggy Sampson lived in that trailer park for over twenty years. It wasn't surprising you found someone who knew her."

"I knew her name before I went to the trailer park," Jaron said, not sure why Devin's disbelief annoyed him so much.

Devin looked at him for a disturbing amount of time, considering the speedometer had reached eighty miles an hour. "Paulo said you grew up there. Maybe you knew her and didn't realize it right away." He looked back toward the road. "Hell, she might've been your babysitter when you were a kid."

Jaron saw no point in arguing with Devin. He folded his jacket and placed it against the glass window before leaning his head against it. "Wake me up when we get closer," he said before closing his eyes.

"Did you really have a seizure yesterday?"

Jaron sighed and kept his eyes shut. "That's what the nurse told me."

"Do the doctors know why it happened?"

Annoyed, Jaron opened his eyes. "Why do you care?"

Devin shifted in his seat. "You could have walked away from this case and nobody would've questioned it. And that was before you ended up in the hospital. Why not quit?"

"It was never an option."

"Because of Paulo?" Devin shook his head. "Don't count on him sticking around after we find Matt. My lieutenant said he would take him back in a heartbeat."

Curious in spite of himself, Jaron said, "You said Paulo only moved here because of the... Jefferson case. Why do you think he'll go back to the State Police once we find Matt?"

"His friends, family, and career are all waiting for him in Springfield."

Jaron had no illusions that the couple of kisses he shared with Paulo would be enough of a motivation to stay. He wondered where Devin included himself in that list. As a friend? Or something more?

"He just needs to get his confidence back," Devin said without looking away from the road. "Finding Matt will help him."

"Did the Jefferson case involve a child?"

Devin nodded. "A father put his baby boy in a lit oven to punish the mother."

Jaron gasped, pressing his hand against his mouth. He was grateful he could only read animal minds. Only humans could be monsters.

"Paulo was in a nearby apartment interviewing a witness, but there was no way he could've known. We tracked the perp all the way to Chicago. He pulled a knife on Paulo and Paulo shot him." Devin tapped his fingers on the steering wheel. "I thought Paulo would get better after he had caught the guy, but he didn't."

An image flashed in Jaron's mind. A haggard-looking Paulo was lying on a bed with bloodred sheets. He was staring at the ceiling, looking dazed. The image was so detailed he could see the stubble on Paulo's cheeks and the dark circles under his eyes. He sensed no animal in the room. So how was he picking up on this image?

"Holy fuck," Jaron said.

"What's wrong?"

"Sheets. What color are your sheets?"

"Huh?" Devin said, before yanking on the wheel to stop the car from drifting into the other lane.

Jaron's pulse began to quicken. "Were you just thinking about Paulo lying shirtless on red silk sheets? It looked like he was staring at the ceiling like it was going to cave in on his head."

Devin slammed on the brakes and pulled the car over, sending up a spray of gravel. "How the hell did you just pluck that image out of my head?" he demanded.

Jaron held out his hands. "I have no idea unless you're secretly a werewolf."

Bear barked, startling them both so much that Devin smacked his head on the ceiling.

"Werewolf," Devin muttered, checking the mirrors and pulling back on the road. "This case has officially been crowned the all-time weirdest. Even weirder than the guy who dressed as a clown 24/7."

Jaron had no response to that horrifying image. He was too busy freaking out.

"Tell me what number I'm thinking of."

"No, that's too easy. You're a perv with porno sheets. Of course you're gonna think of 69."

Devin laughed. "Valid. Let me think of another one."

"How about we don't?"

Devin frowned. "Why not?"

Jaron chewed his bottom lip. "When I'm in the salon, I'm surrounded by the thoughts and emotions of the animals. It's a warm, comfortable feeling, even when they are annoyed by getting their nails cut. Because they know they're being taken care of. Now imagine being at the police station with the thoughts and emotions of everyone in the building bombarding your mind. Would you want that?"

Devin winced. "Hell, no, but I wouldn't think you could just switch off the ability because you don't want it. You've never gotten readings off of people before?"

Jaron remembered the conversation he'd had with Stewie's owner about Chrissy. "I've gotten flashes of information not related to a reading, but I've always assumed it was my subconscious at work. For instance, while reading a Jack Russell terrier, I realized a woman who works at the salon is having money problems. I assumed I must have heard her talk about it without focusing on it at the time."

"I can't imagine Paulo talking to you about my sheets, but even if he did, how could you know I was thinking about that moment? The way you described is exactly what Paulo looked like when he told me he was leaving the ISP."

"Why are you so quick to jump on the believer bandwagon? What happened to lucky coincidences?"

"Tell me the number."

Jaron exhaled loudly. "Five, but I have no idea what you're thinking now, so clearly it's a fluke."

Devin groaned. "I can't believe you really are psychic. There'll be no living with Paulo after this."

"It doesn't make any sense. I've had the ability to read animals my whole life. Why would I suddenly start reading people now?"

"Maybe you blocked the ability to read people as a kid and the seizure knocked something loose."

"I'm not a clogged drain." Jaron pressed his hand against his throbbing head. "And being able to read people won't help me find Matt. Only Pixie can help me do that, and I haven't seen her since before the seizure." He wasn't sure the dream version counted. Even though he wasn't sure why, he didn't think a ghost could invade a person's dream. It felt more like his subconscious pointing him in the right direction, leading him down a path he thought was closed off to him. Had he always had the ability to sense animals' spirits? Stephen seemed to think he had. They'd talked about it throughout brunch. If he had somehow blocked being a medium, could he have blocked other abilities as well?

Devin grinned. "We've got time to kill, so why not try? It might even help if you can get a read on Matt or even Marnie."

Jaron sighed. He didn't want to play poke the psychic. What if he couldn't reconnect with Pixie? The death of one child had caused Paulo to walk away from his position at the ISP. What would happen if Jaron couldn't save Matt?

"WE'RE HERE," Devin said as he turned onto Oak Road.

Police cruisers and other cars lined the narrow residential street. A blue tarp had been erected on someone's front lawn, sheltering several officers from the steady rain. Two officers were looking at something pinned to the table while another talked on the radio.

Devin drove past the group looking for an open spot. Nearly a dozen houses went by before he pulled over and parallel-parked with impressive efficiency. "Wait here until I can track down Paulo." He sighed. "If anyone asks, you're a dog handler with experience in search and rescue."

Jaron nodded in agreement.

Devin released his seatbelt and exited the vehicle.

As Jaron watched Devin hike toward the other officers, his attention was drawn to a one-story cottage-style house. Instead of a porch, there was a cobblestone path that led to the front door before branching out to run along the front of the house and around the corners. Pixie was sitting on the left path.

Whimpering, Bear put his paw on the back of the driver's seat.

Jaron rubbed the Newfie's big head. "I'll be right back." He saw an image in his mind of Bear sitting on top of him. Jaron scrambled out of the car before Bear could carry out the threat.

Looking down the street, Jaron saw no sign of Devin or Paulo. He was supposed to wait, but what if Pixie disappeared? He couldn't risk that. Decision made, he walked along the path, experiencing a strange sense of déjà vu. The path wound around the house to the backyard. Though "backyard" was the wrong word for it. The house appeared to have a dense forest behind it. Seeing no sign of the house's owners, Jaron walked to the edge of the forest. Pixie sat at the base of a massive oak, her appearance faded and unclear.

PAULO WAS glad Peggy Sampson had agreed to let them use her house as a command center before she left with her daughter. This conversation with the Wilsons was difficult enough without the reminder that their child was somewhere in the cold, wet woods. Paulo directed Mrs. Wilson to sit on the couch next to him. Fisher chose to sit in an old recliner.

Mr. Wilson paced in front of the television. "How many people are looking for Matt?"

"We have ten officers searching for Matt on the ground, including a K9 unit. Now that the thunderstorm has cleared, we'll be able to bring in a helicopter to help in the search."

"Why so few searchers? We had two dozen people from our church volunteer to come with us and help search." He glared at Fisher. "But he wouldn't let them come."

As much as Paulo enjoyed watching Fisher squirm under Mr. Wilson's icy visage, he agreed with the decision. "I understand your desire, but we can't have civilians involved. It's too dangerous."

Mr. Wilson raised his chin. "I'm willing to take the risk."

"We know Marnie Becker is off her meds and mentally unstable. She had no qualms about duct-taping a seventy year old woman to a chair and leaving her alone."

Mrs. Wilson rose from the couch and stood next to her husband. "That's why we need to find this woman fast."

"Exactly," Mr. Wilson said.

"What if she has a gun? She's convinced you stole her child. She could use the gun to hurt you or Matt."

Mr. Wilson's voice broke. "There has to be more we can do. He's been out there too long."

"Sergeant Devin Morris should get here soon. He's bringing Jaron to help with the search."

"You're not serious," Fisher said, his disgust coloring his voice. "You're bringing that fraud here?"

Paulo scrambled to his feet and grabbed a hold of Mr. Wilson before he could get his hands on Fisher.

"Bastard!" Mr. Wilson yelled.

Fisher stared at Mr. Wilson, his mouth agape.

Paulo manhandled Mr. Wilson into sitting on the couch. His wife joined him, taking hold of his hand and murmuring words of comfort.

"Can I speak with you for a minute in the kitchen, Agent Fisher?" Paulo asked, willing himself to keep calm. He headed for the kitchen.

Looking sullen, Fisher rose and followed Paulo into the kitchen.

Paulo kept his voice low. "You have too much experience on the job to be this bad at dealing with a vic's family. You know how high emotions run in a case like this. So why don't you tell me what the hell is going on?"

Fisher sighed. "Every time a high-profile case like this comes around, the supposed psychics come crawling out of the woodworks, looking for money or attention. It was only a matter of time before one decided to stack the deck in his favor by perpetrating the crime."

"There's no evidence that Jaron is involved in this case."

"Maybe not directly, but that doesn't mean your boyfriend *isn't* involved. I wouldn't be surprised if we find out that Jaron has been whispering in Marnie's ear. He met her at the hospital, learned about her son's death, and decided to give her a little push in the right direction. He knows about the Healing Paws therapy program, and he has friends in the hospital. Hell, he even knows the vic's father. The best con men can not only convince you to do what they want, but make you think it was your idea."

"Our priority needs to be finding Matt, not antagonizing his father because he doesn't share your views."

Fisher had the decency to look chagrined. "You're right. Now isn't the time. But when we find Matt, Jaron and I will be having a long talk."

A knock on the front door saved Paulo from responding to Fisher's poorly disguised threat. *Please let that be Devin or I'm going to smash in Fisher's face.*

CHAPTER 19

PAULO EXITED the house and joined Devin on the porch, leaving Fisher to the wolves. It was better than the man deserved. He could hear Mr. Wilson ranting about negative energy through the solid wooden door, but not the sounds of a fistfight. Not yet, anyway.

"Why did the Feds send us that fuckwad Fisher?" Paulo grumbled. His prior experiences working with the Feds in the past had all been positive, with agents working with him cooperatively.

Devin chuckled. "Yeah, he's certainly not on the believer bandwagon with our psychic."

Paulo squinted at him. "Our psychic? Since when did Jaron become *our* psychic?"

Devin gave him a toothy grin. "We bonded on the way here. It was beautiful."

"Now there's a terrifying thought." Paulo massaged his forehead as he brought Devin up to speed. "The two rookie first responders went barreling into the forest like a pair of rampaging rhinos. In opposite directions, no less, pretty much destroying our chances of knowing which direction Matt and Marnie went."

"God save us from rookies. Were we ever that stupid?"

Paulo smirked. "Hell, no. The County Sheriff has the area locked down just in case Marnie attempts to run. They are also going door to door since we don't know for sure that Matt went into the woods. He might be hiding somewhere in the neighborhood."

"Jaron thinks he's in the woods."

"And you believe him?"

"We already covered this. After this case, we should bring him back to Springfield and put him on the ISP payroll. Can you imagine how valuable a guy who can read our suspects' minds would be?"

"What do you mean?" Paulo asked, ignoring Devin's assertion that he would return to the ISP. "He can only read animals' minds."

"Oh, he can read human minds too," Devin said, sounding thrilled to be dropping that bombshell. "Not as well as animals, but he hasn't practiced much. I tried thinking of numbers, colors, and even basic shapes. We did it like twenty times before he got tired, and he was right around 75 percent of the time."

"Dammit, Devin, using his abilities drains him physically. That's how he ended up in the hospital."

Devin made a clucking noise with his tongue, making Paulo want to smack him.

"Go babysit Fisher for me while I get Jaron," Paulo said.

"In that case," Devin said, tossing him a set of keys, "get my Taser from the trunk while you're getting our boy."

Paulo snatched up the keys and stepped off the porch, not sure if Devin was serious or not. He could also understand Devin's excitement as an investigator. Even before knowing about Jaron's ability to read people, he'd considered how valuable Jaron could be on an investigation. But it was a little disconcerting on a personal level. What would it be like to have a lover who could read his mind? Even though he knew Jaron wouldn't abuse such a power, the idea of thoughts being private was a deep-seated belief. He hated to think it, but it felt unnatural for someone to have access to another person's innermost thoughts. He gave himself a mental shake. Now wasn't the time to think about it.

Paulo heard Bear before he located Devin's car. The deep, guttural bark made the hair on the back of his neck rise. He quickened his pace, while scanning the area for the source of Bear's distress. As he reached the car, he saw that Bear had crawled into the driver's seat. He moved closer, causing Bear to begin scratching the window frantically.

Paulo peered into the car. "*Foda*," he swore when he realized Jaron wasn't inside. He called out several times, hoping his errant psychic would appear. He pulled out his cell phone and called Jaron. Jaron's discarded jacket began to ring. He swore again and punched in Devin's number. Devin answered on the first ring.

Paulo could hear Mr. Wilson talking about auras in the background. "Jaron isn't here. Did he say anything about checking out the area?"

"I told him to stay put," Devin said, sounding indignant. "I should've handcuffed him to the steering wheel."

Paulo watched a glob of slobber slide down the window. "I think Bear woulda eaten your face if you tried. He's giving me his best Cujo impression. I'm going to take a look around." He looked at Bear. "I'm hoping Lassie can lead me to Timmy."

"I should come with you," Devin said.

"No, I need you here. We need to get that copter in the air. And I don't trust Fisher to coordinate with the additional officers on the way from the local state police."

Devin heaved a put-upon sigh. "Fine, but I'm definitely going to need the Taser, so leave my keys under the driver's side visor."

"You got it," Paulo said before he ended the call. He clicked the key fob and opened the door a hand's width. "Sit, Bear."

Bear obeyed, panting heavily.

Paulo opened the door further and positioned himself to block any escape attempts. "Okay, Bear, we're going to go look for Jaron, but I need you to heel instead of attempting to rip off my arm."

Bear cocked his head.

Belatedly, Paulo realized he should've retrieved the leash from the backseat first. He started to close the door when Bear made his move.

Bear pushed off the seat with his back feet and shoved against Paulo with his front paws. Arms flailing, Paulo fell backward and landed on his ass on the damp ground. Bear's bushy black tail smacked Paulo in the face as he leaped over him and onto the sidewalk.

"I'm going to murder that *cachorro louco*," Paulo muttered as he dragged himself to his feet. He turned around and found Bear standing patiently on a cobblestone path.

Stepping backward, Bear barked several times.

Paulo put the keys in the car and shut the door. "All right, Lassie, lead the way."

THE RECENT rain had made the ground slick with wet leaves and mud. Jaron's sneakers squished and squeaked as he trekked through the thick brush and trees. The frigid temperature made him wish he'd grabbed his coat before getting out of the car, especially since his cell phone was in the pocket. It was a tossup who would be more pissed at him, Paulo or Devin, but it couldn't be helped. He couldn't risk delaying and possibly losing sight of Pixie. He could only hope that Bear would be able to lead Paulo to him. The position of the sun told him that he was heading east. It made sense. The park was shaped like a warped cylinder. According to Devin, there were well-marked trails and camping areas toward the west. If Marnie was with Matt, she would likely avoid such places.

The forest pulsed with life, big and small, a distracting buzzing in his mind. He struggled to keep the blur of white fur in sight as he navigated the thick brush and trees. With every step, his unease grew, making him pick up his pace. Noticing broken twigs and trampled foliage, he wondered if that meant someone had been through here recently. Was it one of the searchers, Marnie, or Matt? The thought shoved an image into his mind so hard he fell to the ground. A sharp twig dug into his palm, ripping open the skin. *Snickers yelled at the boy as he climbed through the window. It was dangerous to go out in a storm.*

Jaron hauled himself to his feet, brushing his muddy hands on his track pants. A trickle of blood trailed down his arm, but he was too cold to feel much pain. He pressed the sleeve of his sweatshirt against the wound. The thick material helped to staunch the blood flow. The cut didn't appear to be too deep.

Pixie barked, apparently unhappy with Jaron's delay.

When she took off, Jaron ran after her. Keeping up with Pixie was easier said than done. Pixie moved through the trees and prickly bushes, leaving Jaron scrambling for a way around on the uneven ground. Thorns scraped at his hands and gripped his hair, but he ripped himself free and kept going. The sense of urgency compelled him to move faster in spite of his burning lungs and aching side. He had to be at least a mile, if not more, from Devin's car. He knew that somewhere in the forest were teams of searchers, but he had no idea where they were. Devin seemed to think he should be able to locate them. But reading Devin's mind had felt wrong. Like Freddy Krueger using his metal claws on a chalkboard wrong.

Brandon! The name reverberated in Jaron's mind, sending him to his knees. He covered his ears with his hands, trying to block out the scream drilling into his brain. Blind panic gripped him, stealing his breath. *Brandon! Brandon! Brandon!* The name acted like a battering ram against his mind. He covered his mouth, tasting blood and mud. If he started screaming, he'd never stop. Marnie was close by, and her fear and grief and guilt threatened to render Jaron unconscious. "Stop!" Jaron shouted. At first the cascade of emotions continued to assail him. But then something shifted in Jaron's brain. The reptilian part of his subconscious where his self-preservation lurked rose, and he could breathe again.

When Jaron dragged himself upright, he froze. "Pixie?" He spun around slowly, trying to spot her. Nothing. Closing his eyes, he took a deep breath, the icy air burning his lungs. He blew out a plume of smoke, trying to calm his racing heart. He opened his eyes. Nothing. Over his gasping breaths, Jaron heard a rumbling sound. He started jogging toward the sound, not sure why. The volume increased as he moved closer to the source. Through the trees, he could see a rushing creek. The recent rain had left it swollen and fast-moving.

Jaron's gaze was drawn to the bank. Someone in a dark hoodie was stepping into the water. *Are they nuts?* Moving closer, Jaron understood why. The top half of a massive oak tree had partially broken off, submerging some of the branches in the middle of the creek. Clinging precariously to one of the upper branches was a young boy. Matt. It was a miracle the rushing water hadn't knocked the treetop loose and sent it and Matt downstream.

A white blur drew Jaron's attention. Pixie ran across the surface of the churning water to where Matt clung to the tree branch. Pixie disappeared as she reached Matt, as if the little dog's energy was being absorbed into Matt.

BEAR REFUSED to get close enough to let Paulo attach a leash, but the Newfie's black coat made keeping him in sight relatively easy as they walked briskly. He wondered if it was Jaron's scent or psychic pull leading Bear through the woods. Or maybe it was both.

His police radio crackled and Paulo answered Devin's call.

"The chopper is in the air," Devin said. "It's equipped with FLIR technology. The infrared thermal imaging will help us direct the search teams. Where are you?"

"I'm heading east. Let's hope Bear is tracking Jaron and not a squirrel."

"We don't have any teams in that direction. Do you want me to tell the chopper to begin there?"

Paulo hesitated. The standard practice was to begin at the last known location and expand out in a square search pattern. He had confidence in Jaron, but how would he explain it to the pilot? "No, stick to the standard pattern. Even if Jaron had been running, he couldn't be more than a few miles away. Tell the spotter to keep an eye out for him. If they spot anyone, have them radio you. All the teams have been equipped with radios."

"You got it, boss."

Paulo winced. Devin was supposed to be the lead on this case. "Sorry."

Devin snorted. "This is what you do best. What you were meant to do."

Instead of working for the SPD, Devin didn't say, but the message was loud and clear. From the moment Paulo had announced a probable location for Marnie, Devin had taken a backseat on the investigation. The manipulative bastard. This case was probably Devin's twisted idea of therapy. Paulo didn't call him on it. "Over and out."

Paulo had worked vandalism and theft cases since coming to Stanton with the kind of apathy he couldn't seem to shake. Until the Matt Wilson case. Damned if Paulo would admit that to Devin.

CHAPTER 20

"WAIT, MARNIE!" Jaron shouted. He raced toward the bank.

Marnie either didn't hear him or chose to ignore him. Almost immediately, Marnie lost her balance, the rough current knocking her off her feet. Her heavy clothes made swimming nearly impossible. Rather than turn back, she continued forward. She slipped again and went under.

Jaron reached the edge of the creek, pulled off his sweatshirt, and then toed off his shoes. His track pants shouldn't limit his movement. *Maybe that's why Pixie kept trashing my jeans?* That was too weird to contemplate.

Matt's eyes were closed as he held onto the branch. Scanning the area, Jaron couldn't see Marnie anywhere. Had the current dragged her away?

"Where's a water dog when you need one," Jaron muttered as he moved up the bank. He hoped the current would push him closer to Matt. Marnie's attempt to move straight across clearly hadn't worked. *What do I do when I get there?* He doubted the tree would remain attached for long if he added his weight to Matt's. He would have to hope he had the strength to make it back to shore. All too well he remembered hearing about good Samaritans who ended up drowning when they attempted to rescue someone. But he couldn't stand by and watch as Matt clung to his lifeline. Even if Bear managed to get here in time, there was no guarantee the Newfie could get Matt back to shore without assistance.

The water was so cold it burned, sending shockwaves of pain up his legs. If he managed to pull Matt to shore, there was still the risk of them both succumbing to hypothermia. When the water reached his waist, Jaron was sure his lungs were about to burst. Goosebumps broke out all over his skin. The rough current made it feel like he was trying to walk on a Slip 'N Slide, threatening to topple him at any moment. Would it be better to swim? Or would he be swept away downstream? He was nearly at Matt's position, but he wasn't over far enough. If he passed by Matt, he wouldn't have the strength to swim upstream.

Jaron gave up attempting to walk and pushed off the ground, kicking his feet frantically. Gasping for air, he attempted to swim. His attempt was more of a doggy paddle than a stroke. He was afraid to put his head under the water and risk losing sight of Matt.

Icy spray splattered his face and he swallowed a mouthful of water. He coughed several times, ingesting more water than he expelled. Closing his mouth, he kicked hard and pushed his way through the churning current. When he reached the tree, he lunged forward, his fingertips grasping a small branch. The branch snapped and he sank under the water. He felt himself moving, the stream dragging him away. Silt clouded the water, making it impossible to see.

Jaron swam underwater. For several long seconds, he didn't move, the force of the water keeping him trapped in the inky blackness. Muscles straining, he began to make progress closely. He stopped when he bumped into something solid: Matt's legs. Lungs burning, he pushed up to the surface. The first breath of air tasted so sweet it made him giddy. Looking at the tangle of branches, he found a large one and took hold of it. The wood creaked but held. A thin strip of wood connected the treetop to the old oak. It could snap any minute or next week. Jaron had no way of knowing.

White-faced, Matt hadn't opened his eyes or reacted at all to Jaron's approach. The blue cast to his lips made him look disturbingly like a corpse. His death grip on the branch was the only sign of life.

Jaron raised his voice to be heard over the rushing water. "Matt, my name is Jaron. Your parents hired me to help find you and bring you home."

Matt opened his dark eyes, directing his gaze beyond Jaron. "She's not my momma."

Jaron looked over his shoulder. Marnie was further downstream, pinned against a boulder.

"I know, Matt," Jaron said, repeating the child's name. Matt's sense of identity had been torn to pieces by Marnie. While Jaron sensed no malice when he touched Marnie's mind, she had hurt Matt in ways that would be slow to heal. Jaron could feel the stress and fear radiating off Matt. And guilt. Marnie had made him doubt his parents' love. But Matt hadn't given up. Was Pixie responsible for the spark of life helping him to hold on?

Hearing Bear's bark, Jaron looked toward the shore. He sighed in relief. Bear didn't even hesitate as he plunged into the water. Newfoundlands had been bred to be water dogs. In the 1800s, they were used to rescue shipwrecked sailors from the ocean. Their webbed feet, great lung capacity, and powerful frame made them strong swimmers. Bear's doggy paddle put Jaron to shame.

"Matt, I need you to let go of the branch and wrap your arms and legs around me."

Matt shook his head. "I'll drown."

"Look, Matt." Jaron pointed to the Newfie. "Bear's a rescue dog. He's going to help us."

When Bear got close enough, Jaron grabbed his collar. Bear placed his massive paws on Jaron's shoulders. He leaned forward and licked Jaron's cheek.

Matt stared into Bear's dark eyes before smiling wanly. "Hi, Bear."

Bear licked Matt's cheek too.

Matt didn't resist when Jaron took hold of him. He wrapped his arms and legs around Jaron in a vise-like grip. Jaron used his right arm to keep Matt in place. Matt wasn't shivering, which was a bad sign. Holding onto Bear's collar with his left, Jaron pushed off the creek bed. He envied Bear his thick waterproof hair as a wave of water stole his breath. He positioned himself to the side of Bear as the Newfie attempted to haul them to shore. Jaron kicked hard, worried his numb fingers would lose their grip.

When Jaron saw Paulo emerge from the trees, he felt a surge of relief. His attempt to call out came out brittle and broken. But it was enough. Paulo zeroed in on them and raced toward the shore. After pulling off his jacket and long-sleeved shirt, he waded into the water. The water was thigh-deep when he reached them.

"Take Matt," Jaron said, not sure he would be able to stand. Bear dragged him forward until they had both landed on the shore.

"Where's Marnie?" Paulo asked as he lifted Matt up. Goosebumps pebbled his skin, but Paulo appeared unaffected by the cold.

Jaron coughed, trying to force air into his lungs. "Further downstream on a rock."

Paulo nodded. "Help is coming," he said, but Jaron knew it might not be in time for Marnie.

Jaron forced himself to stand and walk over to where Paulo was stripping off Matt's wet clothes. Paulo had given Matt his badge to hold. Matt clung to the badge like it was a lifeline. Paulo put his shirt on Matt, the material hanging past Matt's knees. Then he wrapped the boy in his leather coat.

Jaron's attempt to sit next to them was more like a strategic collapse. Paulo rose and retrieved Jaron's sweatshirt. Embarrassingly, Jaron needed as much help as Matt to put it on. Paulo also made him eat the much-hated glucose tablet.

"I wish I had another jacket," Paulo said, rubbing Jaron's arms and chest to stimulate blood flow.

A splash had Jaron looking back toward the creek. "Bear!" he shouted. He scrambled over to the bank. He could hardly see Bear over the choppy water. The Newfie was headed for the rock Marnie still clung to.

Jaron hadn't realized he had stepped into the water until Paulo was dragging him back.

"It's too dangerous," Paulo said.

"He'll drown," Jaron said, desperately trying to pry Paulo's hands from his waist. Even with Bear's swimming ability, the distance was too far. Bear had to have traveled through the forest to reach them, followed by towing Jaron and Matt to shore. Bear's endurance could only last so long.

"You can't help him by drowning yourself. Tell him to take her to the far bank. The distance is shorter."

Jaron wanted to tell Bear to abandon Marnie and head for the shore, but he knew it wouldn't work. To Bear, Marnie wasn't a mentally ill kidnapper. She was someone who needed his help. Jaron didn't want Marnie to drown, but he selfishly valued Bear's life over hers.

Marnie had slipped further down on the rock with her eyes closed.

The force of the water pushed Bear past Marnie by several feet. Through their link, Jaron could feel how tired Bear was, the difficulty of keeping his lungs clear of water as he swam against the current.

Jaron could vaguely hear Paulo talking into a radio, but Jaron was too focused on Bear, sending him a mental pep talk. *Almost there. Save her. She needs your help.*

When Bear finally reached Marnie, he shoved his head under her armpit, causing her to grab hold of his thick coat. Jaron concentrated on sending Bear an image of the far shore. Bear resisted, his instincts telling him to return to Jaron. They would never make it.

"Go there, Bear," Jaron said, falling to his knees.

Paulo followed Jaron to the ground, his grip tight around Jaron's waist.

As Bear reached the shore, Jaron noticed black spots flickering in front of his eyes. And then nothing.

CHAPTER 21

JARON WOKE to the sound of Stephen arguing with someone nearby. A familiar weight had him pinned to an uncomfortable bed. Opening his eyes, it took a moment for Jaron to realize where he was. The windowless hospital room looked similar to the one in Stanton. Was he still in Missouri? He looked at Bear. Bear's chin was resting on Jaron's stomach. His dark eyes were alert and he was projecting his annoyance.

Jaron smiled. "Sorry, Bear." He was surprised the small hospital bed wasn't buckling under their combined weight.

Bear grumbled. It was hard to argue with doggy logic. Bad things tended to happen when Bear wasn't there to keep his idiot human safe.

Laughing, Jaron rubbed Bear's head, noticing he wasn't attached to an IV. A Band-Aid indicated that it had been connected at some point. That had to be a good sign, right?

The door opened, admitting Stephen. "We need to stop meeting like this." His tone was light and mocking, but the tension in his shoulders telegraphed his distress.

"Is Matt okay?"

Stephen nodded. "They're going to keep him overnight. They're worried about him developing pneumonia, but so far he's doing fine. The Wilsons wanted to come see you, but I convinced them to wait until we get back to Stanton."

Jaron sighed. "Thank you." He wondered about Marnie too, but he knew better than to ask Stephen about her. "When can I get out of here?"

Stephen scowled. "I told the nurse to track down a doctor, but I don't know if he'll do it. He was giving me shit about being your medical proxy. So we may need to bust out of Hick Hospital without permission." He picked up a backpack off the floor and tossed it on the bed.

"Thanks for bringing my stuff and driving all the way out here."

"Don't mention it. And I mean never. When we get back to Stanton, I want to pretend none of this shit ever happened."

"All of it, including that kiss you laid on me?"

"Oh, is it time for psychic psychoanalysis? Shouldn't I be the one lying down?"

Jaron ignored the mockery. "You love me, trust me, and even like me. Which is more than you can say about all your ex-boyfriends combined." He took hold of Stephen's hand. "I'm a safe choice because you know I'd never hurt you deliberately."

Stephen rolled his eyes. "Maybe I just want you because of the way your ass looks in your Goodwill jeans."

Jaron shook his head. "You don't have sex with someone you used to have bean burrito fart contests with."

"So sayeth the reigning champ of flatulence." Stephen rubbed his thumb against Jaron's hand. "We're not kids anymore."

Jaron looked down at their joined hands, concentrating on his connection to Stephen. It was easier than he would've thought to connect with his best friend's mind. Stephen's emotions reminded Jaron of a layered cake. Worry on the top layer. Jealousy of Paulo on the next one. Love and affection filled the cake. But on the bottom layer was relief. A part of Stephen knew they shouldn't be together.

"I won't hurt you, Stephen. Even if it means denying you something you think you want."

"Because of Paulo?"

"Because I love you. Because I can't afford to lose your friendship. Because all I've ever wanted was to call you my brother, my family."

Stephen sighed. "Do you love him?"

"We haven't even made it past first base yet. But I care about him a lot. I think we could be good together."

"And if it doesn't work out?"

Jaron refused to give Stephen false hope. He wouldn't make the same mistake that Devin had made with Paulo. Even if it meant potentially losing his friendship with Stephen. "Then I'll expect you to console me with beer and bean burritos."

Stephen squeezed Jaron's hand. "You're damn right I will."

TWO DAYS in this dank motel room had Jaron longing for his room at the salon. The smell of wet dog would be a relief. He knew Stephen would let him stay there. His best friend had been pestering him about it since Jaron was released from the hospital. It made sense to stay there until he'd saved enough for a down payment for rent and found a part time job. It was the smart thing to do. He just couldn't seem to make himself do it. It didn't help that he hadn't heard from Paulo beyond two hurried phone calls. Capturing Marnie was apparently step one to a very complicated process. Jaron knew the other reason Paulo was staying away. To keep Jaron off the press's radar. His musing was interrupted by a knock on the door.

After rising from the bed, Jaron opened the door to find the whole Wilson clan waiting for him.

"Can we come in?" Mr. Wilson asked before Jaron could even open his mouth.

"Uh, sure." Jaron opened the door further and stepped to the side. His cheeks flushed as he closed the door behind them. His room wasn't meant for entertaining.

Matt walked over to where Bear was lying on the floor. He sat down in front of Bear and leaned back, sucking his thumb like a toddler. Bear seemed happy enough to serve as a pillow for the boy.

Mr. Wilson looked uncomfortable. He kept his voice low. "The therapist says it's normal to regress after something so traumatic. We're thinking about getting him another dog."

"Don't," Jaron blurted out. He ducked his head. "I'm sorry. I don't mean to tell you what to do."

"Why not get another one?" Mrs. Wilson asked, looking genuinely interested.

"Pixie's not dead," Matt shouted. Standing up, he clenched his hands into fists as tears formed in his eyes. "She's lost in the woods and we need to find her."

Mr. Wilson knelt down in front of his son. "Sweetheart, we've talked about this. Pixie is in heaven with Nana Wilson."

Matt shook his head violently. "You're a liar! I hate you! Hate you!"

The words impacted Mr. Wilson like a slap in the face. When he stumbled to his feet, Jaron touched his arm. "Can I try?"

Mrs. Wilson gave her assent while her husband stared at his son like the boy had been replaced by a pod person.

Jaron sat Indian-style in front of Matt and patted the carpet. "Can I talk to you about Pixie?"

"M-Marnie gave Pixie to her brother. He was supposta take her to a shelter, but he didn't. He let her go in the woods. I know it."

Matt's insistence made Jaron pause, a half-formed idea taking shape in his mind. "How do you know?"

Matt sat down heavily, his arm draped around Bear. "Marnie found me after I ran away." He lowered his head, petting Bear's thick coat. "We walked for a long time. And then I heard Pixie bark. I ran away from Marnie again to find her."

"Bear was in the woods looking for you that day. Maybe you heard him barking."

Jaron deserved the dirty look Matt gave him. Even if Bear had been inhaling helium, he wouldn't sound like a shih tzu's bark. Could Matt have really heard Pixie? Martin seemed to hear her barking when they were in the alley. Maybe if emotions were strong enough, a ghost could reach out to a person. Jaron had never met another animal medium before. He'd only seen advertisements online of people claiming to have the ability. He wished he knew someone he could ask. "Did your parents tell you what I can do?"

"Daddy said you were a psychic. That's how come you knew how to find me." Matt grabbed a hold of Jaron's sleeve. "Will you go with me back to the woods to find Pixie?"

Matt was one brave little kid if he was willing to go back to the place where they both nearly froze to death. "Pixie isn't in the woods,

Matt. She passed on, but I can make you understand why you feel like she's still here. Close your eyes and place your hand on your heart."

Reluctantly, Matt closed his eyes and put his hand over his heart like he was doing the Pledge of Allegiance.

"Okay, I want you to concentrate on Pixie." Jaron held out his hand, focusing on the energy he still sensed in Matt. He'd watched Pixie's energy being absorbed into Matt. A small spark of that energy remained. "Think about how much you love her."

Matt pressed his lips together and scrunched his nose.

"It's okay to miss her, but you haven't lost her. A part of her will be with you always. Can you feel her, Matt?"

Matt's eyes snapped open and he jumped to his feet. He weaved around Jaron like a pro-baller and hugged his father hard enough to nearly tackle him to the ground.

"I felt her," Matt whispered.

Mr. Wilson ruffled his son's curls. "I'm glad, sweetheart." He picked Matt up and held the boy as if he were still a toddler. "I can't thank you enough, Jaron." He traded a look with his wife before heading for the door.

Confused, Jaron watched them go, leaving Mrs. Wilson behind.

Mrs. Wilson waited until her husband and child had left before speaking. "I'd like to settle our bill."

"Oh, okay. If you want." Jaron walked over to the nightstand. "I was going to type it up and mail it to you. I figured you guys might need some time after everything that happened." He grabbed the invoice form he'd used to write down the date and times he'd worked on the case. After double-checking the math, he signed the bottom of the form and brought it over to Mrs. Wilson.

Mrs. Wilson looked at the invoice carefully. "A hundred and thirty dollars. Is that the grand total?"

"Um, yes?" Jaron had never given a client such a large bill. "I included travel time to Missouri. But technically, I was only working the case on the way down there, so you can knock off thirty."

Mrs. Wilson looked at the invoice again. "You didn't have travel expenses?"

"No, the police drove me where I needed to go."

"You were hospitalized twice while working the case. Is that correct?"

Jaron wondered how she knew about the first time. "Technically the first time was from falling out of a tree. Mostly." He opted not to mention that Pixie might have contributed to his seizure.

"Is that a yes?"

Jaron resisted the urge to squirm under her piercing gaze. She should have been a detective. She could strip answers from someone like a bucket of turpentine on a painted table. "Yes, ma'am."

"Do you have health insurance?"

"I have basic coverage."

She nodded like she wasn't surprised. "So you'll have medical expenses from two hospitals."

Jaron had been trying really hard not to think about it. "I guess." When she raised her eyebrows, he said, "I mean yes."

"Are you hoping for a book deal?"

It took a moment for Jaron to understand what she meant. "God, no. Please tell me you guys didn't mention me to the press."

"No, but I imagine your name will appear in the police reports."

Jaron hadn't thought about what Paulo might put in his report. Would he end up having to testify in court? "I mostly got myself stuck in the creek right along with Matt. Bear's the real hero."

Bear's ears perked up at the sound of his name. Chuckling, Jaron rubbed his furry head.

After folding up the invoice and placing it in her purse, Mrs. Wilson took out her checkbook and began filling it out. She handed Jaron the check. "I'm afraid I can't pay you a hundred and thirty dollars."

"That's okay," Jaron said, looking down at the check. "Just pay me when... uh... there's an extra zero." The check had been written for thirteen hundred dollars.

"You're a lousy businessman, Mr. Greenberg." She placed her checkbook back into her purse. "But you're one hell of a psychic."

Jaron felt a fluttery feeling in his stomach. "This is way too much money. I can't accept it." He held out the check to her.

"Please take it," she said, her eyes filling with moisture.

The sight of Mrs. Wilson's tears wasn't something Jaron was prepared to handle. He looked around the room, hoping a box of tissues would magically appear. No luck. He ducked into the bathroom and grabbed a handful of toilet paper. "Here," he said, desperately holding out his pathetic offering. "Please stop crying." It was unnerving to see someone normally so cool and collected in tears. "I'll take the check." Taking the check didn't mean he had to cash it. He'd give the Wilsons a couple of weeks and then give them back the check.

Mrs. Wilson took the toilet paper and wiped her eyes and nose. She cleared her throat. "I'd accepted that my child was dead. That the most I could hope for was closure. Then you came along and rekindled my hope. And I hated you for it." She took a ragged breath. "Because I knew how painful it was to have my hope stripped away. No amount of words or money can thank you for what you did."

Jaron's cheeks warmed. "I'm glad I could help."

Mrs. Wilson gestured toward a pile of job applications on Jaron's bed. "Can I give you some unsolicited advice?"

"Sure," Jaron said quickly, not wanting to upset her again.

"I'm thankful you have this gift. My child is alive because of it. You need to learn to be thankful too."

Jaron frowned. "What do you mean?"

"A man who charges ten dollars an hour doesn't think he has a gift. He's too afraid to see his own value."

Jaron swallowed hard. "Most of my cases aren't that complicated. I find lost cats and teach temperamental dogs to behave. What I do isn't worth more than ten dollars an hour."

"We paid a dog trainer fifty dollars an hour to work with Pixie when she was a puppy."

"Wow, that explains why I get so many clients that want me to potty train their dogs. But with a trainer they're paying for an expert. It makes sense that I'm cheaper."

Mrs. Wilson nodded. "They have online classes you can take. That would allow you to add certified dog trainer to your business card. Who better to train a dog than a man who can communicate with them directly?"

Jaron had looked up the cost of tuition a couple of years ago. He couldn't afford the three thousand dollars then. It was probably more expensive now. "I'll look in to it."

Mrs. Wilson took out an envelope from her purse and gave it to Jaron. "People from our church took up a collection. They raised five thousand dollars for information leading to Matt's whereabouts." She smiled. "That should cover the tuition costs. Or at least help you move out of this motel."

Jaron stared at the envelope. "I didn't open my business to make money. I love working with animals. This business allowed me to pay the bills and still be able to help my best friend with the dog salon."

"But now your friend's business is thriving. Isn't it time to start planning for your own future?"

Jaron smiled. "Jaron Greenberg: Psychic Dog Trainer does have a good ring."

CHAPTER 22

NOT LONG after dawn, Paulo knocked on the door to Jaron's motel room, wishing he were here under better circumstances.

When Jaron opened the door, he stared at Paulo with sleep-blurred eyes, his blond hair sticking up in all directions. "Paulo?" He stepped back and beckoned him inside.

Paulo made his way into the motel room and closed the door. The cop in Paulo wanted to chastise Jaron for answering the door nearly naked in a shady neighborhood. The rest of him was too busy enjoying the view. Jaron was dressed only in boxer shorts with paw prints, riding low on his hips. His chest and arms had more definition than Paulo would've expected given his lean frame. A scattering of golden hairs surrounded his nipples. The cool morning air had left the buds pebbled. Paulo's mouth watered with the desire to taste them. Bear glared at Paulo from the foot of the bed as if he were a mind reader.

Jaron rubbed his eyes. "Sorry, I was up really late researching."

Looking down, Paulo saw dark bruises covered Jaron's knees and there were dozens of small scratches on his shins. "Come here." He pulled Jaron into his arms. "Are you okay? What were you researching? Are you still having problems with your blood sugar?"

Jaron placed his head on Paulo's shoulder. "My fingers are about to fall off because Stephen keeps attacking me with the Glucometer, but otherwise I've been fine." He told Paulo about the reward money and his conversation with Mrs. Wilson.

Paulo tightened his hold on Jaron. Jaron's skin felt warm and soft. He pulled back and kissed Jaron on the forehead. "You deserve that money." He traced his hand along Jaron's jaw, ending below his full lips. "Do you know how much I've missed you?" As the words left his mouth, he realized Jaron might already know. Had Jaron been born with the ability to read the minds of both animals and people? Paulo had read the police file on Jaron's father. He wouldn't want insight into that guy's twisted brain. Maybe Jaron had buried the ability to read people's minds as a form of self-preservation, until the Matt Wilson case unearthed his latent clairvoyance. Paulo wondered if Jaron was reading his mind right now.

"I'm not reading your mind." Jaron's face fell. "Oh, God, that's what you were thinking, wasn't it?" He flapped his hands. "I can only do it consciously… except for that one time with Marnie. But I think it was because I was trying to find her."

Paulo wrapped his arms around Jaron and pulled him close again. "It's okay."

Jaron pressed his forehead against the side of Paulo's neck. "It's different with animals. They have no sense of privacy. But humans do, so it takes more effort. I read Stephen's mind when I was in the hospital. I wanted to know if he was really in love with me. So I just did it without even considering that I was mind-raping him."

"You're being too hard on yourself." Paulo carded his hands through Jaron's soft hair, massaging his scalp gently. "Give yourself time to learn how to control it. There has to be a way to shut the ability off and on." He couldn't resist asking, "What did you find out?"

Jaron snorted. "Always the detective."

"Hey, we're inquisitive by nature." Paulo's brain supplied other areas he'd like to discover. Like whether the downy hair on Jaron's stomach was as soft as it looked. He wanted to slip his fingers past the elastic band on Jaron's boxers and follow the trail of gold hair with his tongue and teeth. Jaron didn't need to be a mind reader to know Paulo wanted him. Paulo's hardening cock was pressed against Jaron's hip.

Jaron gripped the front of Paulo's shirt and looked up at Paulo through his thick white lashes. "How long before Marnie goes to trial?"

The answer was: Too fucking long. Paulo forced himself to let go of Jaron. "It'll take six months to a year before she goes to trial, so maybe you should get dressed before Bear has to defend your virtue." There was always a chance the D.A. would offer Marnie a plea deal she'd be willing to accept, but he wasn't holding his breath.

An expression Paulo couldn't identify passed over Jaron's features. He released Paulo and turned around to retrieve his jeans from the carpet. Paulo stifled a groan at the sight of Jaron's tight ass stretching the fabric of the boxers.

Paulo concentrated on the morbid décor of the motel to get a hold of his libido. "That's part of the reason I'm here. Since Marnie took Matt across state lines, she could be charged with a federal crime. Chief Tucker is talking to Fisher's superior about handling the case locally, but he wants us to cooperate with Fisher in the meantime. Fisher wants an opportunity to question you himself."

Jaron pulled on a blue long-sleeved shirt. "I already gave my statement to Devin. Why does Agent Fisher want to talk to me?" He scraped a hand through his blond hair. "Stephen said he doesn't like me very much."

That was an understatement. "I'm not sure what is going on. I can't imagine him doing anything to jeopardize the case against Marnie, but I wasn't expecting him to insist on interviewing you again. I don't know if he's trying to make the SPD look bad or if something else is going on. You need to go in there with guns blazing, with every weapon in your arsenal."

Jaron's eyes widened. "You want me to read his mind during the interview. Paulo, I don't think I can... or if I should."

Paulo didn't trust Fisher. Right from the start, the agent had taken this case too personally. "I've worked with the Feds before. It's not like on TV. They don't come in and start throwing their weight around. They work cooperatively with the local PD. Fisher has been an aggressive SOB from the second he got here."

"What do I say if he asks why I was there and how I found Matt?"

Paulo realized he was coming dangerously close to coaching a witness. "You were there because the Wilsons requested you be part of the search. As for how you found Matt, tell him the truth, but only give him the basic facts." He ran his hands through his dark hair. "If he tries to get you to talk about us, don't lie. I won't risk you being brought up on obstruction charges."

Jaron paled. "Devin said you could be charged for being involved with a witness. I don't want you to get in trouble because of me. Can't I refuse to talk to Fisher?"

"He can't force you to talk with him, but refusing him isn't a good idea. It would be better to just answer his questions honestly. Don't worry about me. As far as I'm concerned, you didn't become a witness until Missouri. If it seems like he's trying to accuse you of being involved in the kidnapping, then end the interview."

Jaron sighed. "Just give me a minute to finish getting ready."

THE CAR ride to the police station had seemed endless, the awkward silence painfully loud. Maybe it was naivety, but Jaron wasn't afraid of Fisher attempting to trick him into implicating himself. Rather, he feared saying something that would get Paulo into trouble. Paulo had taken a leap of faith most people wouldn't have when he'd believed in Jaron's abilities rather than dismissing him as a fraud or a freak. Paulo didn't deserve to be reprimanded for that.

As Jaron stepped into the interview room, his sinuses were overwhelmed by the sharp scent of bleach and antiseptic. One look at the cramped room made Jaron want to run back to his fishy motel room. He couldn't decide what was more unnerving: the dirty jumbo mirror or the bolt on the center of the table, presumably for handcuffs. The table and one chair had also been bolted to the floor. A second rolling chair was the only remaining furniture in the room. "Couldn't we do the interview somewhere else?"

Paulo squeezed Jaron's arm. "Devin and I will be on the other side of that mirror. Knowing Fisher, he'll likely leave you sitting in here for a while to make you anxious. Don't let him get to you, and drink your juice if you decide to tap into his head." He handed him a bottle of orange juice.

Jaron attempted a smile, but his reflection showed it looked hideous. "I'll be okay." He didn't even remember meeting Agent Fisher, but the choice of location for the interview couldn't be a good sign. Even his scummy motel was more hospitable. Sighing, he walked over to the table and sat down to wait.

PAULO ENTERED the observation room next to the interview room. He spotted Devin standing in front of the two-way mirror, his gaze directed at the computer that monitored the covert video and audio surveillance equipment.

"Why the hell is Jaron in Interro 3?" Paulo asked. They reserved the room for combative suspects.

Not looking up, Devin said, "Why do you insist on asking questions when you know the answers?" He pressed a side button on the laptop, ejecting the DVD burner.

Paulo frowned—normally a technician set up the equipment, which meant the detective would only have to hit the start button located within the interrogation room. "What are you doing?"

"I told Chief Tucker I would set up the video recording since Fisher isn't familiar with the system. Fisher uses the kind that burn straight to DVD."

Paulo scowled. "You're being awfully helpful to a guy implying you didn't do a thorough enough job questioning Jaron."

Devin placed a blank DVD in the slot and closed the drive. "In Fisher's defense, I wasn't all that thorough. I focused my questions on what Jaron saw and did when he reached the creek. I deliberately avoided asking him how he managed to find Marnie and Matt."

"How Jaron found them is irrelevant. What does Fisher hope to accomplish with this interview?"

Devin turned away from the computer. "I don't know. Maybe he just wants to screw you over by getting Jaron to admit you're banging him."

Paulo gritted his teeth. "I haven't done anything wrong."

Devin snorted. "That's probably for the best, considering his new ability."

"What do you mean?"

"I like Jaron. But working with a mind reader isn't the same as dating one."

"I don't have anything to hide from him." Paulo realized the truth in his words as he said them. He knew Jaron would never exploit the ability, whereas Paulo would use it ruthlessly if he could tap into the brains of witnesses and suspects.

Devin laughed. "That's because you're still thinking with your dick. I know you better than that."

"I'm not saying I'd give him free rein to go poking around in my head, but I trust him."

"Jesus, Paulo, you went running for the cornfields rather than talk to me about the Jefferson case. You're telling me you're okay with a guy who could pry the truth out of your head?"

"The last time I tried to talk to you about that case, I found you entertaining triplets."

Devin held out his hands in defense. "We never agreed to be exclusive, so don't pretend otherwise."

Paulo had no interest in rehashing that argument. He had known Devin's views on monogamy before they got together, but he had arrogantly assumed it would be different between them. Likewise, Devin knew Paulo was a serial monogamist. They'd both acted like idiots. But Paulo had no intention of telling Devin that. Sleeping with triplets was just plain greedy.

Devin loosened his tie. "I'll admit to being a shitty friend. I knew you were upset, but I didn't understand it. We got the bad guy. You put that fucker in the ground."

Paulo took a deep breath and exhaled slowly. "I was cleared of any misconduct, but things changed for me that day. I didn't want him to spend the rest of his life in prison. I wanted him dead. When he went for his knife, I thought, thank God, I have an excuse to blow his head off."

"Dammit, Paulo, you know better. He was armed and dangerous. What should you have done? Shot him in the shoulder or the hand like some ridiculous TV cop show? No, you aim for center mass of the target and shoot. He was a threat to your life. A knife doesn't run out of bullets. It can kill you just as easily as a gun."

Paulo stared down at his empty hands. "It wasn't the first time I'd shot someone or even the first time someone had died, but it was the first time I'd enjoyed it. It made me realize I wasn't cut out for the job." He laughed bitterly. "But rather than quit, I transferred to Stanton, a place where major crime rarely happens. That is, until I got here."

"I read the autopsy results. That baby was alive when he started to burn. I hope to hell that son of a bitch is roasting in hell for what he did. That baby died in agony and you put down the monster who did that to him. Why shouldn't you enjoy it? You shouldn't have to walk away from a job you love for getting him justice." Devin squeezed Paulo's shoulder. "Come back to the ISP."

Paulo looked through the window. Jaron was picking off the label of the bottle of orange juice, his body tense and anxious. Was he nervous about the interview or could he sense Paulo's emotions through the glass? Maybe it would be better for Jaron to pry the truth out of Paulo's brain, because he sure as hell didn't understand his reaction to the Jefferson case. Could you do the right thing, for the wrong reasons? "I wanted revenge, not justice. I wanted Illinois politicians to bring back the electric chair so I could watch him fry."

Devin smacked the back of Paulo's head. "You're not a vigilante. You let yourself get too emotionally involved in a case. It happens. But at the end of the day, you followed procedure. Give yourself a break." He glanced through the window. "You can still see Jaron if you're still interested. Springfield is only a little over an hour away."

Paulo nodded. "I'll think about it."

"HELLO, I'M Special Agent Fisher. Thank you for agreeing to meet with me today, Mr. Greenberg. I read the initial statement you gave, but I have some follow up questions."

Jaron had a hard time matching Fisher's bland expression with the image Bear had projected of the agent sprawled on the ground of the hospital lobby.

Fisher hit a white button above the table before taking a seat across from Jaron. He rattled off the date, time, and location before asking Jaron to state his contact information.

"Jaron Greenberg... uh... I don't have a permanent address. I'm staying at the Lakeside Motel for now."

Fisher smiled. "I imagine that reward money the Wilsons gave you will help you find your own place." He appeared politely interested as he asked Jaron questions about his pet psychic business. When did the business open? Who are his typical clients? What are his rates?

Fisher showed no sign of the contempt Paulo and Stephen had described.

Jaron opened his juice and took a sip, giving himself time to focus. While the ethics of invading someone's mind still concerned him, he also trusted Paulo's opinion of the agent. How did Fisher even know about the reward money? Had the Wilsons told him about it? Paulo saw Fisher as a threat, so Jaron would treat him that way.

Jaron thought he was prepared to touch Fisher's mind. He wasn't. The bottle of juice slipped through his fingers and rolled off the table, splattering to the ground. Fisher's thoughts and emotions crashed into Jaron's mind like a tidal wave. Without thinking Jaron asked, "Who is Emily?"

Fisher's mouth tightened, his bland expression disappearing. He smacked the button on the wall. "Am I supposed to be impressed you've done your research? Or did you have your boyfriend do that work for you? Let me guess. You think Emily is dead and you can help me find the body."

Beneath Fisher's contempt, Jaron could feel grief; it felt like an opened wound. Touching such a private pain was wrong, but he wasn't sure how to stop now that he'd connected with Fisher's mind. "I'm sorry I upset you. I don't know anything about Emily. Her name is ping ponging around in your brain. I don't have the best control right now." Looking around the room, he saw nothing to clean up the spilled juice.

Fisher sneered. "I thought you were a pet psychic. Now you can read people's minds too?"

Fisher's anger made Jaron feel like his skin was covered in blisters, pus-filled and painful. Jaron was vaguely aware that Fisher was still talking to him, but he couldn't focus on the words. He had to figure out a way to block Fisher's thoughts and emotions or he'd start screaming. His heart felt like it was going to burst through his chest any second. He needed to create a barrier in his mind. But what kind? He'd always sucked at analogies in English class. Closing his eyes, he pictured the window from his dream with Pixie. When the window was open, he could see and hear Matt talking with Peggy. When the window had closed, he'd lost the connection. Jaron concentrated on picturing the window in his mind and then slammed it shut. He opened his eyes, no longer feeling the pressure of Fisher's thoughts against his.

Fisher's face was flushed and his breathing heavy. "I had a long talk with Marnie Becker about you today."

Jaron slid the window up just a little as Fisher continued.

"Marnie said you talked to her about her son Brandon. She said *you* pointed her toward Matt Wilson."

Through the mirror, Jaron thought he heard a muffled argument. He doubted Paulo and Devin would be happy with this line of questioning. He focused his attention back on Fisher. If the eyes were the window to the soul, then someone had painted liar across Fisher's. "The first time I ever spoke to Marnie Becker was in the woods in Missouri."

"Tell me why you did it, Jaron. Why did you put that little boy through hell for a lousy five grand? Do you have a book deal lined up? Or maybe a starring role in a TV movie?"

Jaron realized he could play the same game with Fisher that he had with Devin, but it wouldn't matter. He could successfully read Fisher's mind a thousand times and the agent still wouldn't believe. Some supposed psychic had stolen Fisher's hope and he wasn't about to risk losing it again.

"There's nothing more to say." Jaron stood up.

"We aren't done yet." Fisher smacked the table. "Sit your ass down or I'll have you arrested."

Jaron shook his head, seeing the lie painted across Fisher's forehead. "I'm sorry, Agent Fisher. I wish I could help you. I know you loved her very much."

Fisher leapt to his feet and backed Jaron into a corner of the room. "Shut your damn mouth!" he shouted, spittle flying from his mouth.

The door flew open and Paulo came charging inside with Devin close behind. Paulo grabbed the back of Fisher's suit jacket and shoved him aside. "Get the fuck away from him!"

Fisher straightened his jacket. "He must be a great cocksucker for you to toss your career away for him, Silva."

Devin moved to grab Paulo, but he was too slow. Paulo's fist flashed through the air and caught Fisher in a solid blow on the chin. Fisher landed on the tile floor with a splat on the spilled orange juice.

"Enough!" A deep voice bellowed, making everyone in the room flinch.

Chief Tucker stood in the doorway of the room. "Morris and Silva, get the hell out of here." He looked over at Jaron. "You're looking a little pale, son. Do you need medical assistance?"

"I'll get him some more juice," Paulo said. He and Devin shuffled out of the room like a pair of recalcitrant schoolboys.

Chief Tucker closed the door behind them. He then gestured toward the rolling chair. "Have a seat, Jaron."

Agent Fisher climbed to his feet. His face was red and blotchy and his lip split. "I intend to press charges for assault against Detective Silva."

The chief ignored him. "Son, did Agent Fisher accuse you of being involved in the kidnapping of Matt Wilson?"

Jaron slid along the wall to avoid Fisher and sat on the chair. He wiped sweat from his forehead. "Yes."

"Did he advise you of your Miranda rights prior to questioning you?"

"No, sir."

Chief Tucker addressed Fisher. "How about you forget that Detective Silva took a swing at you, and I forget that you turned off the video surveillance to violate Jaron's Miranda rights and physically intimidate him?"

Fisher clenched his fists. "I've been trying to do my job, but Detective Silva has been preventing me from doing so every step of the way. His intimate relationship with Mr. Greenberg has clouded his judgment. Greenberg isn't the hero; he's the orchestrator behind the kidnapping."

Chief Tucker crossed his arms. "Son, you ain't got a lick of proof of that beyond your own prejudice against psychics. Detective Silva was just as suspicious of Jaron when he started this case. He's satisfied Jaron isn't involved in the kidnapping and so am I. Now I can't stop you from pressing charges, but you can bet your soggy ass I'll be speaking to your superior if you don't walk away."

Fisher stormed out of the room with bad grace.

Jaron watched him go, his stomach clenching. "Do you think he'll press charges?" He never should've attempted to read Fisher's mind.

The chief sighed. "If he tries, I'll make damn sure his boss rips him a new one."

A knock on the door signaled Paulo's return. He handed Jaron a bottle of apple juice. "Are you okay?"

Jaron nodded.

"Take a good look at him, detective," Chief Tucker said, "because I don't want you two breathing the same air until this case is resolved. I won't give the defense attorney ammunition."

Paulo swallowed visibly. "I drove Jaron here, Chief."

Chief Tucker snorted. "Back to work, Silva. I'll make sure he gets home."

CHAPTER 23

SLIDING THE key card into the slot, Jaron opened the door and stepped into an empty motel room. "What the hell?" He spotted a pink Post-it note stuck to the deer head on the wall. He walked over to it. A familiar chicken-scratch handwriting had written an address on it. Pulling out his phone, he put in a call to his meddling best friend. When Stephen answered, Jaron asked, "What have you done?"

"I'm staging an intervention."

"I said I was going to find an apartment."

"No, you were going to find some shithole studio apartment. You and Bear would both end up with fleas."

Jaron recognized the address. There was no way he could afford the rent unless Stephen's uncle was giving him a discounted rate. "How did you even know I'd be gone?" He didn't bother asking how Stephen had gotten into the motel room. People had an alarming tendency to bow to his will. Jaron included.

"I had this big speech planned to convince you. If that failed, Shawn agreed to pin you to the bed while we grabbed your shit."

Stephen might be the youngest of the five brothers, but he wasn't the baby of the family. He was the commander in chief of the brood. Like all of the Miller brothers, Shawn was dark blond and built like a brick house. He totally would've pinned Jaron to the bed like a bug at Stephen's say so.

"Scott is on the way to pick you up," Stephen said.

The Miller clan loved the letter "S." Everyone from Great Aunt Stella to Sparky the Golden Retriever had an "S" name. As a kid, Jaron had fantasized about changing his name to Saron. Thank God he'd had the sense to keep that a secret.

"Seriously, Stephen, can't you call him off? I'll find a nice affordable studio."

Stephen laughed evilly. "You wanted to be part of the family. Prepare to be initiated." He ended the call.

A few minutes later, there was a knock on the door. When Jaron answered it, Scott immediately pulled Jaron into a bear hug.

"We've been worried sick about you."

"Hi Scott," Jaron mumbled against the man's wool trench coat.

"I know he's being a pushy bastard, but you've gotta let him help you. He feels terrible about boxing your shit up and throwing you out."

"Can't breathe," Jaron squeaked.

Chuckling, Scott released him. "Sorry, I just can't believe you were in the hospital twice for low blood sugar and he didn't tell us. I wouldn't be surprised if Mom flies in from Florida just to kick his ass. If one of her boys is hurt, she wants to know about it."

Jaron's eyes burned. "It's been a crazy couple of weeks."

Jaron and Scott started for the parking lot. They hadn't taken more than three steps before the grilling began. Stephen and his brothers operated under the assumption that privacy and boundaries were for other people.

"Who's this Pablo Stephen says you're in love with?"

"It's Paulo and I never said I was in love with him. It's only been a few weeks. I can't be in love." Jaron had no desire to turn his new lie detector ability on himself. It would be beyond stupid to fall in love with Paulo. "What did Stephen tell you about him?"

Scott clicked the fob for his metallic Lexus. "That you'd made the horrible mistake of dating a cop," said the local defense attorney. He opened the car door. "And that Stephen would need a lawyer if he broke your heart."

Jaron rolled his eyes and got into the passenger side. The tan leather seat felt disturbingly warm under his ass. "You're not the one defending Marnie Becker, are you?"

Scott took his place behind the wheel and started the car. "No, she's not my case."

Jaron sighed in relief. "That's good. I'd hate to have to face you on the stand."

The seatbelt slipped through Scott's fingers, smacking against the window. "Just how involved are you in the case?"

Jaron attached his own belt to give himself more time. Stephen's family knew about his abilities with animals, but it wasn't something that was talked about often. "I helped the police track Marnie and Matt. Um, should we be talking about this?"

Scott waved off the question. "This conversation is confidential. I won't talk to Marnie's attorney because I apparently have a conflict of interest. Now, is Paulo one of the detectives working the case?"

"Yes," Jaron said miserably. "And Chief Tucker said we had to stay apart until after the trial, so there won't be any dating anytime soon, if ever." He doubted Paulo would still be interested a year from now, assuming he didn't return to the ISP.

Scott cleared his throat. "The D.A. will likely offer Becker a plea deal."

"Why would the D.A. do that if they caught her red-handed?"

"From what I read in the papers, Becker might go for an insanity plea. A grieving mother with a history of mental illness would have the potential to sway a jury. If you were the one to find Matt, how did you manage to stay out of the papers?"

Jaron wasn't sure of that either, but he was sincerely grateful. "I asked Matt's parents not to mention me to anyone. I found Matt, but Paulo and Bear were the ones who got us out of that creek before we drowned."

Scott stared at him. "So that hospital stay Stephen mentioned wasn't just for low blood sugar?"

Jaron winced. "It was mostly because of that."

"Oh, I can't wait to get you back to the apartment so we can drag the full story out of you. Then you can watch us kick Stephen's ass for keeping quiet about it."

PAULO KNOCKED on the door of Jaron's new apartment with a Butter Fern tucked under his arm. It was the only houseplant he could find at the garden center that wasn't toxic to animals. The past two weeks had been grueling as he waited for the D.A. to propose a plea deal and offer it to Marnie.

Jaron answered the door. His eyes widened at the fern Paulo offered him. "Oh, you didn't have to do that." He smiled shyly. "Thank you. But are you sure this date has been approved?"

Paulo's gaze drifted, taking in Jaron's black slacks and blue button-down shirt. He loved the way the clothes clung to his lean body. "I've got a signed note from the chief. Do you want to see it?"

Jaron smiled broadly. "No, I trust you. Come inside for a minute while I give Bear his treat."

Paulo shut the door and looked around at the apartment as Jaron took the plant into the kitchen. The layout appeared to be similar to his place. A small kitchen butted against a decent-sized living room. A couch with a black slipcover faced a worn but high-end wooden entertainment center, which held a 32-inch flat-screen television and a collection of books. "Wow, I've been in Stanton for two months and haven't unpacked, and you managed it in two weeks."

Jaron placed the plant on the counter and grabbed a banana from a bowl of fruit. "Stephen and his family have apparently been conspiring behind my back to get me out of the motel."

Seeing Bear on his dog bed made Paulo laugh. The chocolate brown bed came with matching bolsters and pillows. It looked more like a short couch than a dog bed. Bear grinned at Paulo as if he knew how posh his new bed was. "This is nicer than my place."

Jaron ducked his head. "Too nice, but that's because Stephen's uncle owns the building and I'm getting the family rate whether I want it or not." He shrugged. "The living room furniture has apparently been in storage. The Miller clan has a shared storage container for castoffs."

Paulo reminded himself that he was happy that Jaron was out of that awful motel. That Stephen had been the one to rescue Jaron from it wasn't important. *Dammit.*

"I still can't believe the case is over," Jaron said as he peeled the banana. "Can you tell me the specifics of the deal?"

Paulo nodded. "Marnie pled guilty but mentally ill to aggravated kidnapping and child endangerment. The agreement means she'll be sentenced to twenty years and be given access to mental health treatment in prison. She'll have an opportunity for parole in ten years."

Jaron frowned. "I'm surprised she accepted the deal. She seemed so convinced Matt was her child."

"I know Dr. Roberts asked the Wilsons for photo albums, and that she spent a long time talking to Marnie. She must've figured out a way to convince her." If Marnie had turned to Dr. Roberts when she first saw Matt, then the kidnapping might never have happened. And Paulo likely wouldn't have met Jaron. Even if he had, he doubted he would've been convinced Jaron was a psychic without seeing it firsthand. That was a sobering thought.

Jaron sighed. "I'm not making excuses for Marnie, but I understand why she did it. In that brief moment when I touched her mind, it felt like someone had ripped out a part of my soul, and I would do anything to fill that void again."

"I think the D.A. offered her the deal to avoid her pleading not guilty by reason of insanity."

Bear leapt off the dog bed and raced over to Jaron. He sat in front of Jaron, his tail thumping against the carpet.

Jaron smiled at the Newfie. "Be a good boy while I'm gone." He broke off half of the banana and tossed it to Bear. Bear gobbled up the treat like he hadn't eaten in days. Laughing, Jaron tossed Bear the remaining piece of fruit. "Where are we going tonight?"

"I made reservations at Nat's," Paulo said. Stanton had very little in the way of nice restaurants, but several women at the station had recommended Nat's. He wanted a place where Jaron wouldn't be limited to only a salad to avoid eating meat. He hadn't bothered asking his fellow cops for a vegetarian-friendly establishment. They would've laughed their meat-and-potato asses off.

Jaron rinsed his hands off in the sink. "I've only been there once, but the food was really great." He dried his hands off on a towel. "I'm ready to go."

PAULO DIDN'T find the exterior of Nat's too impressive, but the small dining room they were seated in had a warm, inviting feel. Abstract metal pictures in deep red and rust decorated the walls. The crooning voice of Dean Martin set to low could be heard from the speakers. It was as fancy as a town like Stanton could get.

The waitress arrived within moments of them sitting down. They ordered the house wine as she handed over the menus.

"I've heard the bruschetta is good," Paulo said. "Do you want me to order it?"

"It sounds delicious."

A couple of minutes later, the waitress placed a platter of bruschetta on the table. The scent of tomato, garlic, and basil made Paulo's stomach lurch hungrily. He ordered pot roast for his meal. Jaron select the vegan roasted vegetable pasta before digging into the appetizer.

The grilled baguette crunched loudly when Jaron took a bite. He moaned obscenely as he chewed. The oil made Jaron's bottom lip glisten. "Don't you like it?"

Paulo dragged his gaze from Jaron's mouth and looked down at his plate. They were barely through the appetizer and he wanted to crawl over the table and kiss Jaron breathless. "It smells great." He popped the small square into his mouth. It tasted as good as he expected, but Paulo needed a distraction before he embarrassed them both. "What will you do now with your business?"

"The pet psychic business is on hold for the time being. I'm going to work part-time in the salon so Stephen will have time to train Mel to be the assistant manager. Eventually, she'll manage the salon part of the business while Stephen focuses on the doggy daycare part. And I'm going to enroll in an online dog trainer certification program." Jaron bit his bottom lip. "Stephen thinks we should offer behavioral classes in the backyard of the salon, but I haven't made any promises."

Most of the time Paulo had spent with Jaron, Jaron had been nearing his limit, physically and mentally. Seeing him in the restaurant's soft light, looking happy and relaxed as he talked about the dog trainer programs he'd researched, made Paulo's chest ache. Jaron was beautiful in every sense of the word. The waitress brought Paulo food and he ate it. He couldn't say whether he enjoyed it or not. His focus was on the man in front of him.

As the waitress cleared the plates, she asked, "Can I interest you in dessert?"

Jaron licked his lips. "I don't need any," he said, which wasn't the same as "want."

Stephen had sent Paulo a one-word text message: *Chocolate.*

"We'll have one slice of Xtreme Supreme Chocolate Cake to share," Paulo said.

The waitress's smile faltered. "Would you like a second plate?"

"No," Paulo said, not looking away from Jaron.

She bobbled the plates but managed to hold onto them. "Coming right up."

Jaron's cheeks reddened. "You didn't have to do that."

Paulo grinned. "Now that I have permission, I want everyone in this town to know I'm dating the resident psychic."

"Does that mean you're staying in Stanton? I wouldn't blame you if you wanted to go back to the ISP."

The waitress returned in record time with the three-tiered chocolate cake. She scurried away after placing the plate on the table along with two forks.

Paulo picked up a fork and speared a bite of the cake. "I'm not going anywhere. The Jefferson case might've been the reason I left the ISP, but it's not the reason I want to stay with the SPD. I can make a difference here too." He offered the fork to Jaron.

Jaron snatched the fork from Paulo's fingers and devoured the cake with a low moan. Away from prying eyes, Paulo would love to feed Jaron bites of the rich cake.

Jaron's eyes heated. "This cake is very good, but we should get it to go."

"God, yes."

The most attentive waitress on the planet appeared with the check and a Styrofoam box.

Paulo drank the rest of his glass of wine in one long gulp. He managed to pay the check and pack up the cake in under three minutes. That had to be a record.

Paulo placed his hand on the small of Jaron's back as they headed for the door. As he passed another couple, he heard the man say, "Let's get the cake they had."

Paulo grinned.

CHAPTER 24

BY THE time they'd stumbled up the stairs to Jaron's third floor apartment, Jaron had eaten most of the cake and both their hands were smeared with chocolate. He opened the door, giving Bear a mental greeting and a request to stay in bed. Once they'd entered, Paulo pressed Jaron against the door and kissed him deeply, his sticky hands cupping Jaron's face. Their tongues tangled together until the need for breath pulled them apart.

Jaron snagged the last bite of cake from the container. "Do you want it?"

"Oh, yeah," Paulo said and then opened his mouth.

Jaron found himself pulling the cake away even before he registered why. *Lie.* "I... should wash my hands." He pushed off the door and headed for the bathroom.

Paulo grabbed his arm. "Hey, what's wrong?"

"I'm sorry, but I think this was a bad idea." Jaron pulled away and retreated to the bathroom. After tossing the container in the garbage can, he turned on the sink and scrubbed the chocolate residue from his hands.

Paulo appeared in the doorway. Even with smears of chocolate on his gray button-up, he looked gorgeous. "Did I freak you out? We can take it slower."

Jaron shut off the sink and watched the water slowly drain away. "Since the interview with Fisher, I keep getting these little... psychic flashes, a word or an emotion. If I'm not concentrating on the window, then stuff leaks through like faulty insulation."

Paulo frowned. "What window?"

Jaron dried his hands on a towel. "It's just an analogy for how I try to control these new abilities."

"So open window is receptive and a closed window means you're not receptive, blocking the thoughts and feelings?" Paulo's eyes widened. "You pulled away because you read my mind. What did you sense that freaked you out? It can't be how much I want to get my hands on your ass, because I've been thinking about that since the day we met."

Jaron's cheeks heated. "When someone lies, I can see it on their face like it's written in marker. It's how I knew when Fisher was lying in the interview." Sensing the direction of Paulo's thoughts, he smacked his arm. "Stop thinking like a cop."

"Sorry, but do you have any idea how helpful a walking lie detector would be on the job?"

"The idea of me reading your mind bothers you." Jaron held up his hand. "I know it. And it's totally understandable. I wouldn't like it either. I just wanted us to have a nice, normal date. But my window is leaking and I don't know how to stop it."

"It freaked me out when Devin first told me, but I've gotten over the shock."

Jaron hated to do it, but Paulo would need a demonstration if he was going to understand. "You're jealous of Stephen, worried Bear will cockblock you, and you wish I'd brush my teeth, because you hate chocolate even if watching me eat it turns you on." He exhaled loudly. "Do you get it now?"

Paulo stared at Jaron for several seconds, his expression as unreadable as his mind. "Did you sense anything from the waitress at the restaurant or the other customers?"

"No, but I never know when it's going to happen."

"How about the woman in the stairwell that saw me shove my fingers in your mouth so you could lick off the chocolate?"

Jaron gaped at him. "One of my neighbors saw me doing that?"

Paulo's grin was wolfish. "She looked like she wanted to join in on the fun. All these people were examples of strong emotions, but you didn't sense anything off them. Why not?"

Jaron shrugged. That he could add accidental mind reader to his resume was incomprehensible. He'd never regret finding Matt, but he wished it hadn't meant turning his world upside down. His teeth suddenly itchy, he snatched his toothbrush from the ceramic cup. "So far it's only been Stephen, his brothers, and you that have leaked through accidentally."

"All people you care about and whose opinion you value."

Jaron grabbed the tube of Crest toothpaste and unscrewed the top. "That makes it worse, not better." He shook his head. "Actually, it happened that first time with Devin too. I'd forgotten about that."

"Maybe there's a reason you read their minds. Like a part of you wanted to know even if you weren't consciously aware of it."

"That doesn't make it right."

Paulo maneuvered his way into the bathroom and sat on the closed toilet seat. "I'll say it again. You're being too fucking hard on yourself. You'll never learn to control these new abilities by attempting to nail that window shut. Eventually, it will come crashing open and you won't be prepared for it."

Jaron shivered, remembering what it felt like to be trapped in Fisher's mind. "What do I do in the meantime? I don't want to invade the privacy of people I lo—care about."

Paulo's grin was filthy. "I can think of several ways you can make it up to me, but let's start with you telling me three things you wouldn't have otherwise said out loud."

"How is that supposed to help?"

"Because you feel guilty and confessing secrets will make you feel better."

Jaron squinted his eyes. "Are you sure you're not the mind reader?"

Paulo smirked. "I wish. Now start confessing."

Jaron applied the cinnamon-flavored toothpaste on the brush, trying to decide what to say. He turned on the sink long enough to wet the brush. After opening the cabinet, he took out a spare toothbrush. "I bought this because I hoped you'd spend the night." He placed it on the counter. "And I wish you'd brush too, so you won't taste like dead cow."

Paulo's laugh was deep and throaty. "I asked for that one. In my defense, saying I don't like chocolate is like admitting to being a cannibal to most people. It's just easier to eat the chocolate." He grabbed the toothpaste, squeezed, and licked off the dab of toothpaste, which was both gross and totally hot. After putting the tube aside, he asked, "Now what's the third one?"

Jaron began brushing his teeth, trying to think of another one. "I thought Devin was a male model when I first saw him." He spit in the sink.

"Male model, huh?" Paulo leapt from the toilet seat and pressed Jaron against the wall. He took possession of Jaron's mouth, shoving his tongue inside. He knotted his hand in Jaron's hair as he deepened the kiss, stroking and caressing.

Jaron groaned. He could feel Paulo's hardening dick against his hip through layers of fabric. "Bedroom," he managed to get out before Paulo took his mouth again in another probing kiss.

Paulo took hold of Jaron's hand, dragging him along as he headed for the bedroom. Once inside he pushed the door closed, likely to prevent any Bear interruptions. Not releasing Jaron, he toed off his shoes and climbed onto the bed, sitting in the center with his long legs stretched out. Jaron kicked off his shoes and joined him on the bed.

Paulo pulled Jaron onto his lap and kissed him hard. "I want you to open that window." He untucked Jaron's shirt and slid his hands underneath. His rough fingers kneaded Jaron's lower back.

"That sounds like a terrible idea." Jaron knew he would end up hearing something awful like disappointment over his dick size or something equally mortifying.

"Trust me," Paulo said, the deep purr of his voice making Jaron shiver. "It's your window. Your abilities. Take control."

"What if I can't control it?"

Paulo cupped Jaron's face with his hands. "Trust yourself the way I trust you." He kissed Jaron softly. "Accept that you're going to make mistakes in the beginning."

Jaron nodded in agreement. Rather than go wide open like he had with Fisher, he eased the window up a little. Instead of pain, a warm, fluid feeling settled into his bones. He wrapped his arms around Paulo's neck and kissed him, feeling his desire echoed in Paulo as he inched the window up further and further.

"Can you tell what I'm thinking now?"

"God, Paulo." The sensations pouring through Jaron were too intense. He'd end up coming like a teenager if he didn't get a handle on them.

Paulo canted his hips, rubbing his hard cock against Jaron's ass. "What do I want to do to you?"

Jaron licked his lips. "You want to suck me and then fuck me."

"Hell, yes, but both don't need to be on the agenda tonight."

Jaron pressed his forehead against the side of Paulo's neck. The scent of warm, slightly sweaty skin was overlaid with rosemary. "What if I want both?"

With a growl, Paulo pushed Jaron backward against the mattress, stretching his muscled body against Jaron's leaner frame to hold him in place. Hovering above, Paulo began to unbutton Jaron's shirt. He kissed and nibbled each bit of skin revealed as he opened the shirt. When the last button was undone, he pulled off the shirt and tossed it onto the floor. He lightly traced around each of Jaron's nipples, making the skin darken and the buds harden. "Since there's only one psychic in this bed, you're going to have to tell me how you like it." He rocked his hips pressing their groins together. "Fast? Slow? Deep? Hard?"

Jaron's face heated. "Just… um… the usual."

Paulo made a tsking sound. He moved his hand to the top of Jaron's slacks and flicked open the button. Slowly he pulled the zipper down. "Tell me how you like it."

Jaron's heart pounded against his ribs. He could feel how much Paulo genuinely wanted to know, which made the request all the hotter. "I like it," he said, "slow and deep with lots of suction."

Paulo helped Jaron remove his slacks and briefs. Slowly his hand moved downward, skimming over Jaron's stomach to his thighs. He leaned over and kissed Jaron's stomach, a brief touch from his lips that made Jaron burn. "*Belo*," he murmured.

Paulo scooted down to the end of the bed and spread Jaron's legs. Leaning over, he kissed and nibbled on Jaron's spread thighs. His breath felt scalding on Jaron's oversensitive skin. He ran his tongue over Jaron's balls, one side then the other, making Jaron squirm.

Paulo dragged his tongue up the length of Jaron's cock. He gripped the base of Jaron's shaft and licked the glistening tip. Moaning, he wrapped his lips around Jaron's cock.

Jaron whimpered, his fists clutching the comforter as Paulo took him deeper. Paulo slowly released Jaron's shaft, then sucked it down again. He bobbed his tight mouth up and down Jaron's length, flicking his tongue over the head over and over. The heat and pressure threatened to overwhelm Jaron. He didn't want it to end so soon.

"Paulo, please," Jaron said, his voice breaking. "I want you inside me." He realized the recently purchased supplies were sitting in a plastic bag on the kitchen counter. Why couldn't he have gained telekinesis instead of mind reading? Having condoms fly through the air at his command would be way cooler than accessing people's thoughts. "I have stuff, but it's in the kitchen."

Paulo crawled up the bed and kissed Jaron hard. "Don't move," he said, scrambling off the bed.

Sitting up, Jaron pulled off his socks and resisted the urge to hide under the covers as he waited for Paulo to return. He felt Bear's excitement when Paulo detoured to pet the Newfie and call him a good boy. It was a blatant anticockblock maneuver, but Bear didn't know that. Jaron gave Bear another mental request to stay on his pet bed so this didn't become a threesome.

All the saliva dried up in Jaron's mouth when Paulo stepped back into the room. Between the bedroom and the kitchen, Paulo had managed to lose his clothes. A pelt of dark hair covered Paulo's chiseled chest and flat stomach. His upcurved cock bobbed with each step as he approached the bed. God, he was beautiful.

After tossing the bag onto the comforter, Paulo crawled over to the center of the bed, his heated gaze moving over every inch of Jaron's body. He sat down on the bed and held his hand out. "Come here."

Jaron climbed onto Paulo's lap and wrapped his legs around Paulo's waist. The first touch of skin against skin made them both groan. Jaron dragged his fingers down the curly black hair covering Paulo's chest. The thin layer of hair was softer than it looked.

Paulo slid his hands over Jaron's ass, cupping it before gently pulling Jaron forward, trapping their hard cocks between them. Jaron rocked forward, groaning at the friction.

Jaron heard the squish of the lube bottle and then felt the cool liquid against his entrance. Paulo massaged Jaron's hole in slow, lazy circles. "Can you feel how much I want you, *anjo*?"

Jaron stroked Paulo's cock slowly. "You've called me that before. What does... *anjo* mean?"

"It doesn't translate well," Paulo said, as the word "lie" flashed briefly on his forehead.

Jaron grinned. Looking toward the door, he said, "I bet Google would translate it."

Paulo smacked Jaron's ass. "Brat," he said before kissing Jaron.

Jaron's laugh turned into a moan as Paulo pressed a finger inside his ass. The sweet burn reminded Jaron of just how long it had been since he'd last done this. Leaning forward, he dragged his teeth along the side of Paulo's neck, kissing and nibbling his salty skin. Paulo put more lubricant on and pushed two fingers into Jaron's hole. Jaron rocked his hips to encourage Paulo to stroke his fingers in and out a little faster. Every time he passed over Jaron's prostate, it produced a surge of pleasure. Leaning backward, Jaron retrieved a condom packet from the box of Trojans, tearing it open with his teeth. He stroked Paulo's cock several times before applying the condom.

Paulo moved his hands to Jaron's hips. Lifting up, Jaron lined Paulo's cock up with his entrance and slowly impaled himself on his hard length. He sucked in his breath sharply as he was breached, and he closed his eyes tightly as he forced himself to relax. He could feel how much Paulo wanted to shove inside, but he resisted, not wanting to hurt Jaron. He rose and eased back down until Paulo was fully inside him. The sensation of being completely filled made him shudder, causing Paulo to groan and tighten his grip on Jaron's hips. He didn't know how Paulo managed to maintain control, because he couldn't wait another second. "Fuck me, Paulo."

They moved together in a sinuous dance, hips rolling, backs arching in a choreographed routine. Like Jaron had managed to pluck the rhythm from Paulo's brain, they came together again and again. Paulo gripped Jaron's ass as he increased the pace. Jaron rolled his hips to meet each thrust. He felt the echo of tight heat on his cock, making his balls ache for release.

Jaron wasn't sure where his orgasm began and Paulo's ended. But the result left him on the verge of passing out. Without Paulo even touching Jaron's cock, Jaron came, splattering his seed between them.

Paulo groaned, thrusting into Jaron several more times, his mind so focused on his release that Jaron nearly felt like he was going to come again. Panting heavily, Paulo fell backward onto the bed, taking Jaron with him, heedless of the sticky, wet seed that still covered his stomach, and was now all over both of them. That telekinesis would've made retrieving the tissues from the bedside table much easier, because Jaron was too exhausted to move.

After Paulo pulled out, he encouraged Jaron to stretch out on the bed before tossing the condom in the bedside wastebasket and collapsing next to him. He pulled Jaron into his arms, leaning their foreheads together while their heartbeats slowed. For some time afterward, they lay in each other's arms in a sated haze. Jaron knew he needed to get up and take Bear out and get cleaned up, but he didn't want to leave Paulo just yet.

Paulo kissed Jaron's forehead. "*Anjo* means angel. When I first saw you, I didn't want you to be a fraud. I hated the idea of someone so beautiful and sweet being a con man. Right from the beginning, I wanted to believe in you and that scared the hell out of me."

Jaron looked up at him. "I didn't want you to think I was a fraud either. Normally, I don't care if people don't believe me as long as they're not calling me a devil-worshiper or something. But it was different with you."

Paulo combed his fingers through Jaron's damp hair. "My *amor*," he whispered.

Jaron pressed his hand to his mouth, his eyes suddenly burning. "I… felt that." A tear slipped down his cheek. "Does that word mean beautiful?"

Paulo rolled onto his side, pulling Jaron with him. He pressed himself against Jaron. He kissed Jaron's ear. "I'm sure Google can tell you," he said, making Jaron laugh.

JD RUSKIN writes character-driven romance stories about complex men from a variety of backgrounds. JD is greatly influenced by her time in the Midwest, from the bustling streets of Chicago to the cornfields of rural Illinois. She enjoys writing stories with juicy plots, memorable characters, and smoking hot encounters.

JD's first novel, *When One Door Opens*, was a finalist in the Rainbow Award and the winner of 2014 Epic E-book award. When not writing, she has a passion for traveling, photography, and graphic design.

Contact information

Website: http://www.jdruskin.com/

Facebook: https://www.facebook.com/jd.ruskin.books

Twitter: @JDRuskin1184

WHEN ONE
DOOR OPENS

JD RUSKIN

http://www.dreamspinnerpress.com

ANOTHER HEALING

M. RAIYA

http://www.dreamspinnerpress.com

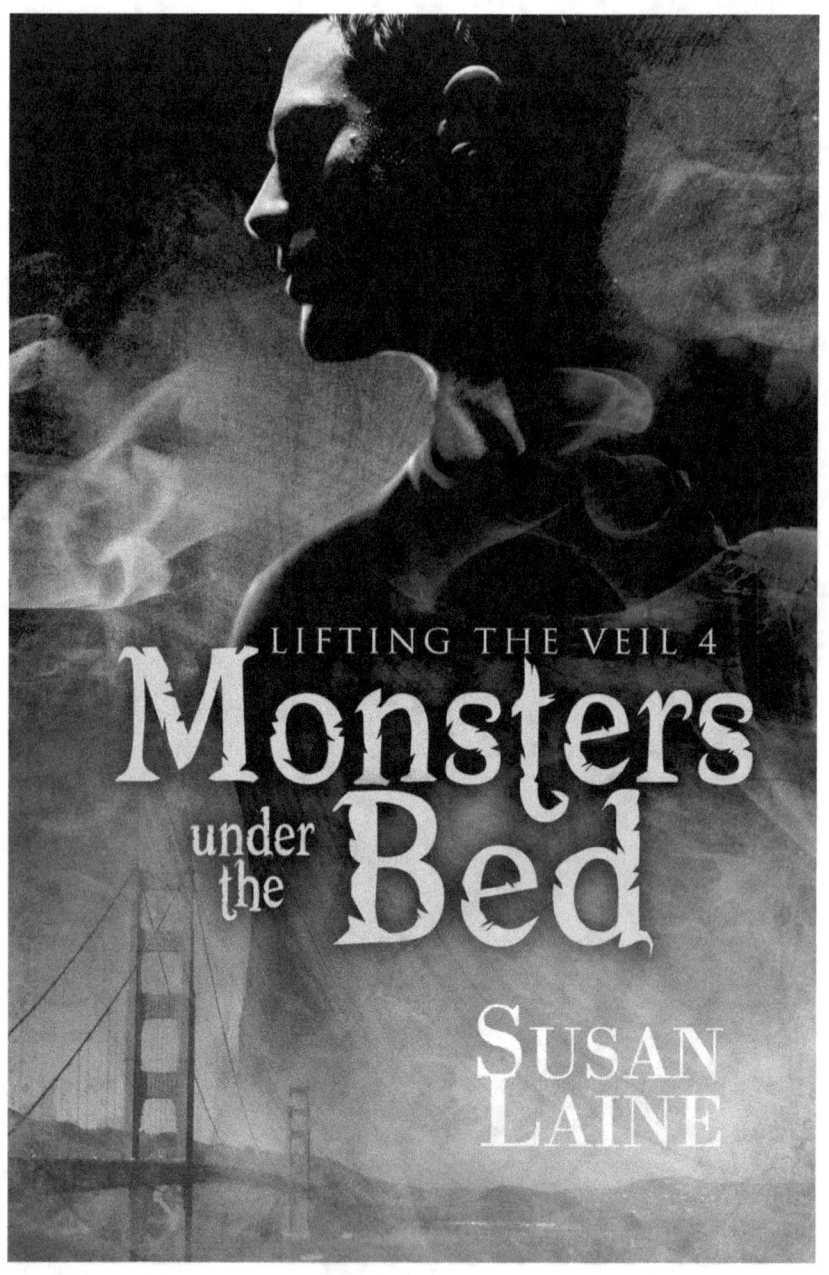

LIFTING THE VEIL 4

Monsters
under the Bed

Susan Laine

http://www.dreamspinnerpress.com

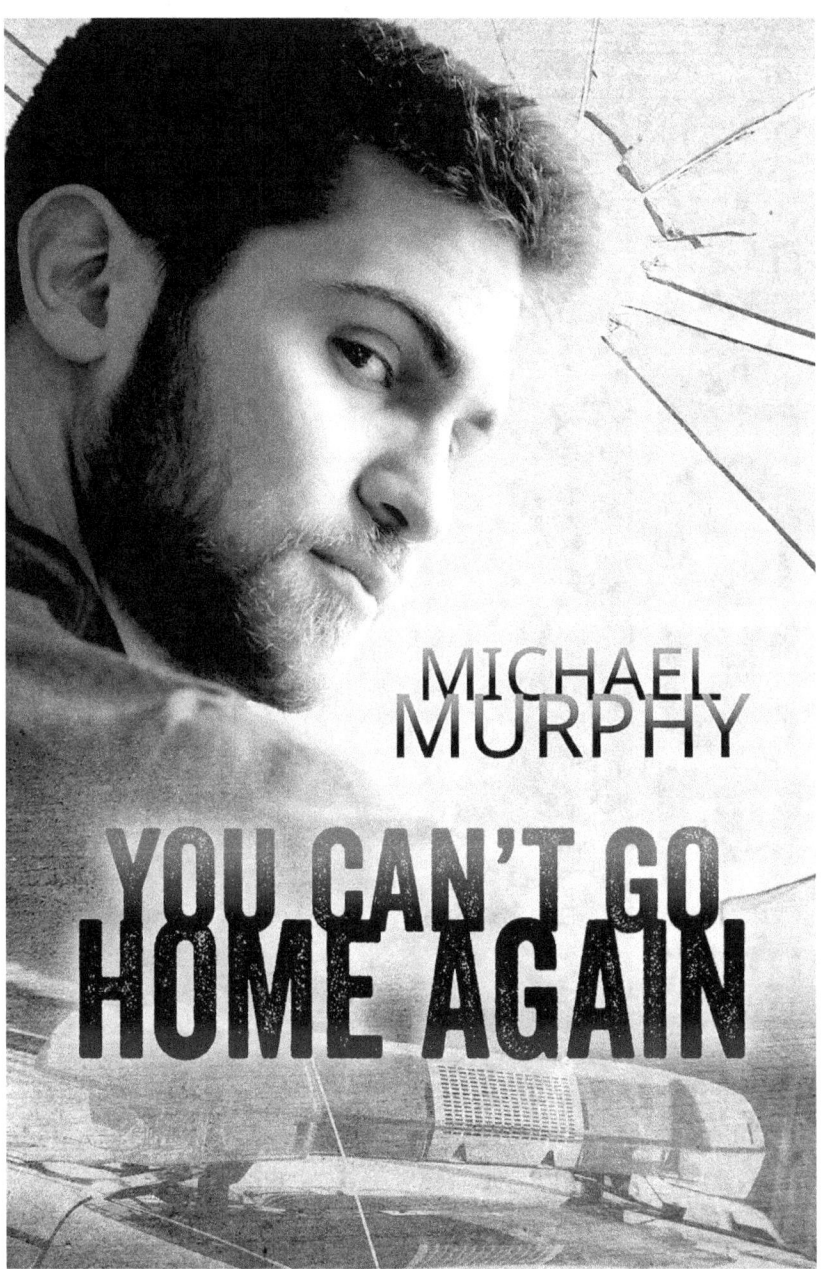

MICHAEL
MURPHY

YOU CAN'T GO
HOME AGAIN

http://www.dreamspinnerpress.com

FOR
MORE
OF THE
BEST
GAY
ROMANCE

Dreamspinner Press

DREAMSPINNERPRESS.COM